High Plains Promise

High Plains Promise

Love on the High Plains: Book 2

Simone Beaudelaire

Contents

Prologue

Garden City, KS 1874

"Wesley, wait for me," nine-year-old Allison Spencer whined as she chased her best friend through the backyard.

"Nope," Wesley replied, stopping long enough for her almost to catch up before he sped off again. "Hurry up, Allie. You're such a girl,"

"It's not fair," she wailed, tossing a sweaty strand of golden hair out of her face. "You don't have to wear a skirt!"

"Allison!" Rebecca called.

Allison stopped in her tracks. So did Wesley. They turned in unison to regard Allison's nineteen-year-old sister, who leaned against the railing that surrounded the back porch of their white, two-story home. "Wesley's mother is here. He needs to go, and Ma says you need a bath before church tomorrow."

Uh oh. We'd better hop to it. Ma won't like it if we dawdle, and she will not *appreciate needing to ask twice.*

Then the entirety of the message dawned on Allison. Wesley giggled as her face flamed.

Sensing his momentary distraction, she pounced, tackling her best friend directly into a mud puddle that had accumulated in the backyard, beside the rosebushes.

"Allie!" Wesley responded with a whine of his own. Thick, sticky green mud oozed up under his arms and between his legs, staining his already messy play clothes.

"Now who needs a bath, stinky?" Allison teased.

"Don't call me stinky!" Wesley howled. He shoved, knocking Allison off his chest so that she fell into the mud herself.

They looked at each other and burst out laughing. *Wes looks like the swamp monster we made up a story about last week, all green and slimy, and from the expression on his face, I bet I look even worse.* She ran a hand through her long blond hair and grimaced at the gritty, wet sensation. *Definitely worse.*

"My ma is going to kill me," Wesley complained when he had caught his breath.

Privately, Allison agreed. *I have a strict mother, but Mrs. Fulton is nothing but a battleax. Sometimes she seems almost crazy. I won't say it though. Wes is defensive about his mother.* Instead, she extended her hand to Wesley, intending to help him out of the mud.

He gave her a sharp yank, sending her sprawling in the disgusting slime.

"I'm gonna get you," she snarled, trying to push herself up. Her hands slipped. "When I get out of this puddle, I'm going to kill you."

Wesley laughed. "You'll have to catch me first, girly girl." He hoisted himself to his feet. "Besides, if you kill me, who will marry you then?" He reached out his hand to her this time.

She considered it warily. "What do you mean?"

"I mean, I always thought we would get married someday, didn't you, Allie?"

Of course, I have. I don't want to end up like my sister. Poor Becky, jilted by her fiancé. It seems like she might die of grief, though what exactly was so special about that boy, I've never been sure. Marrying my best friend is a much better idea. "Yeah, I guess so," she replied, aiming for nonchalance. "Are you sure you mean it?"

"Allie," he said, suddenly solemn, "I promise to marry you when we grow up." He extended his hand, so they could shake on it. She pressed her palm to his, and they shook briefly. Then he pulled, hoisting her to her feet.

They looked each other in the eyes for the span of half a dozen heartbeats. Then Wesley darted in close and kissed her, pressing his lips briefly to her cheek before giving her another hard shove, sending her sprawling before he turned and ran for the gate.

Ten years later

"Oh, Wesley," Allison moaned into her fiancé's mouth. He took the opening of her lips as an opportunity to slide his tongue inside. She let him take the familiar liberty, as he'd expected. This time, though, Wesley pressed his advance a step further, opening the buttons of her snowy white shirtwaist halfway to her navel. He slipped his hand inside and began caressing the bare skin of her upper chest, above the lacy edge of her chemise.

A cool breeze slipped past the broken windows of the abandoned farmhouse, teasing Wesley's heated flesh.

Allison moaned again.

Wesley grasped her stiffening nipple and gently squeezed it. "I want you, Allie," he told her gruffly.

"Oh, Wesley, yes." She pressed her luscious curves against his body.

He lowered her to the uneven dirt floor and covered her, grasping the edges of Allison's chemise and lowering it. "So pretty," he whispered, reaching out to touch one, reverence and awe in his voice and hands.

Allison arched her back, offering herself freely.

It's more than I deserve, my precious virgin's eager surrender, but I want to take it, nonetheless. I will someday, after our wedding, which is surely years away. He frowned. *I will, however, take a taste of all she has to offer, starting with this bounty spread out before me.* Shoving down thought, he touched Allie's again. Stroking her right breast with the tips of his fingers, he caressed the nipple to velvet hardness and leaned down to give it a long, sweet lick.

She squeaked, her hands cupping to the back of his head, holding him against her pillowy softness.

He obligingly opened his lips and sucked little peak into his mouth, tugging gently.

"Ahhh," Allison sighed.

So, she likes that, does she? He moved to the other side and tried again, getting the same encouraging result.

If only I could marry her now, this summer. We're were a little young, it's true, but I've seen it work before if the families are supportive. Alli-

son's probably would be. They like me well enough, and they realize our marriage is inevitable.

He'd had to endure many lectures from Mr. Spencer about treating a woman he loved with respect. *I do respect Allie. No less so, for holding her half-naked in my arms. If only Mother would agree. But, no. There will be no help from that quarter. I'll have to wait on the wedding until I can afford to support my bride.* Which meant he'd have to wait on completing this consummation as well.

Shaking off the thought, he backed up and treated himself to a long, lingering look at his beloved, sprawled on the dirt, breasts bare and glistening in the intense summer sunshine. *This is wrong. We should be on a nice, clean bed. Allie should have my ring on her finger. How can I wait to have her? It will be years. Years, and I'm about to burst with longing.* While his friends had generally had an experience or two by now, the thought of bedding another woman left Wesley cold. *Why would I, when I have all this to play with?*

He leaned down to suckle her nipple again, tugging firmly on the sensitive nub.

Allie made a soft sound of pleasure. Her thighs had fallen open so that she cradled his slender hips. He ground against her, imitating intercourse through all their layers of clothing.

"Oh Wes, please. Let's not wait anymore." She clutched his back and pressed him harder against the apex of her thighs.

He kissed her lips and pulled her clothing back into place. "Allie, I love you. I'm not going to take your virginity here in the dirt, so we can spend the next however many years sneaking around. I won't do it. I want that white wedding and my eager virgin bride afterwards. Don't you want that?"

"It doesn't seem important right now," she replied, a hint of a sulk lingering around her soft, pink lips.

"That's passion talking. When you calm down—"

"I *never* calm down, Wes," she interrupted. "Never. When I wake up in the morning, I'm already on fire. I simmer all day, and by night, I'm burning up. I love you and I want you so bad. Do you honestly think we'll be able to wait years?"

Honestly, I don't, he admitted ruefully, but still, he held firm to his convictions. "I know, sweet girl. I feel it too, and you're right. It will be a struggle, but we should at least try. This is no place for our first time anyway."

Allison's gaze scanned the room, taking in the cobwebs—some complete with spiders—the bare dirt floor, the broken windows and cracked, buckling walls. At last, she sighed and moved as though to stand.

Wesley obligingly climbed off her, though his aching body protested the movement. He lifted her to her feet and pulled her close for a long hug.

"I wish we could get married *now*," she complained.

"I know, honey, but I can't afford it yet. Where would we live? I have to work for a while and save up. The job at the bank is great, and I love it, but to buy a whole house? You know I don't have enough money for that right now."

"I know."

"Better head home, honey. You've been gone a long time. You don't want your folks finding us here."

"Yes, I do," she replied instantly.

"Why?"

"Because they'll make us get married. That's all I want anyway."

Wesley had to chuckle at her matter-of-fact response. "Little spitfire," he said fondly. "It's a good thing I'm not interested in ladylike behavior from my wife." He kissed her again. "Go home, Allison. Don't you have to get to work early tomorrow?"

She sighed. "Yes, I do. We're expecting a shipment of canned goods, and Mr. Heitschmidt wants a space cleared and ready when they get here, so we don't interrupt the flow of traffic around the store for long."

"Have fun." He kissed her forehead, nose, lips, cheeks, and sent her on her way with a firm pat on the bottom.

Alone at last, Wesley began shaking. *She has no idea how close I came to taking her invitation.* The warmth that had sunk into the front of his trousers had nearly been his undoing. He could still feel her there. *She's correct. There's no way we'll succeed in waiting years for the consumma-*

tion, close as we are already. I hope Allie knows how to relieve the pressure. It doesn't fix the problem, but it takes the edge off. He unbuttoned his trousers and reached inside. *If I go home in this state of rampant arousal, Mother will be sure to notice, and she doesn't hold back from commenting.*

His hand closed around his aching erection, and he let his eyes slide shut, imagining his sweet Allie, naked but for a thick gold wedding ring, sprawled in his bed, her thighs spread wide in invitation…

"That's a pretty picture," a familiar, unwelcome voice commented from the doorway.

Wesley jumped. "Oh my Lord, Samantha! What are you doing here? Go away!" His face burned with shame.

The voluptuous blond strolled into the room. "What am I doing? I'm watching the show. Nice. Very nice. Your Allie is a lucky girl. Too bad you'll never get to marry her."

"Oh, shut up," he groused. *I hope Allie never finds out the town tramp watched me touching her breasts. I'm not holding out hope, though. Samantha's almost as big a gossip as she is a slut.* "What the hell do you mean? I'm marrying her as soon as I can save up enough money to buy a little house. Everyone knows that."

"And your mother is a bitch. She hates Allison. If you do manage to marry her, she'll make life miserable for both of you, for the rest of your days."

"Don't talk about my mother like that. She'll get over it, once it's too late to protest. Now please, go away." His hands moved to the buttons on his trousers. *I'll have to work on my arousal later, at home. It isn't ideal there. If I make the slightest sound, Mother will be knocking on the door, asking if I'm all right.*

"What's your hurry?" Samantha asked, nodding to his groin. I like what you've got there. I'd love to see some more of it."

Red-faced, Wesley turned away. *What's wrong with this woman? Does she have no shame?* "Go away, Samantha. It's not for you."

"Only Allison then? How sad for her. If you did manage to marry her, you'd have no idea how to please her. Poor little virgin with a clumsy virgin husband floundering on top of her." Samantha made a tutting sound. Her arms slipped around Wesley from behind, one hand sliding straight through the opening in his waistband and closing around him. Wesley froze with shock. *Who does things like that?* A wicked little voice whispered in his ear, "She has a point. Most men arrive at their marriage bed with some experience."

I'm so aroused already, he reminded himself, daring to validate the temptation, *just from touching Allison the tiniest bit. Getting her naked will leave me right on the brink. That dearly-longed-for wedding night will be over before it starts.*

In fact, he hovered on the brink right now, his body reacting to the confused mélange of sensations. Images of Allison naked in his arms blended with Samantha's expert touches. The breeze touched his bare flesh as she lowered his trousers to his knees. Circling around to the front of him, she knelt. Liquid warmth enclosed his aching sex and he groaned. "Samantha, please stop."

"Imagine I'm her. Let me help you get ready for her."

She sucked him back in and he was lost, lust bowling over his consciousness, drowning his conscience so that when Samantha lifted her skirt to reveal that she wore no bloomers, when she spread her thighs and urged him down, he knelt. When she lined up his thick erection with the opening of her glistening womanhood, he didn't protest. When she urged him inside, he followed her lead. Groaning at the wet, hot sweetness, he gave his innocence to a woman he didn't even like, while the girl he loved made her long way home, unsatisfied.

Samantha arched her hips, taking him to the hilt inside her, and he groaned again. His orgasm began instantly, giving the seed that should have belonged to Allison, his future bride, to this wanton creature.

Chapter 1

Four Years Later

"Melissa, I'm home!" Wesley called.

His beautiful, three-year-old daughter ran to the front parlor, golden pigtails bouncing with every step.

He glanced up the room and sighed. Like the rest of the house, a thick layer of dust lay on every surface. A threadbare sofa with scarred arms had been shoved against the wall. An overturned side table rested on the floor, with the remains of a broken oil lamp strewn in a wide circle around it. One of the panes in the big bay window was also broken, and chilly air funneled into the room, as well as the odd leaf from the messy, untrimmed shrubs outside. His stomach turned when the wind stilled, allowing the stench of rotten food and dirty house to rise up.

"Daddy!" the little girl squealed, jumping into his arms. He cradled her against his side with one arm and planted a loud kiss on her cheek. She responded in kind. *The uncomplicated love of a child makes up for a multitude of other, less pleasant aspects of life.*

"Hello, Wes," his wife said, entering the room.

Oh, good. She looks fairly lucid today, he noted with relief. "Samantha." He hugged her gently with his free arm around her shoulder and pressed a quick kiss to her lips, twirling a strand of golden hair around his finger. "Did you have a good day?"

"I guess," she replied. "What about you? How was your meeting?" Her voice hardened as she spoke the question.

Uh oh. "Fine. We're getting a new pastor."

Samantha shrugged. "Another two-faced hypocrite?" she asked, an ugly note in her voice.

"I doubt it," Wesley replied. "He's young. Younger than me. Maybe he'll be nice."

"Church people are never nice," Samantha said.

The tone in her voice warned him. *Wrong again. We're heading into dangerous territory.* Wesley changed the subject immediately. "So, what did you do today?"

"We went to the store. I bought some ribbons and a dolly for Melissa."

"That's good," he replied, relieved she'd taken the bait.

"We saw a few people there. Your lover was there."

"I don't have a lover," he replied mildly, his pulse increasing as he struggled not to go into full defensive mode. "I don't need one. I have the most arousing woman in town for my wife." He ran his hand over her backside.

She shoved him away. "Don't lie to me, Wesley. I know you're still with that little whore. The look she gave me... and then talking to me all sweet."

Wesley took a step away from his wife. There was no truth in what she was saying. Since the day she'd come to him and told him she was pregnant, up to this very day, he'd been faithful to her. He knew full well she didn't return the favor. He knew what those pitying, knowing looks from the men around town meant. *It doesn't matter. I have to try and keep my family functioning as best I can, for Melissa's sake.*

"Is that where you *really* were, after work today?" Samantha snarled, working herself further into a tirade. "Did you go to your whore? Did you bring her back to that farmhouse and take her on the floor, in the dirt, the way you always wanted?"

And there we go, Wesley thought, suppressing a sigh. *Melissa doesn't need to hear this.* "Princess, why don't you go run and play," he murmured in his daughter's ear, but she clutched tighter around his neck. Her mother's unstable mood frightened her, as usual. He patted the child's back. "Samantha," he said soothingly, "that farmhouse was torn down years ago. It's not there anymore. Besides, I was with James Heitschmidt and the other elders and deacons for a meeting. Nothing more, I swear."

"Liar!" she shrieked.

"Mommy," Melissa said softly, "Daddy loves you."

Samantha snapped. Her arm flew towards her daughter with the full force of her enraged adult strength.

Wesley shifted Melissa to his hip and turned his body to shield her, using his free hand to catch his wife's wrist in a crushing grip. All his attempts to placate Samantha ended where Melissa's safety was concerned. "Don't," he hissed, tightening his grip on her arm, "hit," he went on, almost spitting now, "the baby!"

"Ow! Wes, you're hurting me!" Samantha wriggled in his grip.

He tightened his hand further, unwilling to take the risk. Once, he'd let go and she'd shot out a second blow. "Stop struggling. I'll let you go when I know you've calmed down. Melissa, I think we should go over to Lydia's. See if she has anything to eat. Mommy needs some time to herself today."

That set Samantha off again. Wrenching her arm futilely, she began screaming. "I know where you're really going! You can play house with your whore all you want, but she'll never have you! Not really. She can only be your slut."

"There's only one slut in this town," Wesley replied. He released her arm with a sharp backwards shove, which sent her stumbling. He sailed out the door, slamming it shut behind him and praying she wouldn't follow.

As Wesley reached the street, Samantha clattered on the porch, screaming abuse towards them at the top of her lungs, for all to hear.

He kept walking. *There's no reasoning with her when she's in one of her moods. The best thing to do is stay away until she calms down,* he told himself as he made a sharp turn onto Main Street.

Curtains fluttered at windows and doors creaked open. Wesley sighed. *If only she didn't feel compelled to play out our family drama in public. Everyone knows. Everyone.*

Once out of earshot of the house, he set Melissa on the ground and took her little hand, though his thoughts remained on his marriage. *I knew from the beginning I was taking on a woman of easy virtue, and a rather unintelligent one at that, but I didn't realize the depth of her problems.*

A fragment of memory floated up, of the day not long after his wedding when he first realized just how much trouble he was in.

When the familiar, shabby door of Lydia's opened, heads turned to take in the new arrivals, small-town idleness at work again. This time, however, the good folks of Garden City had more to see than they'd bargained for.

Wesley Fulton, dressed in his brown work suit, tugged uncomfortably on his collar and glanced at the woman on his arm. Samantha, clad in a figure-hugging pink dress she'd stitched together that hung crookedly on her voluptuous frame preened at the attention. She shot flirtatious glances at every man in the room.

"Stop it," he hissed under his breath. "You're a married woman now."

She turned innocent eyes on him. "Stop what?"

Wesley shook his head. "Just remember who you belong to," he said at last.

Subtlety, apparently, meant nothing to her. Shrugging her shoulders, she let him lead her to a table.

Every eye in the room watched them go. And then the whispers began.

"He married *that* one?"

"If he got anyone in a family way, I would have expected the Spencer girl."

"This one's nothing but a tramp. He'll regret this."

"Stop that. The girl can't help being simple."

Wesley ground his teeth. *Simple is right. I knew she wasn't smart before we married, but until a few minutes ago when I took her to buy a ribbon at the general store—and didn't old man Heitschmidt frown at me then, though I can't blame him—I never realized she couldn't even count or handle money. Ironic, for a banker's wife.*

"Cup of coffee?" A slurred voice cut into his dark ruminations. He looked up into the plump, tilty-eyed face of his cousin.

"Yes, please, Billy," Wesley concurred. "That sounds great."

Samantha scrutinized the young man and apparently decided his disabilities made him less than interesting. "No, thank you. None for me."

"But, say, Billy," Wesley continued, "I didn't know Miss Lydia was having you serve too."

"A bit," Billy replied, smoothing his wispy blond hair into place with large, sausage-like fingers. Though strangers sometimes had difficulty understanding the lad, with his thickened tongue muddling his speech, Wesley had no such trouble. The youth grinned, showing a missing front tooth. "She says I can start with coffee, and if I do good, I can serve lunch too, and even maybe run the till from time to time."

"That's great!" Wesley exclaimed, and his cousin giggled quietly at the sincere compliment. "I'm so glad you're getting a promotion."

Billy's grin widened until it almost split his face, and then his expression turned serious. "Can't I get you anything, Ms. Fulton?"

Samantha regarded Billy again. "Just a glass of water," she decided at last. "My stomach is feeling a bit poorly. The baby, you know."

Billy blushed and shuffled off to the kitchen.

"Do you have to say that so loudly?" Wesley demanded.

"What?"

Wesley couldn't restrain his sigh this time. "About the..." he looked around and hissed, "the baby."

"Why not? It's not a secret, Wes. In just a few short months, we'll be parents." She patted her burgeoning abdomen.

Wesley frowned but said nothing.

Into the silence, the whispers began again. "So it is true. I almost couldn't believe it."

"I wonder if this means she'll give up her whorish ways?"

"I wonder if it's even his..."

Wesley tripped on the edge of one of the bricks that made up Main Street, jarring him back to the present as they arrived at the café, a two-story red brick building with a wooden shingle over the door. It was rather too cold, now in late November, to be out without a coat, and Melissa had begun to shiver. Wesley scooped her up again and snuggled her. In the crisis of the moment, he hadn't thought ahead too well. He tried the door. Locked. *Damn it, can I never get even the smallest break? It's too soon to go home and too cold to stay out, so what can I do?*

"Wesley, so glad I found you." James Heitschmidt said, interrupting Wesley's angry mental rant.

He turned to face the tall, freckle-faced head of the elder board and owner of Garden City's general store. "Hello, James. What can I do for you?" he asked, struggling to appear normal. *If my life fell apart every time my wife threw a fit, I'd be unable to function at all.*

"I need some help at the vicarage. It hasn't been lived in for three years, and the new pastor arrives soon. He needs a place to stay."

"I'd be glad to help, but I have Melissa here." He indicated his little girl, who clung tighter to his neck.

"Gentlemen?" A soft, soothing voice broke over Wesley, making him smile. Allison's sister Becky approached, her lovely face set in a serene half-smile.

If anyone knows how to handle adversity with grace, it's Rebecca Spencer. Maybe someday I can learn to face my problems with a sad smile... or maybe not.

James turned to her. "Miss Spencer, how are you today?"

She flushed a little, in the bite of a sudden, icy gust. "I'm just fine, Mr. Heitschmidt," she replied. "Did I overhear you're going to air out the vicarage?"

"Yes," James replied. He seemed about to elaborate, but nothing came out.

"Well, then," the petite, golden-haired woman continued, "why don't I take Melissa with me for a while? I have some cookies fresh from the oven, and I'd like someone to taste them to be sure they're good."

Wesley looked at his little daughter, gauging whether she would be okay parting from him. The child wriggled in his arms. *It's awfully close to dinner time, but how can I say no? She has so little, compared to other children.*

He set Melissa down, and she ran to Becky, who scooped her up. "Thank you, Miss Rebecca," Melissa said, giving her a big hug. "I'm really hungry."

Wesley closed his eyes. It wouldn't be the first time Samantha had refused to feed Melissa when she was in one of her precarious moods.

Becky didn't bat an eyelash. "Well then, sweetheart, let's have a sandwich and then a cookie, what do you say? I wouldn't want you to get a stomachache."

Melissa cheered.

"Thank you, Miss Spencer," Wesley said softly.

"Any time, Mr. Fulton," she replied. Then she turned and carried Melissa away down the chilly street to the Spencer house, a white two-story with lots of gingerbread trim painted black and matching shutters on all the windows.

As soon as they ducked out of sight, Wesley turned. James was still staring at the door of the Spencers' house.

"Shall we go?" Wesley asked.

James shook his head a couple of times, as though trying to clear his mind. "Yes, let's," he said at last, and the two men headed back down Main street, past the commercial center, which consisted of red brick buildings of varying heights—the mercantile, the bank with the telegraph office up front, and the Occidental Hotel.

At last, they came to the church. Unlike its neighbors, it was made of weathered white boards, and boasted an oversized steeple with an ostentatious brass bell. The sound of the bellowing pipe organ could be heard in the street. Wesley grinned wanly. *Sounds like Kristina is practicing for Sunday.*

To the south of the church, a narrow brick path led past a windblighted tree to a tiny, one-room structure. James unlocked the door of the vicarage and the stench of a building that had been unoccupied for several years assaulted the two men.

"Whew, that's ripe," Wesley commented. *Smells too much like home. Wouldn't wish that on anyone else.*

"Open up the windows," James suggested, stepping over the threshold and making a sharp right turn into the sitting area, where he yanked the first glass pane up to reveal the opening beneath. "I know it's cold, but that wind will take care of the stink in short order." Shivering, Wesley turned left and scooted past a small, round table so he could comply. Within minutes the room had turned freezing but undeniably smelled fresher.

James handed Wesley a broom and he worked on warming himself up by sweeping all the dust and cobwebs from the floors and out onto the stoop, where the breeze carried them away.

James, meanwhile, poked at the pot-bellied stove in the corner, making sure it was vented correctly.

Good plan, Wes thought as he paused in the center of the room, wondering what to do next. *Since the new pastor is coming from Texas, he'll need that source of warmth immediately.*

"Wes, take a look at the bed frame and mattress, would you, while I examine the sofa?" James ordered.

Obediently, Wesley approached the bed and swept off the fabric sheet that served as a cover. The bare mattress, while a bit worn, did not contain any holes or tears. He sat down, pleased that only a small amount of dust billowed up. *Not bad, considering it's been unused for so long. Looks like that twice-yearly cleaning did the trick.* He jiggled on the bed, but the frame did not move. "Seems solid enough," he called to his companion.

"Same here," James replied. "I might almost think the Lord had a hand in keeping this place. Reverend Williams must have a special purpose in this town."

"Let's hope," Wesley agreed. "What about linens? This bed looks mighty uninviting, all bare like this."

"The Ladies' Altar Guild will bring sheets, blankets, and towels tomorrow evening. That way, they'll still be nice and fresh when he arrives in the morning."

"Sounds good. And for food?"

"Allison and Kristina are going to stock the cupboards in the next day or two."

Wesley nodded. "Sounds like things are about set. I sure hope Reverend Williams likes it here. We haven't had a pastor in so long..." Suddenly Wesley realized how bad that sounded. "Not that you've done a bad job, I mean... sorry."

"Don't worry, Wes," James replied. "No offense taken. I'm no pastor. I don't have time to devote to the ministry. I'm glad to fill in, but I know the difference. I'm glad Reverend Williams is coming too."

The men returned to examining the vicarage for livability. Crouching on the floor, Wesley verified there were no mouse holes visible in the baseboards. *Provided the new pastor doesn't have fancy tastes, the little house should be serviceable and comfortable.*

"Well, the walls still look solid," James announced. "What about the floor?"

"Smooth as glass. No signs of warping," Wesley replied, running one hand over a shiny, no longer dusty board.

Task completed, they parted ways at the door with a handshake and James headed south, down the street towards his home.

The church had fallen silent, indicating Kristina had finished practicing and left. Silence hung heavy over the little town, broken only by the endless, whispering wind. No people walked down the broad brick road. No conversation rang from open windows.

Dusk deepened, casting long shadows of trees and buildings over the red brick streets. Wesley turned north and walked to the familiar house he'd visited over and over in his childhood. Every time he visited the Spencer home, he felt a pang of sorrow, no less diminished for the four years that had passed since the death of all his dreams.

He knocked on the door.

Allison opened it, looking lovely and as desirable as ever. *It's hell to look at her*, he thought, wincing as though the vision of her robust, blond loveliness hurt his eyes. *Hurts my heart, more like. In some ways, this is worse than the confrontation with Samantha.*

All he could think, every time he saw Allison, was how different his life would be now if he hadn't been so noble with her. *If I took her there, on the floor of that farmhouse, she would have been the one who conceived my baby. My daughter could have had a stable, loving mother, an adoring aunt and lovely grandparents. This should have been Melissa's family.*

"Wesley," Allison said. She tried to sound cool and collected, but a hint of something in her voice betrayed sorrow that equaled his. *It's always there. I betrayed her. Her trust in me is not what it once was, and deservedly so.* Regret chewed on his insides. *I hurt us both for such a stupid reason.*

Without a word, she ushered him into the parlor. She didn't sit, and so he also remained standing. Their eyes met, and Allison flinched. She turned away.

To keep from staring like a lovesick puppy, he scanned the familiar room with its high-backed sofa, upholstered in black, the two wood and blue velvet armchairs, and the pot-bellied stove in the corner of a room encircled with golden tongue-and-groove paneling. *Once, I considered this room more mine than the gracious two-story gingerbread I used to share with my mother.* In the wake of yet another brutal fight with his wife, this lovely and well-appointed room made the squalor of his own living conditions seem even uglier by comparison.

"Have you eaten?" she asked.

"No," he replied.

"Would you like some dinner? I think we have some leftovers. Melissa ate well, and since Dad's away on the Wichita run, we have an extra seat at the table."

"No thank you," he declined. "I need to head home, I suppose."

Allison seemed poised on the verge of saying something, but then she bowed her head and left in silence. Wesley sank onto one of the armchairs, exhausted. He rested his elbows on his knees and his forehead in his hands.

"Are you sad, Daddy?" a childish voice chirped in his ear. He looked up, meeting his daughter's beautiful dark eyes.

"Not sad," he lied, "just tired and hungry."

"They had chicken and potatoes. Do you want some?"

Wesley's mouth watered at the thought of all the Spencer women's delicious cooking. *No. I can't play house here and pretend. I won't be guilty of Samantha's accusations.*

Inhaling deeply, he took in the scent of butter and meat and bit his lip hard against dual burning in his eyes and throat. *It's so unfair. I committed one sin. One. And I've more than paid for it,* his hungry stomach argued, tempted by the promise of a satisfying meal.

No. I refuse to confirm Samantha's accusations by making her suspicions true in the smallest way.

"Let's go home, princess," he said.

Worry flashed in her eyes, beyond her meager years.

How can such a tiny, innocent child know such stress? He scooped her into his arms. "Goodbye, ladies, and thank you," he called as he walked out into the blustery street. Deep dusk had fallen, and the temperature had dropped even further. Wesley cuddled Melissa close, protecting her from the cold as he hurried through the streets.

In the fiery evening light, long shadows cast by the buildings hung ominously overhead, crowding him. He shivered and walked even faster. His long legs ate up the blocks until at last, he reached his home. Opening the door silently, he crept inside, cursing himself for his cowardice. *This is my home, damn it, and I haven't done anything wrong, so why am I sneaking in like a guilty adolescent?*

He set Melissa on the floor. She clung close to his side. Hand in hand, they walked through the dark, silent house. The echoing of their footsteps on the reverberating wood floor lent weight to the growing notion they were alone. A quick check of the first floor confirmed it. Wesley walked Melissa up the stairs to her bedroom, the only well-kept space in the house.

Her low bed with its pink quilt waited invitingly in one corner, hemmed in by a white bureau and a dark rocking chair. Wesley pulled a pink nightgown out of the top drawer of the bureau and gently dressed his daughter for bed. Then he settled in the rocking chair. His belly cramped with hunger, but he would not forgo this time with Melissa.

He folded his big hands around her tiny ones and prayed with her, not a memorized, rhyming prayer, just an honest conversation with God about the day, and then he sang her a lullaby. Glancing down, he saw her eyes closed. He kissed her forehead and tucked her into bed. As he stood to leave, her arms snaked around his neck in a tight hug.

"I love you, Daddy," she murmured. "Everything will be all right."
Wesley's eyes burned. "I love you too, Melissa," he told her, kissing
her cheek.

Her arms relaxed, falling to her sides.

He hurried back down the stairs to the kitchen, where he began to
rummage for food. His wife's haphazard kitchen system had him baf-
fled as usual. Eventually, he found a loaf of bread in a lower cabinet. It
must have been there for ages, as thick blue and white mold covered
the entire surface. Trying not to gag, he tossed it into the backyard.

A more extensive search of the kitchen revealed the fresh bread she
had purchased that day, wrapped in a tea towel below the kitchen sink.
The icebox held sliced meat, some of it not rotten, and some cheese
from which the mold could be cut off. *For this, I gave up roast chicken
with potatoes,* he lamented with a sigh.

Shaking his head, Wesley consumed his unpalatable supper and
cleaned his own teeth, trying without success to remove the taste of the
overly ripe cheese. Then he went to bed. *Wherever Samantha is tonight,
I hope she stays there. I'm not in the mood to see her.*

Allison sat in a straight-backed wooden chair in front of her vanity, running an ivory-handled brush through her golden hair. She'd just
bathed—a Friday night ritual—and now she wanted her hair to dry before going to bed. *Can't let it dry against the pillow or it will be a rat's
nest tomorrow.* The mundane thought helped chase away the shadows
of grief that always threatened to overtake her quiet moments.

A knock sounded at her door.

"Who is it?" she called.

"Becky," her sister replied.

"C'mon in," she said.

Rebecca entered the room, dressed in a loose white nightgown, with
a tan dressing gown belted around her tiny waist.

In some ways we look so much alike, Allison reflected. *Same blond hair. Same blue eyes, but that's where the common features end. Though over a decade older than me, Becky is a head shorter, and slender where I'm robust. She looks almost fairy-like, all but her mysterious, emotion-concealing half-smile. So different from aggressive cheer—though both façades conceal feelings we have reason to protect. Can't let people get too close. That way leads to heartbreak.*

"Here, let me," Becky said in her soft, serene voice, taking the brush from Allison's hand and running it gently through the thick, sunshine-colored mane.

Allison's eyes closed at the tingling sensation in her scalp. She could feel Becky's hand trembling slightly.

"Worried about Dad?" Allison guessed.

"A bit. I hate that he's out there with those train robbers everyone's been talking about lurking in the shadows." Becky's voice wavered.

"I know," Allison agreed, "but you know Dad loves his job. If he doesn't drive the train, what is he good for? He's said that enough times. Thank the Lord Mom convinced him to keep his rifle with him."

"Did you see Wesley today?" Becky asked, changing the subject.

"Hmmmm," Allison said. *Why did you have to bring up Wesley, sis? I don't want to talk about him. It still hurts too much.*

"He looks really bad," Becky continued, "skinny and sad. I feel sorry for him."

"Do we have to discuss Wesley?" Allison asked, swiveling in her chair and wincing as the brush tugged uncomfortably through her hair.

"Sorry," Becky replied. "I thought you were over him. It's been four years, honey."

"I know," Allison replied, "but part of me still loves him. It's hard to see him and remember."

"Then how on earth can you be his friend?" Becky asked.

Allison rose from the chair and plunked herself down on the blue crazy quilt that covered her bed, leaning back against the headboard. She patted the mattress. Her sister set the brush on the vanity and approached, settling at the opposite end, the footboard supporting her as she slouched. Allison couldn't help but smile. *I doubt anyone but me has seen Becky relaxed enough to slump in years.*

"Love is a funny thing, Becky," Allison told her sister, trying to diminish her pain by taking the tone of an old-time storyteller. "When you love someone, really love them, you have to forgive them, even if they make a horrible, life-changing decision. I can't go back and change the past, and I don't want to lose one of my best friends, so I just… made peace with the pain."

"You should find a suitor," Becky said, her expression uncharacteristically fierce, her eyes flashing like sapphires. "Don't let him destroy your future."

"Destroy?" Allison regarded her sister curiously. "What do you mean? Am I destroyed if I remain single? Is that life not worth living? You never married either, sis."

"I know. This is not what I would have chosen, and I sure don't want it for you."

"Becky, can I ask you something?" Allison asked hesitantly, tilting her head in what she hoped looked like an innocent and disarming gesture.

Becky's cheeks flamed. "You want to know why I never married, right?"

"Yes," Allison replied. *I've always wondered why my sweet, lovely sister is single, at the great age of thirty-five.* "I know your beau left with that other girl, but really, there are other men in the world. Did you love him so much?"

Becky shook her head. "I got over whatever affection I had for him quickly enough. That wasn't it."

"Then why…"

"You know the rumors?"

Allison closed her eyes briefly, and then opened them, nodding slightly.

"They're true."

"You really…" She couldn't continue. Couldn't voice Becky's shame aloud.

Becky smiled sadly, with only one corner of her mouth. "Yes. I was a silly girl back then. I didn't think… I thought it wouldn't matter."

"I'm so sorry, honey. That unbelievable bastard! I wish I could cut his balls off!"

"Allison!" Becky exclaimed, aghast at her sister's unladylike language. Then she giggled, willing, as always, to be amused by Allison's antics.

"Anyway, he didn't force me. I was willing enough… at the time. I regret it though. If only…" her eyes went soft and vacant.

Somehow Allison knew there was a man in her heart, a different man. *What a shame. I wish I knew who it was. That might make a difference… but men are so possessive. She's probably right to think her hopes are futile.* "You know," she said, trying to ease Becky's distress, "I'm not the most innocent girl myself."

Becky's gaze focused back on her sister and she raised an eyebrow. "You let Wesley… take liberties?"

"Oh yes," she replied. "A lot of them. We didn't quite… but… well… you know." She broke off, not wanting to describe how her suitor had once opened her blouse and fondled her, and then promptly bedded another woman and got her pregnant.

"What a sorry pair," Becky quipped. "What's wrong with us?"

"We're a couple of hussies," Allison replied. They looked at each other and burst out laughing, granted a little hysterically. *But really, laughter is better than tears.*

That night, Wesley dreamed of Allison, of that afternoon in the farmhouse, which seemed like a lifetime ago. Only in this dream, when she begged him to take her virginity, he did. In his unconscious state, he sank deep into her tight, eager flesh and pumped hard, desperate to avoid some unseen threat. Dream lovemaking led to a real-life orgasm, which stained his nightshirt and the sheets. Waking in a puddle did nothing to improve Wesley's mood. Especially since he was alone in his marriage bed, his wife having spent the night who knew where.

Grumbling, he cleaned up the mess, dressed for a casual Saturday at home, and headed downstairs. *I may not be much of a cook, but at least I'm capable of brewing coffee and stirring up a pot of porridge.* He dished up a bowl for Melissa, set it at the dirty kitchen table to cool, and slurped down a soothing cup of the strong black brew. Then he filled the dishpan with water and soap and put several days of accumulated dishes inside to soak off the crusted grime. This was his Saturday routine, sometimes with Samantha hovering over the process to offer useless advice, sometimes not.

A few minutes later, as he was scrubbing a filthy fork, his little angel trailed down the stairs, barefoot and still in her nightgown, a ragged teddy bear dragging forlornly behind her.

She slumped down at the table and began eating her oatmeal in silence. Wesley smiled. *Even at three, Melissa is far from a morning person. It will take an hour at least for her to wake up properly.*

The front door slammed open and Samantha breezed in, pink-cheeked and smiling. She leaned over and hugged Melissa before slinking to her husband. Samantha planted a wet kiss on his lips, and he caught a whiff of masculine cologne as he embraced her gently.

"My goodness, it's cold outside," she chirped, her full pink lips parting in a wide smile. He noticed she had love bites all over her throat.

"Why don't you have some breakfast and then warm up in a nice bath," he suggested. *Some might say that's too nice, but I don't want to be around her when she smells like her lover.*

"I just ate," she replied, "but a hot bath sounds wonderful. That's a great idea." She kissed him again and waltzed out of the room.

Wesley tried not to grind his teeth. *I should be thankful Samantha's in a good mood. They seem to get rarer as time goes by.* He glanced at Melissa and was pleased to see his little angel smiling into her oatmeal.

Chapter 2

Saturday night, Wesley bent over Melissa's bed, kissed the tiny girl on the forehead, and made his way back to his own room, deep in contemplation over the wild vacillations his life took. *Well, I met the new pastor, Reverend Cody Williams. He's young for his position—only twenty-four—and possessed of a wide, white-toothed smile and a friendly demeanor. I hope we can be friends. I need one. Allie and Kristina... they're wonderful, but I haven't had a male friend since Jesse moved away.*

I wonder how Jesse's getting along. The cholera outbreak hit him harder than most. Slipping out of his clothes, Wesley climbed under the covers and blew out his lamp.

Work is always good. I can slip out of my worries and into a sheet of numbers, and it's like medicine for my heart. Golly, that would sound strange to anyone who heard it. And then another screaming fight with my wife. She stormed out this time, leaving us alone for two days. I wonder where she goes. His mind veered away. *I wonder when she'll come back.*

As if in answer to his silent question, the mattress dipped. Samantha slipped into bed beside him and cuddled up.

He took her in his arms. *She's my wife. This is the only part of our marriage that actually works, and I refuse to deny myself this one pleasure. Besides, despite everything, Samantha is still damned good in bed.*

After the Sunday service, Wesley lingered in the pew with Melissa, not wanting to wade into the throng of people trying to shake hands and meet the new pastor. Sunlight illuminated the rows of stained-glass windows that lined the two long exterior walls along the sides of the building. The illustrations of Biblical scenes created to irregularly shaped patches of colored light on the floors. *Light like hope. Too bad I have none left.* Overhead, the whitewashed ceiling contrasted with row after row of exposed support beams in the same finish as the floor. To the left of the altar, with its long communion rail and plain box of a pulpit, a door led to a storage room. To the right, another door opened into an office. *Our church, simple but lovely, the center of life in our town. Now a new pastor will be presiding over it, one who might at least provide some respite from the hell of my existence.* Exactly how he could accomplish this, Wesley wasn't sure, but something told him the arrival of Reverend Cody Williams would shake everything up... in a good way.

Lydia Carré, owner of the café, approached him. "Hello, Mr. Fulton," she said, her eyes crinkling in the corners as she smiled.

He smiled back and responded to her greeting with a nod. "Miss Carré."

"How are you two today?"

Melissa looked up from the paper she was coloring with a stub of pencil and gave the chef a shy glance. Lydia patted the girl's silky hair and her own expression turned wistful.

I wonder why she never married. Black-haired, dark-eyed Lydia Carré is surely an anomaly around this town, being half French, half Italian, but she's plump, pretty, friendly, and well-liked. It's clear she doesn't want to be alone, though the man she can't keep her eyes off—Sheriff Brody— never seems to notice. Wesley suppressed a sigh. *In the end, no one gets what they want, I suppose.*

Another woman approached, and this time Melissa abandoned her paper with a joyous squeal and pounced.

"Oof," Rebecca grunted softly as she gathered the child up for a tight hug. "Hello, sweetheart. Wesley. Lydia." The two women smiled at each other.

It's no surprise they're close friends. Both spinsters over thirty, both entrepreneurs, they have a lot in common. Plus, they're just nice. I like them. He shook hands with each woman, contrasting their mature beauty. Unlike Lydia's bold, exotic features, Becky epitomized the pale, Germanic loveliness typical of this town. Her small and delicately-shaped features, poised in a perennially calm expression, exuded an air of graceful acceptance. *Nothing ruffles Rebecca Spencer. She's utterly serene. It's no wonder Melissa, with all the turmoil in her everyday life, is drawn to her soothing presence.* Lydia, with her effusive hand gestures and bubbly nature, intimidated the nervous child and received a tepid reception.

James Heitschmidt, arm in arm with his daughter, came towards them. Kristina greeted her long-time friend with a warm hug, but uncertainty lingered in her expression when she met Wesley's eyes.

He regarded her familiar features. Though no great beauty—Kristina's heavily freckled face and short, upturned nose made no concession to fashion—what upset Wesley was seeing the wariness in that smile. *Something fundamental has changed in all my relationships. Will no semblance of normalcy ever return to my life?*

She released him and seemed compelled to turn toward the doorway, where Cody was shaking hands with the snobby Jackson family. Ilse, their adult daughter, eyed the handsome minister with a predatory expression. *Ilse thinks all the attractive, unmarried men in town belong to her. I'm glad I've never been in her crosshairs. I have no interest in that snippy little cat.* He rolled his eyes in disgust. *Of course, I didn't do much better,* he acknowledged ruefully.

"Wesley, would you and Melissa like to come for lunch this afternoon?" Kristina offered.

After eating his own unpalatable cooking all weekend, Wesley accepted with a grateful smile Kristina didn't see. She had turned to look at the pastor again, as though unable to stop herself. His grin broadened. *It's about time Kristina noticed a man and received his attention in return.*

Even from this distance, Wes could see Cody's blue eyes burning as they alighted on his friend. She blushed and looked away.

Interesting.

Turning, he saw Rebecca deep in a quiet conversation with Kristina's father, James. The bluff, blond shopkeeper seemed to be instructing the woman on how to figure profits. Her parents called to her from outside and she faltered mid-word, blushing furiously to the roots of her golden hair. "Thank you, James," she said softly.

She used his first name. That's unusual. Even Ally, Kris and I get funny looks for not saying Miss and Mister when we talk, even though we've been friends our whole lives. I wonder if that means what I think it means.

"Of course, Rebecca," James said. He reached out and clasped her slender shoulder—it might have been because both her hands were filled with Wesley's daughter, though something about his gaze on her blushing face suggested otherwise—and then released her. "I'll stop by tomorrow and help you get that counter constructed."

She nodded, set Melissa on the floor and left, but tossed a backward glance at the group, her cheeks still pink. *Hmmm. Looks like my unofficial big sister might finally have attracted someone's interest. I hope so.*

Lydia shook everyone's hand and headed out. The Heitschmidts and their lunch guests trailed after her.

"See you later, Reverend," James said. Kristina took the young pastor's hand and gave him a confused look, in which attraction blended with irritation. He held her fingers a little too long and gazed at her with unflinching admiration.

I wonder if he even realizes how much of his interest he's broadcasting. Kristina blushed.

At last, Cody released her, and she hurried down the steps and out into the blustery street.

Wesley shook Cody's hand and gave him a warning glance with an arched eyebrow, silently promising all manner of unpleasantness to anyone who hurt Kristina. Cody returned his gaze without flinching. *Good.*

Then, Wesley joined his friends and they hustled down the street. Though the sun shone, the temperature felt more like winter than fall. He carried Melissa so her tiny, mincing steps would not slow them down.

The Heitschmidt house, the most German-looking residence in town, gleamed white. Strips of wood in a contrasting golden color decorated its upper story instead of the more popular frilly gingerbread. The interior reflected the same aesthetic: sturdy, attractive pieces, but no unnecessary accents. Kristina had always liked things plain and simple, just like her mother before her. No fuss. No clutter.

Wesley took a seat on one end of the black upholstered sofa, and James perched in the other. Kristina hurried into the kitchen to put the finishing touches on the lunch. Melissa trailed after her.

"So, Wes, what do you think of the new pastor?" James asked, and the sharpness in his tone told Wesley that his daughter's interest in the young man had not gone unnoticed.

"I've only talked to him a bit," Wesley admitted, "but he seems decent enough. I don't have any reservations about him so far."

"I think he's a good fellow," James said, his expression suspiciously blank.

"Yes, I agree," Wesley replied. "Just what we need, but he won't stay single for long."

"He won't," James agreed. "I hope Kristina doesn't get hurt." The movement of James's freckled face suggested he was chewing on the inside of his cheek.

"Encourage her to be open to him," Wesley said. "He's just as interested in her."

"That's hard for me," James replied, his mouth relaxing into a dejected frown.

"I know. I can only imagine, but isn't it best for her?"

James dipped his chin in a curt nod and let the oblique conversation drop. A few minutes later Kristina stuck her head into the room and called them to lunch.

Chapter 3

"Good morning," Rebecca said softly, smiling her serene smile at her favorite gentleman. *He's so kind to build my new shop a sales counter.* Her stomach fluttered, but she fought not to let her thoughts show on her face. *There's no point dreaming so don't make yourself crazy.*

"Miss Spencer." James nodded, giving her a wry half-smile.

"I really do appreciate your help," she said, though his formality had her wondering.

"Any time."

He set his tool kit on the floor and shrugged off his coat. *So many women drool over a young man, but even though he's mature, James handles his heavy wooden box and its cumbersome load of tools with ease. I suppose all those years of hefting cans, barrels and other oddments in his store have kept him strong.*

He gifted her with a grin, which dimpled his cheeks and set his freckles rolling into the creases around his eyes, before going to work on the crate containing the pieces of medium-sized pine block that would eventually form the basis of her business.

He looked a bit incongruous surrounded by racks of ready-made dresses, shelves of fabric and lace, and little tables littered with sample books. The walls, instead of being adorned with wainscoting or wallpaper, were hung with a soft periwinkle fabric that contrasted cheerfully with the pale pine floors. *I love this place. It's everything a lady might want when selecting new clothes.*

I also really love James being here. If only…

Rebecca sighed. *There's no hope James will ever care for me in that way, so I would be better off simply to enjoy having a handsome man care for me as a friend and help me when I need it.*

Two weeks passed normally. On good days, Wesley walked down the street to the bank without concern. Other days, he treaded lightly around his wife and hoped not to set her off. He was mostly successful; that is, until two Thursdays later.

His mother had come over for an unannounced visit, and her usual grumpy comments about the sloppy housekeeping and substandard food sent Samantha into a flurry of furious despair. After Mrs. Fulton left, the younger woman attacked her husband and daughter in a vicious torrent of curses and vile insults. Then she started hitting. Once again, Wesley gathered up his daughter and fled, this time finding the café open and Reverend Williams inside, sipping tea and looking thoughtful.

The promising courtship between the young pastor and Kristina seems to have fizzled, which makes sad… but then again, my life is sad, so what's one more match on the fire?

The two men gulped hot beverages and munched toasted sandwiches together in glum silence, saying nothing while Melissa chattered on.

At last, Melissa fell silent when a large sugar cookie arrived at the table for her.

Cody finally decided to speak. "Wes, what am I doing wrong with the choir?" he demanded in his soft, Texas drawl, his blue eyes pleading. "Everything else is going so well. Why won't the choir do what I ask?"

I know what Cody means, and I know the answer. I hope the pastor's willing to hear it. "We're too used to Kristina," he told him bluntly, "and to be honest, she's a better director than you. If you want the choir to do well again, give it back to her."

Cody blinked a couple of times. "Is it really appropriate for a woman to be teaching men that way?"

Wesley snorted. "Teaching? Cody, all she does is wave her arms around. It's not indecent, and she's really good at it. I'd suggest you let her do it. You'll never get the results she does. Your gifts are in other areas."

Cody studied him in silence. Apparently, the internal gears that churned out amazing sermons had ground to a halt at this unexpected idea. "I've never known a town like this, for letting women take on men's roles," Cody commented at last, his eyebrows low.

"We're a small community," Wesley reminded him. "Everyone is allowed to do what needs to be done. We don't have enough people to only delegate tasks to the men when there are willing, talented women to do some of them. I'll say it again. If you want a good choir, let Kristina lead it. And if you want to fit in here, don't try to change things that work."

Cody nodded. "That's good advice. Thank you for your honesty. Everyone else I've asked has talked about giving people time to adjust. That didn't feel quite right."

"Because it isn't. You will need to give people time to adjust, but they'll only do it if you focus on what truly needs to be done."

Cody sighed. "You're right. Could you... tell me some more about Miss Heitschmidt? I seem to have gotten onto her bad side, and I don't even know what I've done. It's pretty important for the music leader and the pastor to get along."

I have an opinion about that, too, but I'm not about to butt in. My track record is miserable, and I'd be a hypocrite to say a word. "I think you should talk to her, not me. She's a reasonable woman for the most part, but she has a German temper. If she's frozen up on you, there's a reason, but she won't hide what it is. I've gotten on her bad side a time or two over the years, and this is what I've learned. Just let her say what's on her mind and don't argue with her about it. I think that will help a lot."

Cody considered, and his face took on a look Wesley recognized; the bewildered emotion of someone more than halfway in love and not sure what to do about it. *If Kristina doesn't let that temper of hers take over, she still has a chance.*

Then, a more pressing issue occurred to Wesley. He glanced at his daughter, who focused intensely on the table, where she was using the crumbs of sugar cookie to create a tiny row. "Um, Pastor..." he said in an undertone. Melissa showed no sign of having heard his soft comment.

"Cody, please, Wes," the pastor replied full-voiced.

Wesley touched his fingertip to his lips and indicated his daughter with a sideways movement of his head. The pastor dipped his chin in acknowledgment.

"Cody then. I… um… I'm having some trouble with um… with my marriage." *I hate admitting it out loud, even in a near-whisper, but the situation is beyond me and getting worse. There seems to be no solution. How can I let my princess live like this day after day? It will destroy her in the end.*

"Well, I'm sorry to hear that," Cody said softly, though he didn't sound in the least surprised. Gossip and small towns went hand in hand after all. "I don't know what advice I could possibly give you, though."

"No one does," Wesley replied, "but I would appreciate some prayer."

"Now that I can manage," Cody replied. "I promise to pray for a solution. I really do think God wants marriages to be happy." The young man's blue eyes went misty and far away, and Wesley knew he was imagining what a happy marriage would be like, preferably with a sweet, freckle-faced musician.

As lunch was over, the men had parted company soon afterwards and Wesley headed home, only to find Samantha gone. *I suppose she goes to her lover when she wants revenge on me,* he reflected, *but honestly, I don't care. When she's in that mood, anything is better than having her around. It feels like surrender, but such is the reality of my life.*

She didn't return home the entire weekend, which was the longest she'd ever been gone. On Monday morning, there was still no sign of Samantha, which presented Wesley with a problem: what to do with Melissa while he worked. *Mother's not an option. She told me, in no uncertain terms, that the daughter of 'that stupid slut' will never be her responsibility.* This left only one possibility. To set up some paper and pencils in the corner of the office and keep her there.

She colored happily throughout the morning, and they ate lunch at the café. They were just settling comfortably into an afternoon of the same when the bell above the bank door jangled and Sheriff Brody clomped in, his boots loud on the floorboards. He made a beeline for the open door of Wesley's office, and the grim expression on his face made Wesley's stomach clench.

"Mr. Fulton, I'm afraid I have very bad news for you."

"What is it?" Wesley asked, his voice barely above a whisper. His stomach dropped to somewhere around the vicinity of his knees.

"It's about your wife."

The swooping sensation turned to a queasy churning. *Oh Lord, what has that woman done now? Assaulted someone? I wouldn't put it past her.* "What about her? What happened?"

The sheriff's broad shoulders sagged, and his mouth followed the downward curve of his salt and pepper mustache, into a grief-stricken frown.

A sensation of trembling, icy fear took hold of Wesley. *Something worse than an assault. Did she accidentally kill someone?* He remembered the time she'd waved a knife at him, during an argument while she was cooking.

"She..." Brody stopped, swallowed, and tried again. "She fell through the ice on the river."

Wesley's brain rejected the comment, it was so far from what he'd imagined. "The ice on the river is too thin to stand on. Why would she have been there?"

"I have no idea why," Brody replied, "but the fact is that she was."

"Is she all right?" Wesley shot from his chair and circled the desk to stand in front of the sheriff.

"Wes," Brody said, his heavy hand wrapping around Wesley's shoulder, "she's dead. It looks like she's been there a while, maybe since yesterday morning."

Buzzing sounded in Wesley's ears. *Dead. Samantha's dead. How could she be dead? It isn't possible. She's young, and while her wits are scattered, her body is healthy. Was healthy. Now she's dead. Drowned. A violent, painful end to a painful life.*

Wesley's stomach wrapped itself in a painful knot. "Excuse me," he muttered, before hurrying through the bank to the water closet. He barely made it.

When his fit of gagging finally ended, he staggered back through the spacious lobby of the bank to his office. Sheriff Brody was there, but this time so was Allison, clutching Melissa.

"Wes," was all she said as she threw herself against him. His arms came around her and his daughter and he trembled violently.

"Wesley," Brody said in a grim voice, "I'm terribly sorry, but I have to ask you a few questions."

He numbly looked up at the Sheriff's face, not really taking in what he was seeing.

"Sheriff," Allison said gently, "he's in shock. You don't think he had anything to do with…"

The sheriff cut her off with a gentle wave of the hand. To Wesley, the movement seemed to wobble, as though looking through water… *or ice. Oh, Lord.* He swallowed hard against another retch.

"Of course not," Brody assured her. "That's not what I meant. I just need to know what I should do with the body."

"Bring her home," Wesley told him firmly. "Bring her home. That's where she belongs." His voice broke.

The sheriff nodded and walked out.

Wesley's control slipped again. A sound like the mewl of a kitten crept from his chest.

"Come on, Wes," Allison said. "You need to get out of here."

He scooped Melissa onto his hip, took Allison's offered arm and let her lead him away.

"Wesley's had bad news," Allison called to the clerk. "He's going home and won't be back for a while. You carry on as normal."

Later, he could never remember the details of that walk; whether the wind blew, whether sun or clouds dominated the sky. His only memories were Allison's arms around his waist and Melissa's around his neck. They entered the front door as the Wade Charles, the sheriff's deputy, was leaving.

"Where is she?" Wesley asked.

"In the front bedroom," Charles replied, pointing overhead. For some reason, it seemed vital that he see Samantha *now*. Wesley brushed past the man, manners forgotten, and he carried Melissa up in a rush, Allison trailing behind him.

In the guest bedroom at the front of the house, Samantha had been laid out on the sunny yellow quilt, her hands folded on her bosom, her eyes closed. Her skin was ugly and grey.

The buzzing in Wesley's head intensified and spots floated across his field of vision. Bit by bit, the implications of this event began to dawn on him. *No more violent outbursts. No more wild mood swings. No more pitying glances from my wife's lovers. I'm free.* For a moment, a sensation of relief passed over him. *Life without Samantha will be so much easier... won't it?*

But wait, who will take care of Melissa when I'm at work? And without Samantha's admittedly unappealing cooking, will we eat? Sandwiches and oatmeal will not hold us indefinitely. What kind of man feels relief over the death of his wife? What's wrong with me?

An arm crossed his field of vision. Allison had removed a handkerchief from the bureau drawer and spread it over Samantha's discolored face. It didn't move.

"She's not breathing," he said stupidly. *Of course, she's not breathing, idiot. She's dead!* Overwhelmed, Wesley sank into a chair in the corner of the room, clutched Melissa to his chest, and burst into ragged sobs.

A soft hand came to rest on his shoulder.

"Wes, Wesley..." Allison sought his attention, but grief and guilt had bowled him under. *This is my fault. I knew Samantha shouldn't be left. I knew she was unstable. I failed her, failed to protect, honor, or cherish her. I failed as a husband, and I'm about to fail as a father, too.*

"I'm going to get some help. Wait for me." The sound of Allison's footsteps grew softer as she retreated down the hallway.

Wait for her? As if I'm able to do anything else.

How long he sat clutching his daughter and choking on bitter sobs, he had no idea. It felt like an eternity, but eventually, he became aware of people in the room. A hand grasped his shoulder.

He turned and met the preacher's eyes, but no words passed between them. Wesley felt fragile, far too fragile to utter a word. Allison trailed her fingertips over his back, and he knew what he needed.

He handed Melissa to Cody and rose, grabbing his friend and crushing her to his chest. Inhaling the sweet, familiar Allison-scent of her—like clean laundry and woman—the world came back into focus a little... or rather, she did. *Here's something real, an anchor to reality.* Across the room, he heard Melissa and Cody talking, but didn't take in any of the words. He just concentrated on breathing, on holding Allison and on trying to keep from shattering.

The next sound to register on his senses was the clatter of more boots on the floor planks. "Son?"

He glanced up. His mother swam before his watering eyes, along with Kristina Heitschmidt. *My loved ones are rallying around me,* he realized in dull surprise. "Mama, she's..." he started, but as usual Mrs. Fulton didn't wait for anyone. She took charge, pushing Allison away from him and hugging him herself.

Conversation swirled around him unheeded, and then Melissa thrust herself into his arms and they all stumbled from the room. He allowed arms he did not attempt to connect with faces to lead him back down to the parlor and into a seat. Bodies compressed the sofa on beside him. "This is my fault," Wesley said at last.

"No," his mother's voice protested. The room slowly came into focus and he saw her to his right. "It was an accident. She went through the ice. You know that."

"Why was she out on the ice? Everyone knows it's not safe. The river never freezes hard enough to stand on. It must have been intentional." *Oh, Lord. Did I really say that out loud? I didn't mean to.*

"Wesley," Cody crouched in front of him, meeting his eyes, "that doesn't make it your fault."

"I knew she was... unstable. She's... tried things before. I shouldn't have left her. It's enough I work all day. There's no way I should be doing these other things; going to church, being a deacon. She never liked it," Wesley babbled in an unstoppable gush.

"You could have brought her with you," Cody reminded him.

"She wouldn't go. Called them a bunch of two-faced hypocrites. There was... gossip, about her, at the church. They weren't nice to her there." Wesley fell silent again.

"I'm sorry to hear that," Cody told him. "I would never have permitted it. I promise you, Wesley, she's going to have a beautiful funeral, right there at the church, and I don't care what anyone says about it."

A rattling noise diverted attention to the doorway, where Kristina stood holding a tray of cups and tea accessories in shaking hands. Mrs. Fulton jumped from the sofa and rescued the tea service before Kristina could drop it. Plunking back onto the sofa with the tray on her lap, she poured a cup and handed it to him.

He didn't drink, just held the warm cup in his unsteady hands. "Pastor, I..." Wesley began hesitantly, trying to engage in the reality around him. "What am I going to do? How can I take care of Melissa alone?"

"Wesley, I'm going to be real honest here," Cody replied, and his softly-drawling voice oozed like healing ointment over the raw wound in Wesley's spirit. "I'm not sure exactly how you're going to make your life work now. Things will change, that's for certain, but you'll never be alone."

Wesley handed the untouched tea back to his mother and buried his face in his hands.

"Let's pray," Cody suggested. "Lord God, we cry out to you today for your comfort for Wesley. Help him, Lord. Remind him he's not alone. He has friends and family who love him, and you will never leave him." The young pastor paused, took a breath and began to recite scripture. " 'The Lord is my shepherd. I shall not want.' "

" 'He maketh me lie down in green pastures.' " Kristina joined him. " 'He leadeth me beside the still waters. He restoreth my soul.' "

A third voice chimed in. Allison, holding Melissa, entered into the room and sat down beside her best friend, taking his other hand. " 'He leadeth me down the paths of righteousness for his name's sake.' "

Wesley spoke too, his voice breaking. " 'Yea, thou I walk through the valley of the shadow of death, I shall fear no evil, for thou art with me. Thy rod and thy staff, they comfort me. Thou preparest a table before me in the presence of mine enemies. Thou anointest my head with oil.

Surely goodness and mercy shall follow me all the days of my life, and I will dwell in the house of the Lord forever.' "

Somehow, the familiar words steadied him, as the voices of so many people joined together to care for Wesley. Melissa's arms tightened around his neck, nearly strangling him, but he made no protest. Nor did Allison complain about the tight grip he maintained on her hand.

"Amen," Cody added. "That's where she is now, Wesley. In the house of the Lord. There's no better, safer place for her than there."

Wesley nodded. *Samantha's at peace at last, her troubles over. My own are only getting worse.*

I need something… what is it? That familiar scent wafted over him and he turned, crushing Allison and Melissa in another tight hug and letting the world slip away again.

Chapter 4

Allison stumbled home, blinded by tears, her heart aching with an almost physical pain. *Wesley seems destroyed by grief. My love, my friend, the only man I ever gave my heart to is hurting, and it hurts me too.*

The long steps from the Fulton house on the south side of town, to the Spencers' on the north, seemed to take a year. Icy wind pelted her with crumbled leaves and bits of dirt. She stumbled and nearly fell, barely managing to right herself. Leaning her hand against the slender trunk of an immature elm tree, she stopped moving and gave herself over to tears.

Around her, she could hear people talking, could hear them but could not take in what they were saying. They buzzed like flies on the windowsills of her mind, unnoticed and unimportant until a small warm hand grasped the hand she'd pressed against her cheek. A hug tightened around her.

Opening swollen eyes, she took in the wavery, undulating form of her sister. "Becky?"

"Yes, love. Come on, let's go home."

For such a small person, Becky possessed surprising strength. She wrapped Allison's arm around her shoulder and supported her as they made their way over the uneven street the last few blocks to their house. Becky wrestled her up the stairs and through the door.

Their mother met them inside. "Good heavens!" Mrs. Spencer exclaimed, leaping from the sofa where she'd perched behind her quilting frame. The movement knocked a strand of silver-laced golden hair from her perfect coiffure. It fell into the groove between her eyebrows, and she irritably pushed it away. "What is going on here? Allison, where have you been?"

"She's been with Wesley," Becky answered for her sister.

"With Wesley? For Heaven's sake, why, Allison?" Mrs. Spencer scolded, smoothing a strand of silver and gold hair away from her face.

"Don't you know how unseemly it is for you to be alone with a married man? I want you to stop doing that,"

"We weren't alone," Allison choked. "Reverend Williams and Kristina were there."

"Allison," her mother said, gentling her voice. "Wesley has a wife. You need to stop spending so much time with him. It does you no good."

"Actually, Mother," Becky interjected, "he doesn't."

"What? What do you mean?"

"Haven't you been anywhere today?" Becky asked.

At least that's what Allison thought she'd asked. She sank down on the sofa, face in her hands, and fought down the urge to succumb to hysterics again.

"No, I've been working on a quilt all day. It seemed too blustery to go outside," Mrs. Spencer said. "Why?"

"Mother," Becky rolled her eyes.

As though we have any other weather, Allison's mind added, though her lips refused to cooperate.

When Becky spoke again, her voice dropped to almost inaudible. "Samantha Fulton died. She fell through the ice on the river and drowned."

"Died!" Mrs. Spencer shrieked, and Allison gasped at the sudden noise. "Well, it must have been suicide. Everyone knows she was crazy."

Allison squeezed her burning eyes shut. A little part of her mind, the last bit that was still coherent, whispered to her. "Perhaps, Mother," she rasped, her throat hurting as much as her eyes, as much as her heart, "she didn't know what she was doing. We're all going to assume it was an accident, for Wesley's sake."

The sofa sagged as her mother sat beside her, taking her hand.

"All right," she said gently, at last. "We can assume that, but why does this upset you so very much, Allison? You weren't her friend. She..."

"You don't have to remind me what she did." Allison hissed. "I don't want to think about it now."

"Mother," Becky said, coming to sit on her sister's other side, "I think Allison is hurting because Wesley is hurting. Those two still have a deep connection."

"Bah," Mrs. Spencer scoffed unsympathetically, "that connection should have been cut years ago, the first time Fulton lowered his trousers for another woman."

"Mother!" Becky exclaimed, aghast at Mrs. Spencer's insensitivity.

A flood of images tumbled through Allison's mind: Wesley kissing Samantha, stretching out in bed with Samantha, holding Samantha. All the years that should have gone to *Allison* had gone to that woman. Now, in her death, Samantha had dealt yet another blow to her rival by breaking Wesley's heart.

Sickened, Allison wrenched herself from the sofa and stumbled up the stairs.

"Goodness, Mother," Becky said, sarcasm dripping from her normally gentle voice. "You certainly handled *that* well. Why can't you stop going on about Wesley? He's certainly more than paid for his mistake."

"But has he learned from it?" Mrs. Spencer asked, turning to her older daughter, undaunted by the disapproving tone. "Will he expect Allison to fall into his arms now that he's free? I don't want her to do that."

"You'd rather she remain a spinster, then?" Becky asked. "It's a blessing to them both that Samantha is gone. I know that's a terrible thing to say, but it's true. She should have been in an institution, not married. It's only by the grace of God their daughter is normal."

"If she's even his daughter," Mrs. Spencer pointed out. "I think she must not be. Mrs. Fulton is more than half-crazy herself. A baby from her son and *that woman* would not have been so healthy."

"Mother!" Becky protested, though in the back of her mind she acknowledged there was a lot of truth in what Mrs. Spencer was saying, "that's enough. Don't say anything else about Wesley *or* Samantha. You're going to hurt your daughter even worse."

"You know, I don't understand you," her mother said, her mouth turning down into a sneer. "How can you forgive Wesley so easily, after what he did?"

"I don't know," Rebecca replied, "he's always seemed like such a little boy to me. I'm not surprised he's made some mistakes. You know he's only twenty-four, same as Allison. When he did… what he did, he was barely nineteen. That's the age for making foolish decisions."

Becky glanced at her mother's face. As always, the question lingered, unasked, in Mrs. Spencer's narrowed eyes, the tension around her mouth, but Becky wouldn't answer. She never had.

"I'm going to go upstairs now too. I need to be sure Allison is all right. Besides, it's late. Good night, Mother."

"Good night, Rebecca," Mrs. Spencer replied, her cerulean gaze still sharp as a razor on her daughter's retreating back.

That evening, Melissa cried herself to sleep in his arms in the rocking chair and he tucked her into her bed. Slowly returning to his bedroom, he regarded the rumpled bed and gulped. The sheets hadn't been changed in a while. The scent of Samantha, of the perfume he'd bought her, and their last lovemaking a few days before her death, wafted up to him. She was gone from the guest bedroom now, her body at the church prepared for the next day's funeral. The bedding on which she'd lain had been removed. The bare mattress had seemed to glare accusingly at him, so he'd shut the door, locking it behind him.

Now I have to strip this bed, too. There's no way I'll be able to sleep bathed in the scent of my wife… my late wife. No, I'll have to remove it all.

He folded the sheets and blankets and carried them down the hall to the guest room. Tossing them inside, he shut the door again and returned to his room. Now he had another bare bed to deal with. He began hunting for bedding. *Where do most people keep sheets and blankets? In a linen closet or a clothes press.* They were in neither. *Under the bed?* No. *In the wardrobe?* No. *I know there are more pieces somewhere. Samantha never put anything anywhere sensible.* At last, he opened her bureau drawers one by one and found sheets in the bottom, with piles of chemises on top of them.

Rolling his eyes, he quickly made up the bed before continuing the hunt for more quilts. A sudden memory had him creeping into Melissa's room, where, sure enough, a pile of quilts sat in the bottom of her wardrobe with dirty boots on top. He reached down to the second quilt in the pile, a navy one with gold stars on it, and carried it back to his bedroom. At last, he had a clean, fragrance-free bed to sleep in Yawning, he climbed between the sheets in his long, gray union suit underwear, trying to relax.

"Mama! Mama!" Soft sobs rang through the house. Sighing, Wesley hauled himself out of bed and into Melissa's bedroom. Without a word, he scooped the weeping toddler into his arms and carried her back into his bedroom, tucking her into the bed beside him.

For tonight, neither of us wants to be alone. Just for tonight...

Wesley passed the rest of the week in a daze. On Sunday, he somehow found clothes and pulled them on. He'd managed to give Melissa a bath and dress her, though her hair was a mess. He knew nothing about long hair. They'd eaten oatmeal porridge again, and now were making their way to church.

He'd been there earlier in the week for the funeral. Samantha, wearing her favorite pink dress, surrounded by golden mums, had been laid to rest in a service that was breathtaking in its tender beauty. *Poor Samantha was treated with more kindness in death than she'd ever received in life. And then, after the funeral, the heavens unleashed a torrent of snow that buried the whole town.*

He'd held and rocked Melissa as the storm raged, and then tried to put her down in her own bed again, only to be awakened by her crying over and over throughout the night. About three in the morning, he'd given up and taken her back to his bed. There, they'd succumbed to utter exhaustion until dawn woke them, light sparkling on the surface of the three-foot snowdrifts piled against the sides of buildings.

He carried Melissa through the messy streets to the church, noting how even the sparkling of the sun on the crusty surface of the snow failed to lighten his mood. *Each day grows harder than the one before, and I haven't been back to work yet. Melissa will be content to color in the corner of my office for a day or two, but I can't bring her there every day until she's old enough to start school.* He climbed the church's rickety wooden steps and tugged on the iron door handle, hissing as the cold metal stung his bare hand. *I need help,* he admitted as the warmth of the stove enveloped him in welcoming comfort, *but where can I find it?*

Seated on the red cushion that covered his usual pew, Melissa perched on his lap, he noticed for the first time that the church was decorated for Christmas. A large tree had been adorned with candles and gilded ornaments. The communion rail sported a cheerful garland of evergreen boughs and bright red bows. *Christmas has nearly arrived, and Melissa will have to face the holiday with no mother to care for her.*

The organ began to play the opening hymn, and Wesley shook his head as the lilting whistles of the pipes drowned out his endless ruminations and dragged his thoughts to the present. He sang, a little raggedly, and couldn't help but smile as Melissa fumbled through the semi-familiar lyrics.

Then Cody stepped into the pulpit and began the morning announcements. At the end of the usual committee meetings and prayer requests, he added "Friends, in the short time I've been here, you've made me feel welcome, and I thank you, but no one has done more to facilitate my integration than Miss Kristina Heitschmidt. Therefore, I have decided to make her a permanent part of my life by marrying her. To my very great surprise, she has agreed. More details will be provided later," Cody continued, "and I sincerely hope all of you will wish us well. And now, if you would take your Bibles and turn to Psalm 57. We will read responsively, whole verse by whole verse."

Wesley was still trying to close his gaping jaws as his fingers fumbled to the center of the pew Bible. *I knew from the beginning that Cody and Kristina belonged together, but to become engaged, just like that?* Then he smiled. *They'll be so good together. As good as Allison and I would have been, if only…*

" 'Be merciful unto me, O God, be merciful unto me…' " Cody began while Wesley clumsily fumbled one-handed for the correct page.

" 'I cry unto God most high,' " Wes responded in ragged unison with the rest of the congregation, speaking more by rote than by intention while his mind continued to wrestle with its unsolvable problems.

If only I'd married her, instead of Samantha, he finished, finally completing the thought that had haunted him for the last four years. *But I didn't, and now everything has changed.*

" 'For thy mercy is great unto the heavens…' "

I need a drop of mercy, he thought. *I need a woman in my life, someone to do all the womanly things around the house. Someone to take care of Melissa. She already likes and trusts Allison, and so do I. If Allie would agree…*

Oh, Lord. If she would agree I can finally marry her. Finally have the perfect life I dreamed of for so long. But would she agree?

He stole a sideways glance at his friend as he tucked the Bible back into its pocket on the back of the pew in front of him and found her studying the pastor with an unreadable expression. Images of Allison as she'd once been, years ago before life turned to ashes, danced in his mind, arousing feelings of tender arousal and hope.

I don't know if she'll agree, but I have to find out. Tradition dictates I wait a year, but there's no way I can manage alone that long. I'll have to think about this carefully.

45

Chapter 5

Allison Spencer and her sister sat at the most level of the uneven tables at Lydia's café with the proprietress and Kristina Heitschmidt. The restaurant had closed a couple of hours ago and now the four ladies had gathered in the large, empty room. Outside the rows of massive windows, a stiff wind sent the twigs on the naked, stunted trees whipping, compounding the vision of a bleak, gray early December afternoon. Though the heat of the kitchen warmed the dining room, the chill seeped in around the door and windows. Allison cradled her cup of hot coffee with gratitude while the warm flavor of gingerbread cake heated her insides.

"I still just can't believe it," Lydia said, taking a sip of her tea. "How long have you two been courting in secret?"

"We haven't been," Kristina insisted. "We've been fighting for the longest time, almost since he first arrived."

"Well then, what happened?" Lydia asked.

Allison met Kristina's eyes briefly. *Should I mention the shocking sight I saw at church the other morning?* Kristina, half-dressed, sound asleep in Cody's arms on a pew cushion, which had been laid out beside the fire. *I suppose they behaved, that the snowstorm caught them together inside the church and nothing more, but it looked bad, and they've been talking of marriage ever since.*

She decided not to speak. *Let everyone think Cody and Kristina are marrying because they want to, not because they compromised each other.* From the way the two of them now looked at each other, not to mention the sweet kisses they'd been caught sharing since then, it seemed that was the case anyway.

On one hand, I'm truly delighted for her. Since her teenage years, Kristina has been convinced that no one would marry a red-haired, freckle-faced woman. I've never agreed with her assessment. Now, pink-cheeked and smiling a silly, woman-in-love smile, Kristina was engaged to quite a startlingly handsome man. A man who treated her like the priceless treasure she was. *There's no bad part of, not even the quick pace. A wintertime wedding will be lovely.* Despite her joy, desperate jealousy gnawed on Allison's guts. *Not because of Cody. Handsome though he is, Reverend Williams does not make my heart beat faster. He'll make a perfect husband for Kristina, but I don't want him. I want Wesley.*

All these years after his betrayal, she still loved him with all her heart, with every fiber of her being. Allison suffered another pang of horrible guilt, as she had ever since Samantha's death. *I never liked the woman, never wished her well, and now she's dead, and Wesley destroyed. He must have loved his wife after all, and not me anymore.*

"You know," Becky said, forcing Allison's attention back to the conversation, "it's quite fashionable to wear all white for a wedding these days, and you would look marvelous in it, Kristina."

"I love the idea," Kristina said, blushing furiously at the compliment. "Is there really time to make a dress? The wedding is only a week away, but I do like simple things ..."

"No, there's no time for a whole dress," Becky told her bluntly, "but I know you have white shirtwaists. If you wore one of those, I would have time to make you a white skirt to go with it."

Kristina beamed. "Perfect. I love the idea. I can look like myself, only a little more... dressed up."

"Do you have white shoes?" Becky asked.

"Oh..." Kristina pondered for a moment. "No. I have light grey ones. They'll have to do."

Becky shrugged. "Close enough. It's much too late to order new shoes."

"I like the statement all white makes," Allison commented.

"So do I," Kristina replied. "I mean, you all know what happened, right?"

Oho, so she's going to spill the beans, after all, is she? Allison allowed amusement over her friend's adventure to lift her spirits.

Becky and Lydia shook their heads.

"There's been some gossip," the café owner said, "but I don't believe a word of it. As if you or the pastor would behave in such a way."

"Here's the unvarnished truth," Kristina replied. "I was caught outside in the blizzard and barely made it to the church. I think I nearly froze to death. I was getting sleepy." The ladies shuddered. Everyone knew what that meant. "Cody was inside, and we were trapped there alone together until morning. So yes, we were 'compromised,' but we didn't do anything wrong. We talked, worked out our problems, and agreed that since we would have to get married anyway, we might as well be happy about it."

"Did he kiss you?" Lydia asked, wide-eyed.

"Yes," Kristina replied, cheeks flaming again. "More than once. But nothing more, I swear."

"Oh, well that's fine then. Certainly not worth gossiping about," Lydia said.

"I agree," Kristina replied firmly. "And that makes the white wedding even more meaningful since there is some gossip. I want to make a statement that I have nothing to feel guilty about."

"Yes," Becky agreed, "I think you should, and I have just the skirt in mind. You'll be stunning."

"What about the reception?" Lydia asked. "Will you want to have a wedding dinner? Do you have a location in mind?"

Kristina shook her head. "My house has small rooms. I don't think the reception can take place there. It would be awfully crowded, and as for the vicarage..." She blinked a couple of times.

She's not wrong there. One modest-sized room, and everyone staring at the bed. Allison stifled a giggle. *No, the wedding dinner can't be held there.*

"Then have it here," Lydia suggested. "I can provide some food and the cake. It will be my gift to you."

"Oh, no. I can't let you do that. I'll pay for the food," Kristina protested.

The two women looked at each other, stubborn Italian against equally stubborn German. Then Lydia laughed. "All right, Kristina. Pay for the food. I'll gift you with the cake."

Kristina grinned. "Perfect."

Allison couldn't help but smile, genuinely this time, despite her anguish. *The joy of my friend's happiness is more important than my own dashed hopes.* She looked around the table. Kristina smiled the same, silly smile, her short nose wrinkled with cheer. Lydia's round, pink cheeks showed deep dimples as she grinned broadly. Then Allison met her sister's eyes. For just a moment, deep misery shone like tears in the azure depths. Becky looked as though she might burst into sobs at any moment. Then the sad look disappeared, replaced by the serene smile. *What on earth was that expression?* Allison couldn't imagine, so she forced her attention back to the wedding discussion again.

"Allison?" Kristina addressed her directly. "You will stand up with me, won't you?"

"Yes, of course," she replied. "I'm honored. What should I wear?"

"Something to coordinate with the Christmas decorations, I suppose." Then she chopped the air with her hand in frustration. "You have good taste. Wear what you want."

Of course, discussions of dresses can't interest Kristina for long. She's a musician to the bone, and female fripperies mean nothing to her.

Focusing on the moment, Allison mentally scanned her wardrobe. *A vibrant burgundy skirt and pelisse will do the trick nicely. With black boots and my cameo pin. I'm all set for the wedding.* Except her heart, which was aching that her friend's dreams were coming true while hers never would.

That evening, Allison sprawled in the chair in Becky's bedroom. Becky brushed her younger sister's hair again. *Hmm, what would look best on Allison for the wedding? A twist? A knot? A coronet?*

As Becky contemplated the styles, Allison chattered on, half-heard. *I'm not paying attention,* she admitted to herself. As usual, her silly mind had slipped away to thoughts of James Heitschmidt. *I can't help but wonder how my friend is coping with his daughter's forced marriage.*

I hope to find time to talk to him soon. I've been so busy lately with my shop, and he with the general store, it's hard to get together, particularly as I don't want to appear to be mooning over him.

"Becky," Allison's hand closed around her sister's wrist, startling her back to reality.

"What is it, Allie?" she asked.

"I've been trying to get your attention for a while. Where were you just now?"

Heat prickled across Becky's cheeks, and she knew she was blushing. "Nowhere interesting," she mumbled.

"Ha," Allison replied, "I think it was somewhere *very* interesting. C'mon sis, tell me. You know I won't tell. What makes you go so far away... or should I say *who*?"

Allison sees too much. "I'm being silly," Becky replied. "There's no reason why I should be dreaming about any man. Especially not this one..."

"Ah, so it *is* a man?"

"Yes," Becky admitted. "I'm human. Even though it's hopeless, he's so special I couldn't help falling..." She sputtered to a halt.

"Falling in love with him?" Allison guessed.

Becky nodded stiffly.

Allison shook her head. "Why is that bad, sis? You deserve it, too."

"I don't," Becky replied. "He's a pillar of the community. He deserves... better."

"Better than being loved by the sweetest, prettiest woman in town?" Allison insisted, turning around as far as the chair would permit and meeting her sister's eyes directly. "He's a man, not a god, Becky. So, who is this paragon?"

Becky gulped. "I'd rather not say."

"Please?" Allison begged, suddenly sounding like a ten-year-old child.

In Becky's mind, sometimes she still seemed like she was. *But that's silly. She could as easily be married as I could. She could have been a mother by now if only our lives hadn't veered so far off course.* "Promise you won't tell?"

"I swear."

"It's... well... it's..." she broke off, embarrassed.

"It's whom?" Allison pressed.

"James," Becky forced out at last.

Allison blinked. "James Heitschmidt? Kristina's father?"

Becky nodded.

"Oh wow," Allison said. And then neither of them said anything else.

Chapter 6

Rebecca sat on one of the comfortable upholstered seats in her dress shop, pinning pieces of a pattern to white satin. She sat back in her chair while she worked, her arms fully extended so she did not lean over the fabric. It was an awkward way to sew, but she didn't want the tears that streamed constantly down her cheeks to stain the fabric.

The bell over the shop door chimed, and Rebecca looked up from her work to see James Heitschmidt. She drank in the sight of him: tall and broad-shouldered, with a shock of reddish-blond hair and a firm-jawed face dotted with freckles. Warm, friendly brown eyes wreathed in smile lines met hers. She gulped and wiped her eyes.

Before she could even react to his presence, he appeared directly beside her, taking her hand in his. "Miss Spencer, is everything all right?"

Oh, he's so warm, she realized as his calloused fingers stroked softly over her skin. "I'm fine, Mr. Heitschmidt."

"But you're crying."

"It's nothing. I'm just feeling sorry for myself, that's all." She urged him to a seat in the chair beside her.

"You, Rebecca? I can hardly imagine it. Why?"

She closed her eyes. He'd rarely used her first name before, but it sounded wonderful in that deep, rumbling voice of his. She ran her thumb over his knuckle once. "Well, it's Kristina. Her wedding, you know."

He regarded her with wistful chocolate eyes.

She smiled sadly, knowing what he was feeling. "It's best for her," she said gently.

"I know," he replied, "but I'll miss her."

"The good part is, she's only going two blocks away."

He sighed. "So why does Kristina's wedding make you sad?"

"Can't you guess?" she asked, and her own bitter tone surprised her, as did her willingness to admit something so personal to him. "She's so much younger than me, and she's getting married. I'll never get married. Never have a family of my own."

"I never realized you wanted one." His eyes gleamed with amber intensity.

"Of course, I do, James. I'm not different from any other woman."

"But, Rebecca, if you wanted a husband, why didn't you marry?" he demanded, eyebrows lowered in confusion. "You're lovely, intelligent and kind. Many men would you."

"It's kind of you to say, James, but no one would have me now. I'll never be able to marry." Her cheeks warmed, but she met his eyes steadily.

His eyebrows drew even closer together, an angry, sandy line like a storm riding on a sea of freckles. "But why would they not? The way you say that sounds like…"

She broke eye contact, looking back down at the satin. "Like the truth, most likely," she dared admit, and her blush gave way to pallor.

James seized her hand again. "What happened, Rebecca?"

"Do I really have to say it? I was betrothed. Years ago, when I was seventeen. He seduced me, then he left. Ran away with one of the Fulton girls. I never saw him again. I thought we would be married. I didn't realize he was playing a game with me, but after that, I knew no man would ever have honorable intentions towards me again. Men want a virgin bride, and I could no longer supply that…" She sniffled once and then clamped down on her unruly emotions, squeezing her eyes closed against a sudden burn.

Why did James demand to know my humiliation? And why did I tell him? He's certain to look at me differently now that he knows of my wanton behavior. He's too much of a gentleman to bandy my shame about, but it will affect our relationship. There would be no more kind talk, no more admiring glances.

"Rebecca," he said, his voice tender.

She opened her eyes and met his, confused by the intensity she saw there. "I think you're making too much of that event. I mean, not every man cares if he marries a virgin. Some men marry widows, after all."

"A widow is respectable. She gave herself in marriage. She's not a slut who…"

"A slut?" he interrupted. "Because of one mistake? Hardly. So that's why you never married, then?"

She nodded, looking away.

He grasped her chin with his free hand and turned her back, so she met his eyes. He captured her with them, as though with a magic spell. "Are you opposed to the idea of marriage, Rebecca? I mean, if a man were interested in courting you, would you be open to it?"

She shook her head. "I couldn't. I would have to tell him… what I just told you, and it was hard enough with you, even though you've been my friend for so long. And then it would all be over anyway, so what would be the point? No. I'm not open to being courted." A tear streaked down her face.

James wiped it away with his fingertips. "But you want to be, don't you?"

"Doesn't everyone?" she burst out. "I'm not happy being a spinster. That's the consequence for my bad behavior. I accept it, but I don't like it."

"But, Rebecca, there's every likelihood a man would be willing to overlook such a mistake. I mean, it's long in the past—years past—and you're a lovely and compelling woman. You don't have to be alone."

She turned away again, and when she spoke, her voice filled with anger she could not suppress. "Stop it, James. I don't want to discuss it anymore. I can't dare to hope. It would crush me. Please, don't talk to me about this mythical man who will forgive my mistake and love…" she broke off, not willing to continue. *I've revealed far too much already.*

"It's not a myth, Rebecca," he murmured, his lips so close to her ear, they actually touched the skin. Enticing tingles spread down her neck. "There is a man who cares deeply for you, who would love to court you, with honorable intentions, and would not care in the slightest about your mistake."

She swallowed. Turning, she faced him again, meeting his eyes from mere inches away. "Unless that man is you, I don't want to know any more."

"It's me." He closed the distance between them and laid his lips on hers.

Rebecca's eyes slid closed at the unexpected kiss. James pulled her to stand so he could crush her slender body in his arms. Thankful she had pulled the draperies, shutting out the street, she savored their privacy by slipping her arms around his neck. They kissed for long minutes, savoring what both had thought could never be.

When he finally released her, new tears spilled down Rebecca's cheeks. "Why didn't you ever say anything?" she demanded. "I've... cared for you so long. I thought you weren't interested."

"I'm interested, Rebecca. I have been for the longest time, but I thought you preferred to remain single. I also thought you were too young for me. I know this is an indelicate question, but aren't you just a little older than my daughter?"

"I'm a great many years older than your daughter. There are ten years between my sister and me, and she's older than Kristina. I'm thirty-five, James. How old are you?"

"Forty-five."

"You see, a decade difference between spouses is no great matter..." She sputtered to a halt. *Talking about spouses is a little much.*

He grinned. "You're right. Ten years is nothing. I thought it was closer to fifteen, but even then, I was about willing to suggest..."

"Even if it were fifteen, I would still say yes." She hugged him tight. "You're sure you don't mind about..."

He interrupted her again. "No, Rebecca. I don't mind. I had a virgin bride years ago, but things are different now; I don't need that again. I would choose you even if a virgin were available."

She rested her head against his chest and closed her eyes.

He stroked her back, cradling her in his arms.

Rebecca smiled through her tears. *Life is changing in the most wonderful, unexpected way.*

Wesley woke up early, sitting bolt upright, heart pounding. *Did I have a nightmare? What happened? Why do I feel like I'm forgetting something?* He inhaled deeply, trying to calm himself, but the feeling didn't fade.

Did I dream something unsettling? He wracked his brain, but nothing came to mind. *It seems like there really is something happening today, something I need to be part of, but what is it?*

Light and shadow shifted over his face as clouds passed between the sun and earth, and then a wintery ray broke through, beaming in his window with a flash of inspiration.

The wedding! Kristina and Cody's wedding. I need to be there. I'm the best man.

As he dressed in his black trousers, white shirt, and coat, he couldn't help thinking about Allison. Though he'd decided a week ago that he needed her, needed to ask her to reinstate the engagement he'd shattered years ago, he had not yet spoken to her. *She was hard to find— preparing for the wedding, I suppose—but I'm not giving up. Perhaps afterward I can talk to her in private.*

Conversation swirled around the cozy interior of Lydia's Café, where Kristina's friends stood in small groups, eating sandwiches and drinking coffee. Wesley leaned against the wall in the corner near where Melissa sat on the floor, picking little bites of cheese from inside her sandwich, but avoiding the ham. Scanning the room, he found his favorite lady, clad in a striking burgundy suit, her long, golden hair wrapped in a loose bun, smiling as she chatted with the bride.

Kristina has never looked so beautiful, he admitted to himself, *mostly due to the glow of joy on her face.*

Cody approached and pressed a cup of coffee into her hand, then wrapped his arm around her waist, leaning over to kiss her temple. Kristina's cheeks turned pink.

I've never seen her this happy. Cody's a lucky man and I hope to be half so lucky. As he watched, Kristina took several steps away from the milling center of the room. A gaggle of young women gathered into a knot. Kristina threw her bouquet of white roses directly to Allison, who, taller than the others, plucked them easily out of the air.

Perfect. "Stay there, princess," Wesley said to Melissa. She didn't acknowledge him, intent as she was on picking every scrap of cheese from her bread. He shook his head and approached Allison from behind, closing his hand around her arm.

She jumped.

"Sorry," he murmured in her ear. "Can you please come with me? I need to talk to you in private."

She turned to look at him. "Yes, all right."

"Are you ready now, or would you like to spend some more time here?"

Allison glanced at Kristina, just in time to see Cody scoop her up and carry her out the door to the cheers of the crowd. Blushing, Allison turned back to Wesley. "Let's go."

He gathered up his daughter and the three of them bundled on their coats and left the party. In the gathering darkness, the chill sank right through to the bone, and they hurried through the icy wind to Wesley's house, Melissa a dead weight in his arms.

Once they reached the entryway, dimly lit by the moon shining through the open door, he realized she had fallen into a sound sleep. *Precious little angel.*

He carried her up the stairs to her bedroom and stripped off her shoes. *This dress,* he realized, eyeing the scratchy pink lace concoction Becky had whipped up for the wedding, *will be no good to sleep in.* Already the places the stiff fabric touched Melissa's skin had reddened. *How do I get it off her without waking her up?*

Allison took the decision out of his hands, removing a flannel nightgown from the bureau and pulling Melissa's fancy dress from her plump little body. The little girl woke up as Allison tugged the nightgown over her head.

"Mama?"

"It's Aunty Allie, honey."

"Oh." Melissa wrapped her arms around Allison's neck. She burst into noisy tears. "I want Mommy," she whined.

"Hush, darling," Allison soothed, natural as any loving aunt. "Your mommy is always with you."

Unable to watch any more, Wesley left the room. *Allison has things well in hand, she always does. She's better with my own daughter than I am.*

Relieved, Wesley walked into the kitchen, hunted down a kettle and a cup from their strange locations, and brewed tea. The homey task kept his hands busy and his mind blank, though he couldn't stop his heartbeat from ticking off the seconds until he would initiate the second most difficult conversation of his life.

Leaning against the banister at the bottom of the stairs with the cup, he stared off into the darkness down the hallway, trying to plan his words. Soft footsteps on the scuffed treads attracted his attention. "Is she sleeping?" he asked, as Allison descended the stairs.

She grabbed his cup of hot tea and took a sip. "Yes. She's sleeping now."

Claiming his cup with one hand and her fingers with the other, he led the way into the parlor and urged her to sit on the sofa.

"Thank you, Allison. I don't know if I could take another night of her crying for her mother." Wesley admitted.

She slipped her arm behind his back and hugged him. "I'm sorry."

He shrugged, guilt and sorrow temporarily overwhelming his goal.

"How are you holding up," she asked.

He shook his head.

"Come on, Wes. We've been friends forever. We used to be engaged. Who else are you going to talk to?"

"I don't want to talk. I want to… do something. Anything. But what can I do? Sam is dead. She's dead, Allison. I failed her. I should have done more."

Allison's fingers threaded into the hair at the nape of his neck, softly stroking. "There's nothing more you could have done, Wes. She's gone.

That part is over. You can't worry about her anymore. The question is, what are you going to do for Melissa and for yourself?"

"Damned if I know," he replied. "I have to be back at work two days after Christmas. Missy's three. She's not even in school yet. Who will watch over her while I'm at the bank? Who will cook and take care of the house? I don't even know how to do those things. What can I do, Allison? I'm barely hanging on now. If I have to be at work all day…"

"What about your mother?"

He quirked an eyebrow at her, willing her to take the hint.

Her ferocious frown told him she understood. "I know, but at least she could watch over Melissa for a while as you figure out what's next."

"I already asked her," he said coolly.

"She didn't refuse?" Allison's lip dipped sharply downward.

Wesley nodded. "She said she's already spent enough of her life taking care of children and isn't going to use her 'golden years' to do more of the same. Especially not with 'that woman's child' "

Allison shut her mouth so tightly, her lips compressed into a disapproving line. "Wes, don't take this wrong, but I really don't like your mother."

He grinned wryly. "She doesn't like you either, Allie."

She lifted her shoulders briefly. "It used to worry me, but I don't care anymore."

"Are you sure about that?" he pressed. A heavy sensation flared in his chest, and the skin on his forehead prickled in spite of the cold.

Allison lowered her eyebrows. "I'm sure I no longer care whether your mother likes me. Our engagement ended when you married Samantha. Why on earth would her opinion matter to me now?"

"Well…" *This is too much,* he realized, nausea churning suddenly in his stomach. *I shouldn't even ask it of her. It would be taking advantage of our connection.* "No. Never mind." His eyes veered away from her face as his courage broke.

"What is it, Wes?" Allison placed her hand against his cheek and turned him back to face her. The warmth of her fingers sank soothingly into his skin.

He opened his mouth, shut it, opened it and tried again. A croak emerged, and he surrendered, again, to the impossibility of what he was about to suggest. "No, I can't, Allison. You shouldn't even be here alone. Your reputation…"

"Let me worry about my own reputation," she said. "What did you want from me?"

Wesley opened his mouth and closed it again.

"Wesley Fulton, for heaven's sake, speak. What is going through that mind of yours?" she demanded.

Out with it, Fulton. She wants to know, and she's a grown woman, not a child to be protected. Let her decide for herself. "It's just… well… I need a wife, Allison. I can't work and raise my daughter and take care of the house alone. There are only two women in the world I trust with Melissa, and Kristina just got married so…"

"So?"

"So, would you consider… reinstating our engagement?" *Good Lord, that sounds even worse than I expected. I'll be lucky if she ever speaks to me again.*

She blinked. "You mean when your year of mourning is up?"

He exhaled. The blast of his breath blew a wisp of golden hair back from her forehead. "No. That's too long; I need you now. I need you to care for my home and for you to be here with me. I need you after Christmas, to care for Melissa when I go back to the bank. Hell, I need you before Christmas, just so her first holiday without her mother isn't a total disaster."

She just looked at him, eyes wide and jaw slack.

"I know it's a lot to ask, but would you consider it, Allison? I need you."

She shook her head, not to say no, but as though to clear it, and put her hands over her face. "When?" she croaked.

"Tomorrow? Sunday? Whenever Cody can do it."

"Oh, Lord, Wes. You want the pastor to perform a wedding the day after his own?" She dissolved into hysterical giggles.

He turned away and regarded the window. Outside, black night had settled over the town. *Of course she would say no. It was a stupid idea.*

She pulled him back around again, forcing him to look into her eyes. *She has always had the most beautiful eyes.*

"Yes, Wesley."

A loud buzzing sounded in his ears as her lips formed the words. "Yes?" he croaked, the bullfrog returning to his throat.

"Yes. On one condition."

Wesley rubbed his jaw and temples, trying to get the buzzing to stop. It sounded like a thousand bees inside his head. "What condition?"

"It has to be a real marriage. I refuse to be your glorified housekeeper. It's all or nothing, Wes." Her pink cheeks told him she knew what she was saying. Then, for the first time in four years, she leaned forward and kissed him, briefly.

"Are you sure you want to do this?" he asked.

"Oh yes," she replied. "I agreed to marry you five years ago. A year later, I lost you. Now I have this opportunity. I'm not letting you go."

Wesley nodded.

"But if you go to bed with another woman, ever again..."

"I won't. I swear!" He grabbed her and kissed her, trying to tell her everything, all the confused, contradictory emotions roiling through him. She was the solution to all the problems he had and several he wasn't ready to admit to.

That night, Allison knocked on her sister's door. Becky answered, her long, blond hair tightly braided and hanging over her shoulder.

"Is everything all right?" she asked.

"Can I come in?" Allison pleaded. "I need to talk to you."

"Of course, Allie." Becky ushered her inside, shutting the door and urging her to a seat on the bed. "What's happening?"

"It's...well, it's Wesley." Allison's hands shook.

Becky noticed and grasped them. "What about him?"

"He..." She gulped. "He asked me to marry him."

Becky's serene smile remained firmly in place. "Well, when's the wedding then?" she asked, her eyes glazing over as she contemplated… something.

Probably dresses, Allison thought, *if I know anything about my sister.* "Sunday, after church, if Cody will agree."

Becky blinked several times, as though a vision had faded from her view. "Sunday? Like, the day after tomorrow? What will Mother say?"

"Oh, please, Becky, don't tell her," Allison begged. "She'll make a big fuss. This is meant to be, and exactly what I want."

Becky seemed to consider for a long time.

Allison began to feel like squirming with nerves.

"Fine," she said at last. "Far be it for me to get in the way. Just be careful, please?"

"All right," Allison agreed, though exactly what she was supposed to be careful about, she wasn't sure.

Chapter 7

Allison wasted no time putting the rash plan into effect. First thing in the morning, she hurried into a warm woolen dress and raced down the stairs with the finesse of an overly-excited child.

"Allison," her mother called from the kitchen, "are you all right? Do you want any breakfast?" The scent of coffee accompanying the words made her pause. *No. Too much is at stake. No time to dawdle.* "Sorry, Mom. I have to get to work," she replied, deliberately cryptic. Then she hurried out the door before any further arguments could be offered. *Or any further discussion,* she added to herself. *I have no intention of telling them what I have planned until it's irrevocable.*

She turned left onto Main Street and headed south toward the church, straight into a blast of cool—though no longer icy—wind. *They will not be pleased,* she admitted, tugging fragments of leaves from her hair as she moved forward toward her dreams, *but I've waited far too long for Wesley. Now that he wants to marry me, I'm going to make it happen, no matter what anyone says.*

Far down the street, she saw her soon-to-be husband's familiar, dark head appear from a side street, hair instantly blown into disarray. He emerged, holding Melissa's hand. Allison crossed the street heedlessly and ran to the vicarage in the shadow of the big church steeple. Wesley and his daughter hurried north to join her.

As they approached the door, Allison began to realize the potential awkwardness of their actions. *Cody and Kristina married yesterday. They might well be... busy, doing intimate things together. Oh, dear.* Her lifted hand faltered.

Wesley glanced at her, then knocked himself.

Blessedly, when Kristina opened the door, she was dressed and looking... almost her usual self. A hint of color in her cheeks suggested an interesting night, but she acted normal and not too flustered.

"Is Reverend Williams in?" Allison asked. "Sorry to barge in on you, but we need to talk to him."

"He went over to the church to prepare his sermon. I think he was distracted." A hint of a smirk appeared on Kristina's lips, and then faded into a blush.

"I'll go," Wesley offered.

"You two come on in," Kristina urged, opening the door wide and leading them into the cozy, single-room dwelling. "It's too windy to stand in the street. Would you like some tea?"

"Yes, please," Allison said eagerly, following her friend into the vicarage. Even given Kristina's tidy nature, the place seemed unnaturally clean, as though to hide the evidence of some kind of mischief. The bed had been made up too precisely, like an oh-so-innocent grin.

Allison looked away. *I guess Kristina lost her virginity before me. Good for her, but who would ever have guessed such an outcome?*

"No tea," Melissa pouted, tugging on Allison's hand. "Auntie Allie, I don't like tea."

"Of course not, darling," Kristina reassured her, approaching and crouching down to the child's eye level. "Let me get you a cookie instead. Here, have a seat at the table." She boosted Melissa into a chair and walked over to the cabinet. Pulling out a tin, she retrieved an oatmeal raisin cookie and brought it back to the child. "That's all right, isn't it?" she asked Allison.

And rightly so. If all goes according to plan, I'll be Melissa's mother soon. "Yes, it's fine."

As the girl nibbled the cookie, the two ladies sat down to cups of tea on the sofa.

"So, what's going on, Allison?" Kristina asked. "I assume you're here for a reason."

"Yes. Um, Wesley... he... he asked me to marry him."

Kristina quirked an eyebrow. "Are you sure you want that after... everything?"

So it begins. Everyone will ask this question, I have no doubt, but I can't blame her for checking. She, at least, is no busybody but a genuine friend who cares about my wellbeing. "Kristina, I've waited so long for this. You can't imagine how bad I want to marry Wes," she reminded her friend.

"I know you do, hon, but are you sure it's best for you?" The look of concern on her friend's freckled face made Allison want to cry.

"How could it not be?" she asked, firming her jaw into a look of intense stubbornness.

"Well, it's awfully fast..."

"I don't think you're one to lecture me about too fast," Allison interrupted archly, giving her friend a stony look.

Kristina's full lips compressed into an expression that might have been annoyance or might have been hiding a grin. "Fine. Cody and I did marry fast. You know what you want, I suppose, but have you considered this? He's not the same Wesley we knew as kids."

Allison blinked. "What do you mean?"

"He's been through hell," Kristina reminded her bluntly. "Can you imagine what it must have been like, being married to Samantha all those years? And he's a father now. So much of the innocent young man you fell in love with is gone."

Allison shook her head. "I don't care. He's still Wesley. Before anything else can happen, before anyone can come between us, I want this done. Kristina, if I can't have him, I don't want anyone." With every word, her pace quickened, and her pitch rose.

Melissa looked away from her treat to regard her honorary aunt with a startled expression.

"Calm down, Allison," Kristina said, lifting a hand as she attempted to soothe her friend. "I'm not trying to tell you not to do it, just making sure you've considered all the options."

Allison replied staunchly, "No matter what anyone says, I will marry Wesley. I never thought I would get this opportunity. I'll never give it up."

The ladies fell silent, contemplating the situation. A few minutes later, Cody and Wesley entered the front door, wearing matching grim expressions. It appeared Kristina was not the only one who feared union was as likely to lead to disaster as joy.

Discussing a wedding should be a joyous event, Allison thought, dismayed.

"Hello, darling," Kristina said to her husband.

"Mrs. Williams." He leaned down and touched his lips to her cheek before taking a seat in one armchair. Wesley perched in the other.

"Well," Cody said, "does everyone know what's going on?"

"Yes," Kristina replied, "Allison has been filling me in. What do you think?"

"I think there are some potential problems with this scenario," Cody replied soberly, "and I'm not going to give my opinion until I've heard from the bride. Miss Spencer, can you please tell me your take on all this?"

Allison spoke in her firmest voice. "It's simple. I want to marry Wesley. What more is there to say?"

"You want to marry him," Cody clarified, "knowing he's still grieving his wife, knowing that he's in… a bad state. You're willing to take him on as-is, daughter in tow, *and* a mother who doesn't like you?"

"Yes." She folded her hands in her lap and challenged Cody with a direct look.

"Why?"

"There's nothing I would refuse him," Allison replied with brutal honesty. "This is not the worst thing he could have asked me." She lifted her head and turned away from him to meet Wesley's eyes. Guilt flashed in his expression.

"What do your parents say?" Cody pressed.

"I haven't asked them. I'm twenty-four years old, Reverend Williams. I want to get married. My best friend has asked me. I'd like it done as soon as possible."

Cody's broad shoulders sagged. "How soon?"

"Tomorrow."

A clatter from beside Allison attracted her attention.

Kristina had overturned her cup, spilling the dregs of her tea into the saucer.

Guess she didn't realize what a short timetable we want.

Kristina rose and carried her dishes to the sink.

When she returned, instead of sitting next to Allison, she stood behind Cody's chair and laid a hand on his shoulder.

The moment Wesley realized the space was unoccupied, he claimed it, taking Allison's hand in his. She curled her fingers around his, holding him tight.

Cody gave them a long look, and then he turned to face the table. "Melissa," he called.

The little girl raised her head. Crumbs dropped from her lips and chin with the movement.

"Can you come here please?"

She scrambled down and ran across the room, climbing onto his lap. He brushed the remaining bits of cookie from her face. "How are you, Melissa?" he asked.

"I miss Mommy," she replied, lip quivering.

"I bet," he agreed, his accented voice softly soothing. The child visibly relaxed, "but your mommy is always with you. Melissa, would you like a new mommy? One you can see?"

The child considered. "Can it be Auntie Allie?"

Allison held her breath. *Melissa wants this as much as Wes and I do. That's more important than I realized it would be.*

"Yes, Melissa. It can be," he told her, defeated by the child's wishes.

Allison exhaled in relief. *Now everything will be all right.*

On December 23rd at noon, Allison and Wesley stood before the pulpit of the church. The service had ended fifteen minutes ago, and the congregation had gone home. All but Cody, Kristina, Melissa, and the two of them. They had taken no time for fancy preparations. Allison wore only a skirt in sage green, a white shirtwaist, and a black shawl. Wesley wore a black suit like he did any other Sunday. Melissa had on a woolen dress in a shade of dark rose. Nothing about their apparel suggested the solemnity of the event.

Allison held Melissa's hand with one of hers, Wesley's with the other, and looked deep into his eyes as Cody softly read the wedding service from the prayer book. *He sounds so nice, with his soft, low voice and soothing accent. What a lovely memory.* A sense of a presence behind her called attention to Kristina, acting as both bridesmaid and witness.

But neither the pastor nor his wife could keep Allison's attention for long. She returned her gaze to Wesley, noting he looked strained, as though he might be about to crack.

She squeezed his fingers, reminding him that she wanted what he was offering.

He gave a weak smile.

"I now pronounce you man and wife," Cody said.

Allison closed her eyes. *I did it. I'm Wesley's wife. My lifelong dream has finally come true.*

"Auntie Allie, does this mean you're my mommy now?" Melissa asked, hugging her legs and nearly knocking her to the floor.

"I would like to be, Melissa. Is that what you want, too?" her heart swelling with the child's approval and her own blossoming joy.

"I don't know. Do you think it will make my other mommy sad?"

"Your other mommy is an angel now," Allison said diplomatically. "I think she'll want whatever makes you happy."

"Maybe I'll call you Mamma Allie instead of Auntie."

"I think that will be fine, sweetheart." Allison bent and kissed the little girl on the cheek.

"Shall we go home, Mrs. Fulton?" Wesley asked softly.

"Yes, fine," Allison replied, "but we have to go back to my… to my parents' house. Let them know what happened, where I'm going…"

But there was no need. The door of the church burst open and Mrs. Spencer charged in, her bosom heaving, yelling at the top of her lungs. "What the devil is going on here?"

"Mrs. Spencer," Cody said in his most soothing voice. He never got to continue.

"Tell me it's not too late. Tell me you didn't just marry my daughter to this…"

"Mother, stop!" Allison said loudly.

"We're married, Mrs. Spencer," Wesley told her, his voice calm. "It's what I should have done years ago."

"No!" she shrieked. "You bastard! How dare you foist your illegitimate daughter and all your mess on my innocent child? If only my husband were here, and not on that damned train, he'd make you pay, you…"

"Mother!" Allison yelled. The room fell silent. All eyes focused on Allison. "I love Wesley and I love Melissa. This is what I've always wanted."

"I'll get it annulled," Mrs. Spencer said, her voice dangerously soft.

"You can't." Allison met her mother's eyes, her voice like steel. "I'm of age whether you like it or not, and there are no grounds."

Mrs. Spencer's pale face turned purple with rage. She opened and closed her mouth several times, but no sound came out.

"Mrs. Spencer, why don't you come to the vicarage with Cody and me," Kristina said soothingly. "I'll make us some tea."

"No thank you, Mrs. Williams," Allison's mother said in a tight, brittle voice. "I think I'll just go home. Mr. Fulton, I had better never hear that you've mistreated my daughter in any way." She spoke through clenched teeth, her molars grinding audibly with every word.

"No, ma'am," Wesley vowed. "I'll be good to her, I promise."

Mrs. Spencer swept through the door. The four young adults loitered awkwardly in the church, giving her a few minutes to get away. Then Allison took Wesley's arm, scooped up Melissa, and left as well, more than ready to go home.

Back at the Spencer home, Rebecca sat in the parlor on the black sofa, sipping tea. James perched beside her, his cup ignored on the table. They sat a respectable distance apart, as any friends enjoying a Sunday visit might, but every now and then, his hand slid across the seat to touch her fingers or rest gently on her leg.

Odd that Mother isn't here, she thought, after he touched her for the fifth time. Though she didn't yet realize the couple needed a chaperone, she did tend to watch Becky like a hawk when any man was around. *And no wonder. If I'm honest with myself, I have to admit I need it.*

After their passionate interlude at her store, James had been a frequent visitor both there and here. Nothing further had been said between them, or to anyone else. They chatted like any old friends, enjoying each other's company, but the heat in his eyes reminded her there would be more to come, and these frequent little touches also helped.

He reached across again, laying his hand on hers. She squeezed his palm gently and then stroked her fingers over it. He lifted her hand and touched his lips to the soft skin. She inhaled deeply. He nibbled one knuckle.

And then Mrs. Spencer burst into the room in a flurry.

James dropped Rebecca's hand and shot to his feet.

"What's wrong, Mother?" Rebecca asked, rising quickly and darting toward her mother, alarmed at Mrs. Spencer's flushed and disheveled appearance.

"That sister of yours! You won't believe what she just went and did."

Rebecca thought for a moment. "She married Wesley, didn't she?"

"How did you know?" Mrs. Spencer demanded, rounding on her older daughter with a ferocious glare.

Rebecca pinned her evasive, serene expression in place. "I've been wondering since Samantha's funeral if she would. Or rather, how long it would take until she did. It's not a surprise, Mother."

"But he already broke her heart once…"

"And it's her heart," Becky reminded her. "If she wants to risk it with him again, that's her choice, isn't it?"

"Why are you taking his side, Rebecca?" Mrs. Spencer narrowed her eyes at her oldest child.

Rebecca returned her mother's gaze mildly, unruffled by the display of temper. "I'm not, Mother. I just think that since this is all she's ever wanted… well, why shouldn't one of us have the chance at happiness?"

Her mother gave her a long, speaking look, and then flounced out of the room.

"Rebecca," James said softly, "she isn't the only one with that chance. Do you want me to talk to them?"

She reached out her hand and he grasped it, drawing her close. "Not today, James. I think Mother's reached the limit of what she can handle today. But soon, please?" *I'm begging. I hate that. I sound like a child.*

James glanced at the closed door to the parlor and pressed one brief, chaste kiss to her lips. "Oh yes, Rebecca. I'll talk to them soon." He smudged her lips with his once more.

Chapter 8

Melissa had been tucked into bed for the night. Allison had retrieved her clothing from her parents' home while Becky kept Mrs. Spencer occupied. Now her possessions were stashed in Samantha's bureau and wardrobe. Wesley's late wife's clothing had been added to the empty guest room, to be dealt with later. The bed had been turned down earlier and awaited them. Wesley sat on the armchair in the corner of the room.

Allison approached, and he pulled her onto his lap.

This is it, he realized, *the moment I've waited and longed for so many years. The night I finally got to make my virgin bride into my wife.* Suddenly, he didn't want to. *Cody was right. Mrs. Spencer was right. I'm taking advantage of her willingness, and I'm in no condition to give anything good back to her.*

"What's wrong, Wes?" she asked him, perceptive as usual.

"Everything," he replied honestly, his heart aching. "This isn't right."

"Wesley, this is the first right thing we've done in years. It's perfect." She put her hands on his cheeks and leaned in to kiss him. "There. Now things are just as they should be."

He looked at her, confused.

"We didn't get to kiss at our wedding. It felt… incomplete. Now I really feel married."

"You really are," he said. "I wish I could be better for you."

"You will be. For now, Wes, let me take care of you. Later on, when you're better, you can return the favor."

What an angel. He claimed her lips for another sweet kiss, turning her so she straddled his lap. Pressing her down onto the growing rigidness of his sex, he realized she felt strange to him. For four long years, he'd been caressed by eager, experienced hands. Allison, it seemed, had no idea she should touch him and encourage him. Her hands stayed planted firmly on his shoulders. She didn't grind herself against him or rub her breasts on his chest. Her lack of experience confused him.

He tried again, easing his tongue into her mouth. She submitted but did not respond.

He sat back, defeated. "What is it?" she asked.

"This just feels wrong. I mean, it's not you, Allie. You're still the right girl, the same sweetheart I wanted so badly four years ago, but I'm not the right man anymore. I dreamed about this perfect wedding night, the two of us giving our innocence to each other, but I ruined that dream. For the last four years, I've been experiencing passion. And now... I have no innocence left to give."

"Then give me your experience, Wes," she urged. "I don't know what I'm doing, but I want you as much as ever. Teach me to be the wife you want. Teach me how to please you."

"It's not that, Allie, I..." He broke off as she kissed him again.

This time she unleashed her innocent passion, driving her tongue deep and running her hands over his shirt. She caressed her way down his arms until she could lace her fingers through his. Then she lifted and placed his hands on her breasts. "Please, Wes. Don't stop. Make me your wife right now."

"Oh, Lord, Allie," he groaned. "Is that really what you want?"

"It is, darling. Touch me."

His hands curled involuntarily, cupping the luscious globes. Eagerly, her nipples rose to meet his touch, and he grasped the tender peaks through her shirtwaist.

"Oh yes," Allison sighed as Wesley's restraint once again shattered.

I have no willpower where women are concerned. Good thing I'm finally married to the right one. "Kiss me, Allie."

She laid her mouth on his and he worked the hard nubs, rolling and twisting them until she was panting with pleasure.

"More," she begged.

Obediently, he opened the buttons of her blouse and slid the garment off her shoulders, dropping it onto the floor. Her chemise quickly followed, leaving her eager breasts exposed to his touch. She lifted his hand back to her breast again. He tenderly chafed one nipple while leaning down to take the other in his mouth.

"Oh! Oh!" she whimpered. She ground her mound against him.

Soon she will be ready for direct stimulation there, and then penetration. I'm ready, but my darling virgin will need more caresses before I breach that untried portal. And I will breach it. I know that now. It's inevitable, not just because I'm terribly aroused, but because she's correct. Nothing has been right in the last four years, until this moment.

Wesley's hands left Allison's breasts, and she moaned in disappointment, but then sighed with relief as he lifted her skirt.

There are too many layers of clothing separating us, and I need to be more than close. I need us finally to be one. For as long as he could remember, it was all he'd wanted. Now, with her straddling his thighs and his thickly erect phallus pressed against her, he wanted to hurry the moment. *She's with me,* he realized. *She feels no fear, only eagerness.*

Wesley opened the drawstring of her bloomers and reached inside, cupping her sex with one hand and pressing inward. He felt her copious moisture and eased through the folds to enter her tightness with one fingertip.

"Sweet virgin bride," he whispered, stroking her maidenhead. "You deserve a better husband."

"I have the husband I want," she gritted out, between gasping sobs of pleasure. Then she whimpered as his questing fingers pulled back, just far enough to stroke an erect nub of sensitive tissue.

"All that for one little touch," he asked, amazed at her responsiveness. "What sounds will you make if I do this?"

He began to circle her clitoris, and with his mouth, he returned to her nipples, sucking each one in turn until the stimulation proved too much and she squealed in wild pleasure, arching her back as her orgasm overtook her. Warm fluids flooded her delicate folds, and he knew she was ready. He stood, his free hand supporting her bottom, and carried her to the bed.

Allison watched with slumberous eyes as he eased her skirt and bloomers from her sated body and removed his clothing. Though the first time she'd seen a naked man, in this small farming community she'd seen animals mate a time or two and knew what that swelling of the male organ meant. At the sight of Wesley's heavy erection, she smiled. *He wants me as badly as all that, does he?* It didn't seem possible that such a thick penis would fit inside her, but she was ready for him to try, nonetheless. *It's time to be his wife, past time.* Allison opened her thighs wide.

Wesley knelt between them. He parted her lips with one hand and with the other placed the head of his sex against her untried opening. "I'm taking you now, Allie," he warned her.

She opened wider, presenting her innocent sex for his plundering. "I love you, Wesley," she said sweetly. He thrust into her, splitting her hymen and filling her completely in a single fluid movement.

Allison gasped at the flash of pain, her hands fisting in the sheets. The sharp sensation of her deflowering faded, though the stretched feeling remained as he pulled back and pushed, sliding his erection in and out of her delicate passage.

Though Wesley had bedded his first wife hundreds of times in their brief years of marriage, this felt marvelously different. He had never experienced the tightness of a virgin. *Allison is every bit as eager as I hoped that long-ago day in the farmhouse.*

Once she recovered from the sting, she began to squirm around, pressing herself upwards to meet the slow, easy strokes that claimed every inch of her for himself. He lowered his body on top of her, embracing her as he increased the intensity of his thrusts.

Allison whimpered, and he studied her lovely face. *Is she in pain? No, it's pleasure. She's building towards another orgasm.* With all the willpower he had, Wesley restrained his climax.

Her head turned to one side and he nipped her neck. The unexpected sting brought her the rest of the way to a shivering, sobbing peak, which had her contracting hard around him. Her pleasure triggered his, and before he even realized it, he flew over the brink, growling.

Wesley slowly returned to awareness, relaxed on top of Allison's prone body. She, too, appeared alert, looking up at the ceiling. He realized suddenly how rough he'd been with her. "Are you all right?" he asked, staring down into her eyes.

"Oh, yes," she sighed. "How lovely. Thank you, Wes."

"It was my pleasure, Allie, believe me." He touched his lips to hers.

"When can we do it again?"

He choked at her question, which caused him to slide from her body. "Aren't you sore?"

"No," she replied. "I feel fine, and I have years to make up for."

"Tomorrow," Wes promised. "I haven't got anything left tonight."

"All right then," she replied.

He pulled the blankets over them and cuddled her close. In their utter satiation, neither one remembered to pull on nightclothes before drifting into deeply restorative sleep.

Chapter 9

A few days after Christmas, Wesley walked down the street to the bank with the winter sun shining brightly on his head. He felt quite marvelous and at peace with the world. As he walked, admiring the attractive collection of houses and businesses lining the brick streets, his mind replayed the lovely week he'd spent with his new bride. *Allison is absolutely everything I hoped she would be. Put simply, a proper wife.* The morning after their wedding, she'd taken one look at the haphazard kitchen and taken everything out of the cabinets and drawers. All day Christmas Eve she'd worked, discarding moldy bits of food and rusted implements. Then she'd washed everything and put it away sensibly, where anyone would be able to find it.

Christmas morning, after a few gifts and a hearty breakfast, she'd attacked the rest of the house, placing linens in the linen closet, clothes in the bureaus and wardrobes, and quilts in a hope chest she found squirreled away in the attic.

The third day she'd cleaned and dusted and waxed and polished. She'd pressed Wesley into service washing the windows inside and out and then trimming the trees and hedges. Soon the exterior of the house matched that of the neighbors for orderly attractiveness, and the inside smelled clean. The only room she refused to deal with was the guest room, where all Samantha's belongings had been housed. She'd gone in to retrieve a few items that seemed to have been stashed there at random and then shut the door, leaving it to be the keeper of Samantha's memory.

For the first time in he couldn't remember how long, he had been able to get up and dress, eat breakfast and leave the house and his daughter, knowing both were in capable hands and would be well cared for while he was gone.

I'm in capable hands too and have been well cared for this week. Yes, Allison has a lot to learn, but her enthusiasm makes up for it, and she's picking up skills quickly. Suppressing a guilty grin, Wesley began to whistle as he walked along.

Quiet hung heavy over the bank when he arrived. No customers. His teller, George, behind his paneled counter with jail-like bars above, looked up at him and waved hesitantly. In the telegraph office, housed in the bank's vestibule, young Christopher Fulton, another of Wesley's many cousins, looked up from his table of mysterious black boxes, an uncertain expression on his face. Wesley hadn't been back to work since that terrible day, and neither of the other men knew quite how to act. *Who can blame them? Am I a widower or a bridegroom? Should they be somber, or joyous*

Wesley didn't know either, so he waved, crossed the pale pine floor to his office, and closed the door behind him. Rolling up his sleeves, he attended to the mountain of paperwork that had piled up in his absence.

"What's next, Mama Allie?" Melissa piped, hopping down from her perch on a chair, where she'd been 'helping' Allison wash the dishes.

Allison set the stained and tattered dishcloth aside, leaving the clean plates in the sink to drain. "I suppose we should start dinner."

"Yay!" the child cheered. "I love dinner. What are we having for dinner?"

Allison poked turned away from the sink and regarded the kitchen. *All in order now, and clean. Goodness, that was hard work. It looked like a herd of pigs had rooted in every corner.* After half a week of laborious cleaning, the cabinets gleamed on shiny, freshly-oiled hinges. A clean cloth covered the table in one corner. Though some of the stains on the floorboards had sunk deep and remained, the floor itself had been stripped of hunks of unidentifiable gunk, swept and mopped. A spice cake cooled on a rack on the counter, waiting for its layer of icing. *I didn't find much food in the house when I was hunting for ingredients,* she realized. *There's a ham, but nothing to go with it.*

"You know, Missy, I'm not sure," she replied at last. "Maybe we should go to the store and pick up some ingredients."

"Store!" Melissa shouted, tossing her dishtowel into the air. It came down onto the top of her head, covering her eyes, and she peered out from beneath the folds, giggling.

"Come on, silly goose," Allison urged. "You need to put on your real hat. It's cold today."

"All right." Melissa dragged the towel off her hair, making it stand up in all directions, and threw the fabric rectangle to the floor.

"Pick up the towel, please," Allison admonished. "The house only stays clean and pretty if we do our part."

Melissa stuck her lip out, but obediently retrieved her towel and hung it up on the edge of the sink. Then, she rushed to the entryway. Allison pulled Melissa's blue pea coat from its hook on the coatrack in and handed it to the child, who dressed herself and fumbled with the buttons. Though they gaped in their misalignment, Allison complimented the child. "Look at you, you did it yourself!"

Melissa beamed.

Allison's own brown jacket hung there as well, and she dressed quickly, before kneeling to slip a knitted cap—the only kind of headwear the Kansas wind couldn't steal—over Melissa's messy blond head.

Then Allison pulled on her own mittens and wrapped a scarf around her head. "Are you ready?" she asked her stepdaughter.

Melissa nodded and reached out one hand. Together they walked out into the cold and made their way north.

"Look, Mama Allie," Melissa urged. She blew out a lungful of air and the chill turned it white. "I'm a dragon."

"That you are," Allison agreed with a laugh. "I'm a mama dragon." She blew out her own stream of 'smoke'.

"Let's fly!" Melissa shouted, racing forward so she tugged at Allison's hand.

"Yes, let's," she agreed. Ignoring the stares of stuffy matrons, they raced through the street to the store and pushed open the door, setting the bell clanging. *Poor Mr. Heitschmidt will need someone new to help him out,* Allison realized, examining a thin layer of dust that had settled on the shelves. *It's too much work for just one person.*

While Melissa stared at the display case, Allison selected a length of ribbon for Melissa's hair and a remnant of fabric to make a new dress for her baby doll. Also some laundry soap. *It looks as though the washing at the Fulton home has been neglected for a while. There's so much to do, the tasks seem overwhelming.*

Of course, it's going to take a while to establish order in a household that had never had any, she reminded herself as she walked along the aisle between a row of heavy barrels and a shelf of merchandise in boxes and cans, *It's part of what I knew I was taking on when I married Wesley. I didn't realize the appalling extent of the mess, though. It's shocking.*

Melissa had slipped free of Allison's line of sight, and she turned, wondering what the child was up to. No surprise, she was eyeing the candy.

"No, love," Allison admonished, "it's almost dinnertime. And don't forget we have cake for dessert."

"I want candy," Melissa pouted. "Mama always bought me candy."

Allison considered. *If that's the girl's habit…* She shook her head. *It's not a good habit.* "No, Melissa. Not today. No candy." She piled her purchases on the counter in front of her former boss, noting that he, like his store, looked a little worse for wear. The wrinkles around his eyes had deepened, so his freckles looked like a fleet of ships on a stormy sea. A few new white streaks had stolen the color from his strawberry-blond hair. "Can you put this on a tab for me, Mr. Heltschmidt?"

"Sure thing, Miss—uh—Mrs. Fulton."

She beamed. "Thank you. Melissa, I said no," she reminded her young charge, as the child sneaked out a hand to touch the peppermint taffy.

The little girl began to whine.

"Well, Mr. Heitschmidt, I guess our shopping is done for today," Allison said. "Come on, Melissa. Time to go."

"I don't wanna go," the child wailed.

She seems to be building up to a tantrum. Definitely time to leave.

"Mr. Heitschmidt!" The sound of noisy boots clomping on the wood floors broke through Melissa's increasing whines.

"What is it, Sheriff Brody? What's wrong?" The mercantile owner sounded as alarmed as Allison felt.

"We're forming a posse. There's a train robbery in progress. I need all the help I can get," Brody barked. His luxurious mustache seemed to vibrate with the tension that stiffened his broad shoulders. His hair stood on end as though he'd raked fingers through it several times.

Suddenly Allison felt a chill, as a horrible realization dawned on her. *Cody and Kristina are on a train today, heading to Wichita for a brief honeymoon.* "Mr. Heitschmidt," she gasped. He realized the implications instantly.

"Lock the mercantile, Allison. Just a moment, Sheriff. Let me get my coat. And my shotgun."

Allison grabbed Melissa with one hand and the keys from their spot behind the counter in the other and locked the door. *The men can go out the back.* Then she scooped up the little girl and ran, fast as her legs would carry her, down the half block and across the street to the bank, where she flew into the lobby, babbling before her brain could even process the scene. "Wes, did you hear about the... Oh, Sheriff. Thank God!" She turned to her husband. "You have to go, Wes. You have to."

"Calm down, Allie. What's going on?"

"Kristina and Cody are on that train."

Wesley's face blanched and for a moment she could see conflict chase across his features, then a visible wave of fear. At last, steely determination narrowed his eyes and tightened his jaw. Without another word, Wesley pulled on his heavy coat, kissed his wife and daughter and ran for the door, Sheriff Brody close on his heels.

Trembling, Allison sank to the floor in a swirl of cranberry-colored skirts. She clutched Melissa, whose tantrum had stopped abruptly at her first sight of the sheriff and prayed for all she was worth that everyone would come home all right.

So many people I love are in danger, and there's nothing more I can do. Please, God, don't let him be hurt. Don't let any of them be hurt.

Wesley walked home slowly from the vicarage. Night had long since fallen, illuminating his dark thoughts with a sliver of moonlight. *Thank God, Cody and Kristina are all right. By some miracle neither were injured in the robbery or the resulting shootout, but they sure are shaken up.*

It had taken both Cody and Wesley to walk Kristina into her home, she was trembling so hard. *Cody was none too steady himself, so I had to half-carry her to her bed, which is something I never would have imagined.* Cody had slipped in after her, taking her in his arms and shutting out the world before Wesley could even shut the door.

Truth be told, I'm not doing so well myself. The carnage on the train as the worst I've ever seen. Tornados have fewer casualties. Twenty passengers shot in cold blood by the train robbers. Only the ones in the car with Cody and Kristina were spared, due to their quick thinking. Only nine survivors.

Of the robbers, two had been killed, one captured, and two escaped. Somehow, Kristina's long-lost brother had been on the train. He hadn't survived, but he'd played a role in saving his sister. *For that, he'll always be a hero. Poor Calvin. The kid was only twenty-one. James is going to take his loss really hard. I don't envy Sheriff Brody having to tell him the sad news.*

Wesley's front door loomed suddenly in front of him, and he jumped at its unexpected appearance.

He opened it slowly, almost not sure which way the handle turned or whether to push or pull. *Hmmm. I must be slightly in shock.*

In the parlor, Allison sat in the rocking chair by the stove, cradling Melissa in her arms and murmuring into the child's ear.

Wesley took in the two golden heads. *Melissa looks enough like Allison to be her child. It's a good thing because Allison will be the only mother Melissa remembers.* He shut the door a little harder than he intended, and the two of them looked up at the unexpected noise.

"Daddy!" Melissa chirped, jumping down and running to him.

He scooped her up and kissed her.

"You see, darling," Allison said. "Here's Daddy, safe and sound."

The little girl smooched a loud, wet kiss on her father's cheek.

"All right, pretty girl, it's time for bed." He swayed. Allison sidled up against him. He wrapped his arm around her and together they carried his daughter up to her room and tucked her into bed. Then he let Allison lead him away.

As he changed clothes, cleaned up, and prepared himself for bed, she hovered close to his side, obviously wild with unasked questions. *I'm glad she's holding back a bit.*

Sure enough, as soon as he had slipped under the covers, Allison blurted. "Are they all right?"

"Yes, love," he replied. "Cody and Kristina came out without a scratch. I took them home. A lot of people weren't so lucky, though." He choked at the memory.

Allison didn't say another word. She simply wrapped her arms around her husband and hugged him tight.

He cupped the back of her head in his hand and drew her to him for a rough, hard kiss, and then another, and another, on the brink of losing control. *I need my wife, need her badly, but she's still so new to passion.* Forcing himself to slow down, he softened his kiss to one of aching tenderness.

Eager as always, Allison returned her husband's embrace. She held his head, fingers laced in his hair. His hands wandered scandalously over her body, stroking her full breasts, her narrow waist, her round soft hips.

She moaned softly at his touch.

This is going to be good.

Rebecca heard about the robbery the next day through the gossip grapevine; that is, Ilse Jackson. The unpleasant young woman had long since appointed herself the keeper of all information in Garden City, and what she didn't know, she quickly ferreted out. So, when she pushed open the heavy wooden door of Rebecca's shop, setting the brass bell dancing in a flurry of metallic jangles, the proprietress knew from the expression on Ilse's face she was not here to discuss the color of gingham she wanted her new dress made out of.

"Have you heard?" the girl asked without preamble.

"Heard what?" Rebecca mumbled around a mouthful of straight pins she was using to attach a delicate white sleeve to the bodice of an infant's christening dress.

"There's been another train robbery." Ilse smirked. "Was your dad on the train?"

Rebecca removed the pins so she could speak safely. "No, he was under the weather and switched with another driver. Did anyone get hurt?"

"Oh, yes," Ilse replied eagerly, bobbing her head until one black curl sprang free of her coiffure and slanted across her face.

There was a little girl who had a little curl... Rebecca thought to herself, suppressing a grin. "Well, go on," she urged. "Tell me all the gory details." *The sooner the story's told, the sooner Ilse will go away, and that's a goal worth pursuing.*

"They say over twenty innocent people were gunned down in the train. Only nine survived. They're calling Reverend Williams and Kristina heroes." That last had a sarcastic edge and no surprise. Kristina had little patience for Ilse's unfortunate personality, and that had been before the girl made a play for Cody. They politely despised each other.

"What do Reverend Williams and Kristina have to do with it?" Not wanting to appear too interested, Rebecca returned to pinning fabric.

"They were on the train."

Rebecca glanced up sharply. "Are they all right?"

"Yes," Ilse replied, with deflated enthusiasm. "They're fine. But…" Her eyes lit up again. "But, well, you remember Kristina's brother, don't you?"

"Calvin? Of course. Cute little boy. What about him?"

"He was there, I hear. He was shot."

A strange sensation of cold gripped Rebecca's insides. *Calvin Heitschmidt? James's son?* She swallowed. "Is he all right?"

"He's dead," Ilse crowed.

A ringing sound began to reverberate around the inside of Rebecca's head, drowning out the girl's inane chatter. She rose without a word and walked from the shop. Despite her reputation for serenity, today she forgot her dignity. Her walk changed to a trot, and then a full out run as she covered the distance between her place of business and the general store.

Maybe it's lies. Just ugly gossip. Maybe that little cockroach got it wrong. Please, God, let her be wrong. Let Calvin be fine.

She banged through the open door of the mercantile and her boots thundered onto the echoing floorboards. James stood, examining a display of canned peaches, his back to her. At the noise, he turned.

Rebecca took one look at his lost, despairing expression, and her heart cracked. She could feel it breaking. She turned back to the door, pulling it shut behind her and twisting the key in the lock, before flying into her beloved's arms.

He crushed her in a trembling embrace.

"Oh, James," she whispered, "I'm so terribly sorry."

"I..." His voice broke. "I never got to make things right. I never got to say... to say I was sorry."

"He knew, darling. I know he did."

James sank to the floor, apparently unable to stand any longer. Rebecca stayed with him, planting herself on his lap and clinging to him. He lowered his head, hiding his face against her shoulder.

Chapter 10

Three months later

"Kristina, how does a woman know if she's pregnant?" Allison asked as she and her sister and her best friend sat in her sparkling parlor with tea and cookies. The broken furniture had been repaired, the window replaced, and the whole room aired out by the refreshing, early spring breeze. Outside the window, the sun shone brightly.

Used to Allison's blunt, uncouth word choices, neither woman seemed surprised.

"I'm not sure," Kristina said. "I know I'm not expecting." She colored.

"Don't look at me," Becky added. "I have no idea either. You'll have to ask someone who knows... like Mother."

"I don't want to ask her, not yet. I'll get her hopes up, and then what if it's nothing?"

"Good point," Becky replied. "Since you and Wesley married, she's talked of nothing but the imaginary grandchildren she thought she'd never have. Do you suspect something?"

"Well, yes," Allison said. "I didn't have my woman's time last month, and it's late this month. I know it's always been irregular, but two months seems like a lot. That, and things are starting to smell funny."

Kristina looked at her askance. "What do you mean, smell funny?"

"It's hard to explain. They smell the same as always, but suddenly the same old aromas bother me. Like the scent of peppermint around the candy counter at the mercantile." At the very thought, she gagged. Swallowing the urge, she glanced at her friends and saw them looking at each other.

"I think you might be right," Becky said. "Better check with the doctor to be sure. Mother will be delighted."

"How do you feel about the possibility?" Kristina asked.

"Scared," Allison admitted. "I'd given up on ever having children, and now..."

"I think you gave up too soon," Becky commented. "I mean, you're only twenty-four. That's not such a great old age to find a husband and start a family."

"Oh, I know it's not," Allison replied. "I just… well, when Wesley was married before, there was no one else I could imagine being with. It wasn't my age."

"Ah, yes," Kristina said. "We both thought there was no one for us, didn't we? But the Lord had a plan all along. We just needed to trust Him." Her freckled cheeks turned pink, though not with embarrassment.

She gets that little flush of color every time she thinks of her handsome husband. Allison couldn't help smiling. Kristina, who had always straddled the line between cute and homely, suddenly looked pretty all the time because of her happy glow. *Marriage suits her very well. In fact, as often as she and her pastor have been caught stealing kisses, it's a surprise she hasn't conceived yet.*

Allison's gaze turned to her sister. *There's a new… something in Becky's expression. Her usual mask of a serene smile seems to have deepened. Something's lurking beneath the surface, and I want to know what it is, but I'll ask later. In private.*

"Have you heard any word on the train robbers?" Becky asked.

"No," Allison replied. "Let's hope they've gone for good."

"They haven't," Kristina interjected with a shudder. "Lydia told me that Sheriff Brody told her, they're still lurking somewhere across the Colorado border. Their old hideout near Liberal was raided, but no one was there. Some of the marked bills from one robbery have been circulating around Pueblo and Colorado Springs."

"You would think Colorado law enforcement would be able to track them down," Allison said.

"That's what Lydia told me the sheriff says. He's really frustrated."

"What about the one they caught?" Becky asked.

"Oh," Kristina replied, shaking her head, confused emotions chasing across her features, "the trial was a few weeks ago. Don't you remember? He's going to be hanged."

The three women fell silent. They had all known this of course. In such a small and isolated town, a hanging would be a public spectacle. *Bloodthirsty wretches, wanting to watch some poor fool kick his last breath away.* The gorge that remained always on the verge of Allison's awareness tried to rise. She gulped it down and patted Kristina's knee. "I know that must be uncomfortable for you. No one will blame you if you don't go."

"I don't plan to. It's terrible. He killed my brother, you know." Her voice wavered, and Becky rose from her chair, setting aside her teacup and wrapping her arms around Kristina.

"Mama Allie!" a little voice chirped from upstairs.

Allison sighed. "Sounds like Melissa is up. She's going to want a snack. You two are welcome to stay, but I'll be back in mommy mode."

"It's really great how you've taken to caring for Wesley's daughter," Kristina commented, her voice had steadied, but red now rimmed her turquoise eyes.

"She's my daughter now, too," Allison replied fiercely.

"Of course, she is," Becky said, "and you're doing a wonderful job with her. It must be a relief—to her *and* to Wesley—that she's in the care of someone so capable."

"I don't feel capable," Allison admitted as the sound of little feet thundered down the staircase. "I feel out of my depth and scared, and if I really am expecting, things are only going to get more complicated." She placed a hand on her belly and wondered, *Is Wesley's baby really growing in there? What a wonderful, terrifying, exciting thought.*

Then Melissa raced into the room, blonde pigtails flying. She jumped into Allison's arms for a hug. "I'm hungry, Mama Allie," she announced, and Allison gave her guests a 'what did I tell you?' look.

"All right, Missy Moo, let's go get you a snack," she told the little girl, carrying her towards the kitchen. Before she could reach the doorway, a knock sounded at the front door.

"Come in," Allison called, and the door opened to reveal Cody's black hair and attractive face. Kristina suddenly looked like she was about to melt. She hurried to her husband and threw her arms around him. He touched his lips to her forehead.

"Are you all done with your sermon?" she asked.

He nodded. "I was heading home, and I thought I would stop by and see if you were ready." The couple lived next door to the church, and the Fulton house was blocks out of his way, but Cody shrugged like it was nothing. Wrapping his arm around his wife, he led her out. She called a brief goodbye over her shoulder and was gone, the door banging shut behind her.

The two sisters looked at each other and laughed. "I'd better go too," Becky said, "I have to head over to the shop for a little while. I'd like to get the last of my pinning done before it gets dark."

Melissa squirmed out of Allison's arms and ran to her Becky, squeezing her tight around the knees and almost knocking her over.

"Oof," Becky grunted. "Come here, little one." She peeled the toddler off her legs and picked her up. "If you need to go see Doctor Halvorson, let me know. I'll look after Melissa for you."

"Wonderful!" Allison said. "That will be a big help." She glanced at the window. "Now, you'd better hurry. It's starting to look a little ominous out there."

Becky glanced out the parlor window at the darkening sky. It did look like some nasty weather was moving in. She gave Melissa a tight squeeze and set her down. "See you later, Allie," she said before hurrying out into the growing darkness.

"Come on, Melissa," Allison said, scooping up her stepdaughter and carrying her into the kitchen. "Let's get you some bread and jam."

Becky bustled around her shop folding fabric remnants. A massive pile of paperwork covered her sewing table, taunting her. It competed with her sewing time and ensured she never got as much done as she wanted or expected.

Other expectations were also not panning out. *Three months after promising to talk to my family about our courtship, James is still seeing me only in secret. He stops by and kisses me or touches my hand. Sometimes, he comes to dinner, but none of that's the declaration I want.*

It seems impossible that a man of his maturity and status in the town would be playing games with me, but then, what's he waiting for? When I asked him to wait on talking to my parents, I didn't mean forever. If he wants to be with me, why isn't he broadcasting it to the whole town? I want it to be known, to be seen on his arm and have people whisper speculation about whether we belong together.

She shook her head, sinking into the chair beside her sewing table and staring blankly at the catalog order form in front of her. *I don't understand what he's doing, but it's too hard to ask, so here we stay, stuck in limbo. Courting in secret as though we're doing a shameful thing... as though I were one...*

BOOM! An explosion rocked the shop, shattering the big plate-glass windows and tearing the door from its hinges. Becky was thrown to the floor, her head slamming the counter as she went.

James strolled along the street toward Becky's shop. *I hope she's in. Late afternoon, her hours become a little erratic, what with church meetings and dinner with her sister, but I want to see her. Who am I fooling? I always want to see her.* His pretty lady filled up the empty places in his heart quite nicely.

He passed the church just in time to see his daughter walk past, arm-in-arm with her husband.

"Dad!" Kristina exclaimed, running over and hugging him.

"Hello, Kris," he replied. "Cody."

"Afternoon, James," the minister drawled, shaking his free hand. "How's everything going?"

"Well enough," he replied, "but it looks like we're in for a bit of weather." They all glanced at the sky. Heavy black rain clouds billowed across the polished silver surface of heaven. The scent of moisture hung heavy in the still air. *When the wind stops, it's going to be bad. I had better hurry.*

Away up the street, a figure dressed all in black clattered across the bricks on a bay horse and stopped in the downtown area. The three of them stared at the unusual sight. The man made a throwing motion with one arm before turning and racing back the way he had come. An explosion, far louder than the loudest prairie thunder, rocked the streets. Windows cracked and a few shattered as flames belched out from a small structure nestled between the bank and jail. James drew in an unsteady breath, frozen for an endless second. Then he ran as he had never run before, Cody and Kristina close at his heels.

They arrived at the front of Becky's burning shop as a shaken-looking Sheriff Brody staggered from his office. Patrons and employees poured out of the bank into the street, wanting to know what the ruckus was about.

Please, Lord, let Rebecca be away from here. James peered into the shop, trying to see if anyone was inside. The shattered panes impeded his vision, and the thick black smoke concealed the interior from view.

"What happened?" Brody asked.

"Someone firebombed the shop," Cody replied grimly. "We all saw it."

At that moment, the heavens opened and a deluge of blinding, icy rain poured down on the crowd.

Several of the milling onlookers squealed and ran for their homes. In the midst of the commotion, a heart-stopping sound cut through. A woman's scream of utter terror.

Oh Lord, no! Rebecca! Without thought, James ran forward. The inferno had already engulfed the door, barring his way. Shifting his eyes frantically to one side and then the other, he realized the glass had mostly broken out of the left-hand display window. He vaulted through.

Inside, black smoke choked out the oxygen. James dropped to the floor, pulling his wet shirt loose and up over his nose.

"Rebecca?" he called, his voice muffled by the damp fabric. The crackling of the fire drowned out his voice, and the thick smoke prevented him from seeing. *How can I find her?* "Rebecca, where are you?" He crawled blindly. *Where is she? Oh God, please let her be all right!*

Move, Heitschmidt, it's a small space. Don't stop. Find her. He crept further into the inferno. "Rebecca!"

A flaming beam fell from the ceiling, landing inches from his hip. For a moment, self-preservation threatened to send him back through the window.

"Come on, man," he said aloud, and then choked on a lungful of smoke. Even close to the floor, breathing was growing increasingly difficult. He pressed on. *I have to find her. No turning back. Not without Rebecca. Oh, God, I haven't even told her I love her. Please don't let her die! Please, God, let me find her.*

"I'm coming, Rebecca!" he called, as he inched his way forward, groping blindly through the choking smoke until his head hit a solid object. He touched it. *Wood. The counter. What if she's behind it?* He felt his way along the half-wall to its opening and passed through. Reaching out with one hand, he connected with a slim ankle.

The heat was growing unbearable. Flames licked all the walls. Luckily the floor and counter had not caught yet, but there wasn't much time. A hesitant hand touched his, and he grabbed and pulled, reversing Rebecca's direction so she headed the same way as him.

"Stay low," he hissed in her ear. Then he began guiding her in a crawl across the floor, covering her body with his. *It's a good thing she's so petite.* He urged her forward, in what he hoped was a straight line, back towards the broken window.

The instant they arrived, he knocked several spear-like shards of glass out of the bottom of the wooden frame with his elbow before he boosted her out, following close behind.

Free of the burning shop, but still hidden from view by the smoke, James found Rebecca had collapsed. He scooped her into his arms and carried her away from the blaze.

As they emerged into the rainy street, he noted in passing that a bucket brigade was throwing water… not on the shop, but on the jail and the bank. *At least the other buildings can be spared. The rain will help put out the flames.*

Coughing, James sank down to sit on the sodden brick walkway, Rebecca cradled close to his chest. She lay still as death, her eyes closed.

"Rebecca," he said quietly. "Rebecca, are you all right?"

"Dad?" James looked up to see Kristina standing over him. Drenched from head to foot, she sank to her knees, heedless of even more water soaking into her skirt. She threw her arms around his neck and nearly strangled him with an enthusiastic hug.

"Easy," he urged, prying her clutching arm away from his windpipe.

"Sorry," she said. "When you went through that window..." Her voice broke and he looked up to see tears streaming down her face. *Poor Kristina. She's lost her mother and her brother, but in spite of that, I wouldn't have done anything differently. The risk was necessary.*

His daughter visibly pulled herself together. "Is Becky all right?" she asked.

"I don't know," he replied. "She seems to have passed out." He shook the woman gently. "Rebecca. Wake up, love. Rebecca." Nothing. He looked up at Kristina and found her eyes had narrowed. James sighed. *The cat's out of the bag now. Oh well. It's time anyway.*

"She's breathing," Kristina observed. "Why don't you take her home, Dad? Being out in this rain won't do her any good."

James nodded. He lifted his precious burden, cradling her against his chest.

"Kristina!" Cody appeared suddenly, grasping his wife's hand. "Come on, let's get you out of here before you catch your death." He led her away.

While the bucket brigade attempted to control the fire that was quickly consuming Rebecca Spencer's shop, Sheriff Brody hurried back into the jail.

A deliberate arson, a firebombing, seems like a diversionary tactic. Sure enough, the jail had more inhabitants than it should. A man, a bandana over his face, was attempting to pick the lock on the barred door holding the criminal captured in the train robbery.

"You there," Brody said, "stop, right now. You're under arrest."

The bandit froze, then whirled around, dropping his lock pick and grabbing at the holster on his hip, but Brody had already drawn. He leveled his revolver at the criminal.

"So help me," the man said, "if you hang this man, you'll bring disaster down on yourself. There are a lot more of us than you realize, and we will take down you, your friends, the whole damned town."

"Ha," Brody replied, unimpressed. "Just try it." He cocked the gun. Despite the roaring of the fire next door and the noisy downpour, the sound of metal striking metal resounded ominously through the stone room.

The criminal responded to the threat in a way Brody had not anticipated. He jumped him, hitting him low on the legs and knocking him to the floor. Brody balled up a fist and swung but connected with nothing. The moment the two of them had hit the floor, the criminal had taken the opportunity to flee, bounding out the door like a startled jackrabbit. Before he fled, before Brody could regain his feet or even aim his revolver, the bandit said, "Remember, if you hang him, you're dead."

Then he was gone.

Chapter 11

James carried Rebecca down the street to his house. Inside, he kicked off his wet, muddy shoes and then stood, just past the doorway, in a quandary. Water dropped from both his and Rebecca's hair and clothing onto the wood floor. She had not regained consciousness yet, which was beginning to alarm him. *A mere faint shouldn't have lasted this long. I hope she hasn't sustained serious lung damage.*

"Rebecca!" he shook her with greater vigor than he had in the street. "Rebecca, wake up. Open your eyes, honey."

She stirred and moaned, turning her face against his shoulder.

"No." He shook her again. "Wake up. Come on, Rebecca."

She groaned and raised her head. "Wha... what happened?" Then she broke into a fit of prolonged coughing.

James held her while she expelled the smoke residue from her lungs. Heedless of their sodden, dripping garments, he carried her through the house to the kitchen. Carefully setting her on a chair, he brought her a glass of water.

She sipped the cool drink and then sighed as it soothed her aching throat. "What happened?" she asked again, her voice raw and harsh.

"There was a fire," he replied honestly, if not completely. *No need to frighten her with the idea of intentional arson.* He watched the memory dawn on her. Her face crumpled and a rough sob clawed its way from her throat.

James moved to her side faster than a heartbeat, setting her cup on the table and pulling her forward into his arms. Her wet hair hung half unbound in long, straggly strands. He removed the pins and stroked the sodden mass tenderly. "You're fine, Rebecca," he soothed. "You're safe."

"My shop?" she choked out.

"I'm sorry," he replied, setting off a flood of fresh tears.

"Oh no!" she moaned. "All that time and money. My fabrics. The dresses I had almost finished. How will I ever come back from this?"

"You will, Rebecca. They're just things. They're not your whole life."

"They are!" she insisted, lifting her face and meeting his eyes. "How will I make a living now? I was counting on the shop for my future!"

She must still be confused. "You don't need that, remember?"

She shook her head, looking as lost as he felt.

"I'm here, darling," he told her. "Let me take care of you."

Something about his words seemed to cut through her, and not in a good way. Her confusion gave way to even greater sorrow. She buried her face in her shaking hands. Her whole body seemed to vibrate with cold and misery.

Women are beyond my comprehension. Giving up the conversation for a calmer time, James helped Rebecca to her feet. He took her hand and guided her through the house to the guest bedroom.

"James, what are we doing here?" she asked, that serene expression and tone firmly back in place, though tears stained her eyes and little hiccups interrupted her words.

"You need to get out of those wet clothes. Some of Trudy's are here. They might be a little loose, but at least they'll be warm and dry."

Rebecca stood frozen and trembling.

Without thought, James reached for the buttons of her sodden blouse. He had her mostly undressed before he even realized what he was doing, and then awareness dawned. Rebecca stood before him clad only in her damp, transparent bloomers.

He froze, eyes riveted on her frame. *What a tempting body she has. Slim, not excessively curvy, but so pretty.* His hand rose of its own volition and gently touched one pert, upright breast. Her little brown nipple reacted instantly, hardening beyond the cold in the room, and she made a soft sound. Her skin felt still cool, but silky soft. He squeezed gently.

And then madness descended. Though James had not set out to seduce his beloved, conscious thought had shattered. He acted on pure instinct, holding out one hand. She, it seemed, possessed no more control than he. She stepped close to him, pulling his mouth down to hers.

His fingers closed on her nipple, gently rolling it.

Rebecca gasped and ground her lower body against him. He pulled her to the bed and collapsed, bringing her with him. They stretched out,

James cupping the slender curve of Rebecca's bottom, and pulled her close, and groaned as her soft belly compressed around his sex. *It's been an eternity since I held a woman in my arms. I want those luscious breasts against my skin.* He reached for her and realized Rebecca wanted the same thing. Her fingers wormed between them and worked the buttons of his shirt. He skimmed off the garment and tossed it aside before pulling her close again.

They kissed tongue to tongue, a fiery embrace of the sweetest passion as they pressed their bodies together. James urged Rebecca to her back and leaned over her, studying the tableau of her lovely, naked curves. Then his hands returned to her breasts. She urged him on, with not a hint of shyness, arching her back to offer herself to him. He fondled and caressed one small, pale globe while he took the other with his mouth.

Rebecca drew in an unsteady breath. Her hips squirmed beneath him, providing enticing stimulation that made his sex ache. *How eager and responsive she is. Some of the best qualities a wife can have. I can scarcely wait to make our relationship permanent. I can't wait. I have to have her now. Rebecca is mine, and I almost lost her.*

Suddenly frantic, he pulled the drawstring of her damp bloomers and tugged the garment down her body. She kicked it away.

His own trousers and drawers joined the pile of discarded clothing, and at last, he was able to stretch out atop his woman with nothing between them. She opened her thighs, but he didn't immediately press for penetration. Instead, he touched her with his fingertips, feeling the wetness of her feminine folds and slipping inside. Her passage clung tighter than he'd expected. *Whatever that fool did to her didn't leave much of an impression. I'll fix that.*

He trailed his fingers the short distance to her clitoris and began to stroke the erect nub. Rebecca let out a surprised squeak at the intense sensation. *I wonder if she's been caressed here at all. She seems so startled, but no matter, I'll teach her to accept a man's pleasuring.*

He feathered light touches on her heated flesh until Rebecca's squirming increased to a constant, eager movement. Her head tossed on the pillow.

She's getting close… so close, but I want to feel her peak.

As he continued building her pleasure, he aligned himself and arched his hips. The tender portal yielded to his entry and he worked his way through her clinging passage until they were fully joined.

Rebecca's muscles locked, and a cry of pleasure seemed to tear itself from her lips. He kissed her, drinking in the soft sounds. The clenching of her internal muscles caressed him deliciously and he only managed a few thrusts before joining her in ecstasy.

Years of built-up tension led to a long orgasm, but eventually, James relaxed. He stretched out on top of his beloved. Their bodies remained joined, though he held his weight on his arms.

"Hmmmm," he hummed. "Sweet Rebecca." He kissed the side of her neck as he gently withdrew.

She turned to her side. He cuddled up against her back and realized her trembling had increased. *Is she cold? No,* he realized, *she's crying. Probably a reaction to everything that had just happened.* "It's all right, love," he murmured against her ear. "Everything is all right. I'm here."

"Nothing's right," she said, her voice catching on every word. "What have I done? Oh God, what have I done?" Sobs overtook her.

What on earth does she mean? "What, this?" he asked, running his hand along her naked arm before hugging her close around the waist. "It's not as terrible as all that, love. I mean, yes it would probably have been better to wait, but we're getting married anyway."

"Are we?"

The question cut him to the heart. "Do you think we're not, Rebecca? Did you change your mind?"

"You changed yours. I know you did. Or maybe you never intended to…"

"No," he snapped, offended anger flaring. "What kind of talk is this? We've been talking marriage all along. That's the point of courtship. What else would it be?"

She shook her head, rejecting his words. "Another seduction. God, I'm stupid. Why do I trust men?"

Pain and confusion drove off the lingering sweetness of their loving. "Seduction?" James growled. "I didn't see that you had to be manipulated, Rebecca."

"No," she agreed, her voice filled with regret. "I didn't have to be manipulated. I guess I'm wanton after all."

"Stop it," he told her harshly, "you're being ridiculous. I don't know where you get these foolish notions, but there's no truth in them. You're not wanton. Just a passionate woman who needs a husband to take care of her. I want to be that husband. I have all along. I'd intended a proper courtship, but I got a little… overwhelmed by the fire and the thought that I'd almost lost you. That's all that happened. I still intend what I always intended. To make you my wife."

"I don't believe you," she choked, bitter sobs wracking her slender frame.

Icy fury overwhelmed him. "And just why the hell not? You've known me for years, Rebecca. I don't seduce women. I never have, and I never will. What have I done to make you distrust me?"

"You said…" her voice broke. She struggled with herself for a long moment and then finally managed to force the words out. "You said you would talk to my parents soon. Three months isn't soon, James. You're keeping me a secret. Are you ashamed of me?"

Ashamed? She thinks I'm ashamed of her? Dear Lord. His anger drained away in a heartbeat. "No, Rebecca, I'm not ashamed. Not at all. I just…" This time he broke off, words abandoning him. *How can I explain something that, when I analyze it, doesn't even make sense to me? I've been stupid. No wonder she's upset.* He tried anyway. "Listen. I… I've only courted one woman before you. I assumed… I guessed that you would want the same things Trudy did. She made me wait for ages, almost a year before we announced our engagement. She enjoyed having the secret. I didn't want you to miss out on anything. And then Calvin." This time, James's voice wavered.

She touched his cheek, giving him sympathetic eyes, but her words returned them to the point. "James, don't you think, given my… history, that I might not want to keep secrets or wait a long time?"

Of course. It's obvious if only I'd stopped to think. She's been hurt, betrayed. She has trouble trusting. Naturally, she will want to tie her man to her in a very visible and obvious way. The delay has not helped any of that, and the lovemaking we just shared only increased her doubts. "I'm sorry," he told her, kissing her cheek. "Please don't think of it that way. I didn't intend to hurt you, and I'm not ashamed of you. Quite the opposite. I love you, Rebecca, and I will marry you. Can you try to believe that?"

She shook her head. "I can't."

Her words stung him, but he tried to squash it down. "Well, let's see what we can do to fix that. Get dressed, darling. We're leaving."

"Leaving where?"

"To your home. We're going to bring this out into the open, right now. We're telling your parents everything."

"Everything?" She demanded, eyes wide and voice a breathy whisper of panic.

"Not about making love, of course, but everything else. It's time. Past time. Up, Rebecca." He helped her to her feet.

The knocker on the front door pounded, so James quickly pulled on his trousers and shirt and hurried downstairs. He arrived in time to see Kristina, her hair damp and her shoes dark with water, just shutting the door behind her.

"Dad? So you are here. Where on earth is Becky?"

"Rebecca is here," he replied, trying not to blush.

Kristina took in his disheveled hair, misbuttoned shirt, and crumpled trousers and her eyes widened.

"She's here? Why is she here? And since when do you call her Rebecca?"

"You told me to bring her home. I did."

"Yes, Dad. To her home. Her folks are worried sick. No one knows where she is."

James blinked. *I certainly misunderstood her intention.* "She was all dirty and wet. I brought her here to change. And I've called her Rebecca for a few months. We're… courting, you know."

If Kristina's jaw had fallen any farther, it would have hit the floor. "You... Becky... what? Dad, what do you mean? You're courting... planning to marry... one of my best friends?"

"Yes, Kristina," he told his daughter. "That doesn't upset you, does it? She is eleven years older than you, after all."

"And ten years younger than you. I guess... I guess I'm not upset, just surprised. But I was thinking about you, how you've been alone these last few years and... well, I was thinking Lydia..."

James shook his head. "There's nothing wrong with Miss Carré, but I'm not interested. Besides, she's younger than Rebecca, did you know?"

"I guess, because I've known Becky my whole life, she seems younger. I suppose it's not a problem, but, Dad, you'd better not go out looking the way you do. People will talk."

He looked down at himself. *Kristina's right, I'm certainly not my usual put-together self. I can't go and talk to the Spencers like this. I'll have to tidy up my clothing and comb my hair.*

A soft swish of fabric drew his eyes to the top of the stairs and his heart melted at the sight of his Rebecca, hastily clad in ill-fitting garments, a stain of pink embarrassment on her cheeks as she faced her friend with the guilty knowledge that she'd just been rolling naked in bed with that friend's father.

She'll have to get used to it, because I aim to change this around completely, now.

"Oh, there you are, Becky," Kristina said, trying to sound normal. "Everyone is wondering where you've been. You'd better head home before your parents worry themselves sick over you."

"Oh, yes, of course," she replied, her voice uncertain.

"Just a moment. I need to tidy up," James said, "and then I'll walk you home."

She nodded, and he pounded up the stairs. Back in his room he straightened his buttons, smoothed his trousers and added a collar. He ran a comb through his hair and glanced at himself in the mirror.

Somehow, the years had crept up on James unannounced. He had celebrated his forty-fifth birthday only a few months before. He didn't feel middle-aged, though. He felt like himself. *Now, suddenly, what I feel is young.* Grinning at his reflection and ignoring the silver gathering at the temples of his red-blond hair, James returned to the parlor where his intended and his daughter sat opposite each other in black leather armchairs. The old friends were, for the first time ever, awkward with each other. They sat in silence so uncomfortable, he could feel it.

"Rebecca?" he said softly, and she shot to her feet. "Come on, let's go. Kristina, would you like to squeeze under my umbrella? It's still raining pretty hard." He indicated the window where a silvery downpour rendered the town nearly invisible.

"No thanks," she replied. "I have one. Bye, Dad, Becky. I… I'll try to get used to this. I'm sure it will be fine."

She fled into the darkening street without another word. Rebecca gave James a stricken-eyed glance. "How upset is she?"

"She'll be all right," he replied, evading the answer. Then he slid his arm around her waist and led her out the door.

They walked through the pouring rain, getting their ankles and feet quite soaked. Rebecca shivered with cold and nerves. *I may be more than of age—an established spinster—but facing my parents with my intended on my arm…* Bubbles of nervous terror churned her stomach into nausea. Only by leaning heavily on James was she able to keep moving forward. The blocks between them and her home stretched out, seeming to lengthen in the growing dusk. *Will we never arrive? Will the promised conversation never come? It feels like a nightmare.*

Eventually, the cheerful house loomed up out of the darkness and they hurried to the door. Inside, after wiping their shoes carefully on an already soggy mat, they greeted Mr. and Mrs. Spencer, who were waiting in the parlor.

"Rebecca, thank the Lord! Where on earth have you been?" Her mother jumped to her feet and crossed the room in a flurry of navy skirts. She pulled her daughter into a warm, motherly embrace.

Rebecca nestled there for a moment. *I just nearly died in a fire.* That truth, which had been subverted under all the momentous events that had followed, rolled over her in a wave, and she began not just to tremble but to shake violently.

"Suh... sorry, Mom," she stuttered. "There was a fire." Then, abruptly, it was all too much, and she succumbed to deep, quiet sobs.

Her mother rubbed her back, squeezing her with one arm. Her father approached and joined in the embrace.

"We heard about the fire," he said. Concern wreathed his rugged, heavily lined face. His salt and pepper hair stood on end where he'd run his fingers through it. "Where were you, Rebecca?"

"James..." she started, turning to look at her intended. He stood awkwardly by the door.

Her parents also glanced at him, then back at her, with matching questioning expressions on their faces.

She swallowed hard and steadied herself with a deep breath. "James rescued me from the fire," she said at last, and her voice sounded firmer, less shaky. "He went into a burning building to save me."

That didn't answer their question. Both of them still regarded her with puzzled eyes.

"He... we..."

"I've been... spending time with Rebecca lately," James said, taking over the conversation. "It's time to come and speak to you formally." He crossed the room and laid a hand on her shoulder.

She stepped away from her parents and took his arm.

"Mr. Spencer, Mrs. Spencer, I would like to ask your blessing to marry your daughter."

Rebecca froze. *Marry? Did he say marry? I expected him to ask their permission to court me, but apparently, he was more serious than I realized.*

Her gaze returned to her parents.

They looked at each other, stunned, and then turned as one back to the couple. She could see approval in her mother's eyes. It made Rebecca a little angry. *Yes, James is a fine catch, being a prosperous, well-*

respected member of the community, but that's not why I love him, so put that greedy face away, Mother.

I love him, and I haven't told him, she realized. He told me, but I didn't respond. I'll have to fix that right away.

"Well..." her father began, "that's certainly a bombshell." He winced at his inappropriate word choice. "I'll consider, but the question remains, what kept you? The... event took place over an hour ago. Where have you been?"

"Sorry," James replied, a hint of guilt in his tone. "Rebecca was a mess from the... incident. I wasn't thinking clearly. I took her back to my house, so she could clean up and get warm. I gave her some dry clothes to change into. I'm sorry we worried you."

Her father pursed his lips, looking somewhat less than convinced.

"Rebecca," her mother said suddenly, "those clothes don't fit you, and you're soaked around the ankles. Why don't you go put on something dry and... yours?"

Rebecca nodded, glad for the reprieve, and hurried out of the room.

"Have a seat, Heitschmidt," Mr. Spencer said, in a voice that told James it was not a suggestion. He sat on a sage green, high-backed armchair and the Spencers took the sofa, giving him matching bemused looks.

"Tell me," Mrs. Spencer began, "when did this happen?"

"About three months ago," he replied. He could see this answer did not please them.

"So why didn't you say anything?" Mr. Spencer asked the obvious question.

"I intended to, several different times. Something would always come up."

"Something?" Mrs. Spencer raised her golden eyebrows until her forehead crinkled.

"First it was... her sister's unexpected wedding."

Mrs. Spencer's rosebud lips compressed into a thin line, creating deep grooves on either side.

He hurried on. "Then the train robbery... my son..." he broke off. "I got a little... sidetracked by that."

"Understandable," Mr. Spencer interrupted his awkward rush. "All right. So, you've been secretly courting Rebecca for three months, and now you want to be betrothed to her?"

"Yes," James replied simply.

"You know," Mrs. Spencer began. Her husband laid a hand on her arm and gave her a warning look. "He has a right to know," she told him. "He wants to marry her. Mr. Heitschmidt..."

"James, please," he urged them.

"James then. There is a possibility that Rebecca might not be... chaste. After her former fiancé jilted her, there was talk. She's never said, and we've never asked, but... I think you should know."

James met the woman's blue-eyed gaze steadily. "I don't care," he said firmly, laying all such pointless speculation to rest once and for all. *My lands, these people and their focus on chastity. No wonder Rebecca has no confidence. As though a youthful transgression should sully her reputation and destroy her prospects forever.* He shook his head in disapproval of the gossipy comment.

That seemed to settle the awkward issue, and they all dropped the subject. The look of relief on her parents' faces matched what he felt.

I really don't want to discuss my role in her lack of chastity, he admitted to himself, though he kept his expression frozen, warning them that he'd appointed himself her champion.

"So then," her mother changed the subject, "do you have a timetable in mind?"

"Oh, I don't know," James replied. "I suppose it will depend on what Rebecca wants."

"Soon," a soft voice came from the doorway. Comfortably dressed in a black wool skirt and a white blouse, her hair neatly restrained in a bun, his lady scarcely resembled the beautiful wanton who'd climaxed so sweetly in his arms only a short time ago.

James rose from his seat and collected Rebecca, escorting her to the chair he had just vacated and standing beside her. "How soon, love?" he asked.

She looked to her parents and then to him. "I want to be married before my next birthday."

"And when is that, Rebecca?" he asked.

Her parents glared.

With everything that had just happened, it took him a while to interpret their angry stares. He turned to Rebecca and saw a dismayed look on her face. *Wake up, man. Not only have you been head of the elder board and lay pastor of the church for years, she's also your daughter's close friend. THINK!* "Right, June. Sorry."

Rebecca's lips turned up in a wan smile. Mr. Spencer visibly relaxed.

"No," her mother said firmly. "That's not enough time. It's already mid-March. We cannot plan a wedding at the beginning of June and expect to be ready."

"What kind of wedding are you thinking about, Mother? Because I want something small. Just you two, Allison and Wesley, Cody and Kristina, and Lydia." She slipped her hand into James's and he squeezed her fingers gently. I just want to say my vows and maybe have a little tea and cake. Nothing more is needed. I'm an old woman. There's no reason for a big fuss."

"You're not old, princess," her father told her.

"I'm old to be unmarried," she replied.

"If you want a small wedding or a large one, I don't care either way. We'll do exactly what you prefer," James said, injecting his thoughts into the conversation. *My bride will have the wedding she wants. I'll make sure of it, whether her mother agrees or not.*

"That's what I want," she said firmly. "A small, simple wedding at the end of May or beginning of June."

Her parents nodded.

It seems when Rebecca insists on something, she gets her way.

Chapter 12

Allison paced the parlor of her home. Every surface gleamed in the afternoon sunshine. In her nervous agitation, she'd polished, dusted, washed windows and generally tidied up. Now the room had never looked cleaner, but the frantic activity had done nothing to quell her nerves. The slight nausea she'd been feeling threatened to rise into full-blown sickness, and she swallowed convulsively.

The door banged open and Allison jumped.

"Hi, hon," Wesley called. "Sorry if I startled you." The fragrance of spring sunshine and prairie flowers trailed him into the room, perfuming the parlor with a sweet, clean, nausea-quelling zephyr.

She inhaled deeply. *Hmmm. Kansas and Wesley. My favorite scent.*

"It's okay, Wes. I was only startled for a moment. What's going on?"

He bounced on his toes, but a grim frown turned his lips down. The strange juxtaposition only made her own swirling thoughts worse.

"Well, there was a little excitement downtown earlier. Sheriff Brody called a town meeting. Remember that robber who was arrested?"

She dipped her chin.

"Well, apparently, the firebombing of your sister's shop was a ruse to try and break him out of prison." His odd demeanor remained.

"And?" Allison pressed, frustrated.

"And nothing. He didn't succeed. Brody thwarted the jailbreak, but before he ran, the other robber made threats against the sheriff and the town if his friend is hanged. He claimed—and Brody believes him—that there's a whole gang of criminals still at large, not just the few who escaped the train robbery."

"What will happen?" Allison asked, nervous at the thought of a band of murderous thieves coming against their town in force.

"Nothing much," Wesley replied, looking conflicted. "The execution will go forward as planned, but Brody wants everyone on alert. Any suspicious activity anywhere in town is to be reported immediately, and he wants us all to be armed when we go out. Do you still have your pocket pistol?"

Allison nodded, remembering the tiny, serviceable weapon he'd given her for her seventeenth birthday. "Yes, of course, and I know where the shogun and shells are too." *If anyone threatens my home, I'll be ready.*

And then a sudden image flashed through her mind, of a young man with a rope around his neck, falling, jerking, twitching. Overwhelmed by the sudden, gruesome thought, nausea rose again. Gagging, Allison ran for the door, circled the stairs, and threw up in a large shrub growing below the parlor's bay window.

"Allie?"

She wavered, and Wesley took her arm to steady her, handing her a handkerchief. She accepted it, knowing the only reason he had a clean one was that she tucked it into his pocket each morning.

"You all right?" he asked, a concerned look crossing his features.

"I…" she broke off, swallowing down another retch. "I'm not feeling the best." *Chicken liver, what are you doing? Tell him the truth.*

But she didn't speak again. There was no time because Wesley continued. "Sorry to hear that. Come on, let's have you lie down. Anyway, I talked to Brody." He walked her back up the stairs and into the house, and then up again to their bedroom, chattering all the way.

Wrapped up in her own thoughts, Allison only paid the slightest attention to his monologue.

"He says he's sure there's going to be trouble later. It's going to take a lot of vigilance to prevent a tragedy, because these are evil, unscrupulous men, as you know. He needs a new deputy and asked me if I knew of anyone. I suggested Jesse." Wesley paused. "I know Jesse said he was never coming back, but he's been out there for several years, and maybe he's about ready to change his mind, even if it's for a short time. It never hurts to ask, right? So anyway, I thought… Allie? Allie, are you listening to me?"

Allison shook herself out of her reverie to find herself standing beside her bed. "Yes, Wesley, I'm listening," she said. "Sorry, I have a lot on my mind. It's a bit hard to concentrate."

"What can you possibly be thinking about that's bigger than a band of train robbers attacking our town?" he asked, clearly exasperated.

"I…" *Okay, Chicken Little, spit it out.* "I went to the doctor today. I've been feeling poorly for a while."

"Oh?" Suddenly Wesley's face was in hers, his eyes focused on her, filled with concern. "What's wrong, Allie?"

"I…" She gulped. "The doctor says I'm… expecting." Her voice wavered.

Wesley's face went ashen, and his eyes widened until they looked like saucers. Then his eyebrows and mouth drew down, and when he spoke, his voice sounded harsh and angry. "That is hardly an appropriate way joke, Allison."

She blinked in shock. "Joke? Wes, it's no joke, and it's no surprise either. We've been… passionately married for months. Did you think this wasn't going to happen sooner or later?" Her voice rose on every syllable until she was nearly shrieking.

"I…" he cleared his throat. "Don't shout, please, Allie. I… It has occasionally crossed my mind, but… later, not so soon."

"Wes, I don't think the decision was ours to make. It happened as the Lord willed. I had no control over it."

He made a face as though to speak, but in the end, remained silent.

"Wes, please, say something. I'm scared."

His lowered eyebrows shot toward his hairline. She knew why. *I'm pretty sure he's never heard me admit that, but spiders are one thing. This is so much more… so much more.*

She waited, but still he didn't comfort her or take her in his arms. He didn't say a single word. He stared at her for a long, tense moment, and then turned on his heel and left the room.

"Come on, Mama Allie," Melissa squealed. The rain had finally cleared away and late March sunshine had dried the marshy soil. Now the little girl, frustrated at being cooped up in the house so long, wanted to run and play.

Allison groaned and hauled herself to her feet. She looked at the chamber pot beside her bed. *I really need to deal with that.* She reached for the pot, but the sight of the vomit inside nearly set off another round. *Pregnancy is hell. Absolute hell. I've hardly gone a week without throwing up. It's growing increasingly difficult to keep up with Melissa, all the household chores and Wesley.*

Her gaze veered away from the chamber pot to the bed, and the urge to sleep nearly overwhelmed her. *No, don't nap now, Allison. Little children need to play, and maybe the bracing air will do you some good too.* She left the pot with its unpleasant contents for later and staggered out of the stuffy bedroom.

Downstairs in the kitchen, Melissa was prancing around the table where a plate contained a fragrant pile of molasses and spice cookies that perfumed the air. Allison's mouth watered. She grabbed one and offered another to her stepdaughter.

"Can I have two, Mama?" she asked.

"No, Missy. Only one."

Melissa pouted.

"Let's go outside," Allison said, effectively distracting the little girl from her impending tantrum. Melissa hurried into her coat and they stepped into the backyard.

The cool breeze soothed the heat in Allison's face, and the food finally settled her stomach. *Mom promised the nausea would pass eventually.*

While the little girl skipped through the garden, examining the prairie flowers that had popped out in the last week, Allison thought back over the three months she'd been married. *While everyday life has settled into a routine, there's still a great deal of tension in both my husband and her stepdaughter. I'm not quite sure what to make of it. I knew there would be grief as the two came to terms with Samantha's loss, but there's also a sense of… something. I can't put my finger on it, but they both seem almost to be holding their breath, waiting for something unspeakable to happen.*

Allison had no idea what that was about, and so she simply tried to make life as normal as possible. She'd established a routine they seemed to find more comforting than she could account for. Meals at regular times, a clean home to live in and chores on a schedule. *Typical, normal chores. Something most families have to a certain extent, but to Wesley and Melissa, the routines seem like... like a lifeline.* Even the tiniest deviation sent them into hysterics. With Allison's early pregnancy wearing her down, deviations were becoming more common, with unpleasant results.

Wesley is not happy about the baby.

Allison tried to tell herself that his deadpan reaction to the news had been surprise, and that his continued tense negativity didn't mean anything, but it was getting harder and harder to believe. *He doesn't want me to be pregnant.* Allison sniffled. *I was so excited about carrying Wesley's child, but he doesn't feel the same.* Every sign of her condition elicited a stony stare. He hadn't laid a hand on her since she'd made the announcement. *Marriage is so much harder than I expected.*

Allison shook off her unhappy contemplations. *Melissa. Focus on Melissa.* She scanned the yard, finding it suddenly empty and silent. *Drat. The child moves like greased lightning. Where on earth did she go?* The yard was fenced all the way around, so the only place she could have gone was back into the house. Allison mounted the steps and pushed open the back door into the kitchen. There, under the table, the little girl sat cramming one cookie after another into her sugar-crusted mouth.

"Melissa Elizabeth Fulton!" Allison exclaimed, wresting the plate out of the child's hands and setting it back on the table. Melissa attempted to flee, but Allison caught her by the shoulder and delivered one hard swat to the back of her pinafore. "I told you that you couldn't have another," she scolded. We'll be eating dinner soon. It was very naughty of you to take more."

Melissa burst into noisy crocodile tears. "You're a bad mommy," she wailed. "I'm going to tell Daddy you hit me."

"Tell him," Allison shrugged. "You can also tell him how you disobeyed me. You're going to spend some time in the corner, little girl."

She marched the child to the spot where two walls met and faced her away from the room. "Now you stand there and think about what you've done."

Melissa tried to leave, squirming in Allison's grip. Allison spanked her bottom once more, hard enough to sting, but not enough to do any lasting harm. *Goodness knows I received enough such swats in my own childhood.*

Melissa stilled and submitted with no further protest. Meanwhile, Allison hunted down the broom and swept the cookie crumbs from the floor, muttering under her breath. "It's still cold enough that rodents might creep inside and be attracted to them, as well as insects, which are starting to awaken. Leaving the sugary bits behind is an invitation to creatures of all kinds to invade our kitchen, and goodness knows, they're already used to living here."

As she worked, luscious aromas soothed her agitation. Rich beef stew with vegetables simmered on the stove. A loaf of fragrant, homemade bread cooled on the counter, ready to be devoured with a smear of butter. Her mouth watered. *I hope Wes comes home soon. If I delay eating…it will have the opposite effect from what I want… to calm my husband with a delicious supper and lure him to bed.*

She added a handful of peas to the stew and set the table. Just as she began to make her way back to the corner to release her stepdaughter from her punishment, the front door banged open.

"Daddy! Daddy!" Melissa yelled, leaving the corner without permission and running through the house to her father.

"Hello, princess." Allison heard her husband say.

"Mama Allie was naughty today. She hit me."

Allison pushed open the door, amused by the child's tattling. Then she saw her husband's face. His eyes, narrow, his jaw tight, he seemed to radiate a violent rage. "Allison, Melissa says…"

"I heard," she said, her voice light.

"Is it true?" His voice sounded like two stones rubbing together.

"I didn't 'hit' her, Wesley. She disobeyed me. I gave her one swat. She disobeyed me again and I gave her another. That's all. Two swats on the bottom. That's all that happened. Why is that a problem?"

Wesley set his daughter on the floor and advanced on his wife. Anger radiated from him. His fists clenched, causing his biceps—thicker than they had any right to be on a man who worked behind a desk—to flex into a palpable threat.

She took one step backwards, involuntarily, but then firmed her resolve and stood her ground.

He grabbed her arm in an iron grip. "Don't hit the baby!" he gritted out.

"I didn't hit her. I spanked her. She deserved it." Allison forced her voice into a flat calm, but inside, her heart pounded, and nausea churned her stomach again.

Wesley's hand drew back, closing into his fist as he snarled, "You said you were better than *her*, but you're not. You're just the same. Are you a whore like her too? Is that even my baby you're carrying?"

Allison ignored the details of what he was saying, focusing on preventing the deadly blow that seemed imminent. "Wesley Fulton, so help me, if you hit me, I'll have Sheriff Brody lock you up. DON'T!"

They remained frozen in that posture for a lingering moment, Wesley threatening violence on his wife, who stood firm, not backing down, meeting his rage with the appearance of calm.

Then he took a deep, shuddering breath and lowered his hand. The bruising grip on her arm relaxed.

"My God, Wes. What on earth has been going on here?" she asked softly. Now that the crisis had passed, Allison began to tremble at the awareness of just how close they had come to disaster.

"Allie, I..." he broke off. Turned to leave. She grabbed his arm.

"Wes, don't go. Don't run from me."

"I almost hurt you, Allie." Even the hunched posture of his back spoke of despair.

"I know, but you didn't. You stopped. You can't run away, Wes. We have to talk about this."

He shook his head.

She ran around the front of his body, taking his arms in her hands and placing herself directly in his line of sight. "Do not walk away from me, Wesley. You are my husband. We have to deal with this. And you're frightening Melissa."

His gaze went to the child, who crouched, frozen like a rabbit, her eyes huge.

The sight of his daughter seemed to shake Wesley loose of whatever had seized hold of him. He crossed to her swiftly and scooped her up.

She hugged him, her little lip trembling. "I'm sorry, Daddy."

"Sorry for what, princess?" he asked her.

"For eating all the cookies. Mama Allie said no, but they were so yummy, I couldn't stop."

"So, you were naughty then?" he asked gently.

She nodded, looking contrite.

"And did Mama Allie hurt you, or spank your bottom?"

Melissa refused to answer. Wesley visibly relaxed.

A little thread of anger flared in Allison. *He didn't believe me. He's known me his whole life, and yet he thought it possible I might hurt his child… or any child. He'd had to get the truth from Missy in order to believe it. What the devil had gone on in this house?*

Wesley kissed Melissa on the cheek. "If you're naughty and Mama Allie swats you, you deserve it. Don't tattle on her again," he said, his voice stern. "Now go play with your dollies in your room. We'll call you to dinner soon."

The child scampered off, glad for the reprieve. While she couldn't possibly have understood what had just happened, she clearly realized that on some level, she was responsible for the terrifying scene she'd just witnessed.

As soon as she was out of earshot, Allison cornered her husband. "All right, Wes, you'd better spill it. What the hell just happened?"

Her husband flinched at her harsh, though not-unexpected language. "I… well, um…" he stammered, getting nowhere.

"Did she hurt Melissa?" Allison demanded, refusing to let him off easy. *I have to know what I'm was up against, what memories I'm fighting.*

"Sometimes," he replied. "I tried to make her stop."

"And yet you left them together," Allison was appalled, "knowing what could happen?"

"What choice did I have? Sam was her mother. What else could I do?"

"Anything else," Allison insisted. "She's *your* daughter too. How could you leave her in danger? What's wrong with you?"

Wesley's jaw clenched. "I didn't know what else to do. There was already so much talk... I... I don't know."

"Talk," Allison scoffed. "As if gossip is more important than her safety. For shame, Wesley."

That dangerous rage flared on his face again. He gritted his teeth and clenched his fists, though they remained at his sides.

This time Allison took a step back.

Wesley's shoulders sagged. "I never knew what to do. You can't imagine, Allie, what it was like, living with her from day to day. We could never guess if she was going to be sweet or violent. It changed like the wind changes directions. There was no predicting her moods."

"And she was unfaithful too, wasn't she?" Allison asked gently.

He gave her a stony look.

"Hey, I need to know!" she reminded him. "You have long-established habits that don't make sense to me. I need to understand why."

He nodded, his expression exhausted. "I have no idea how many lovers she had, but it was more than one."

Allison shook her head. "Will you ever be able to let go of the hurt?" she asked. "Or will I be competing with the memories of a dead woman forever?"

"I don't know," he told her honestly, his face bleak. "I know it seems impossible, but I loved her on some level. Loved her as much as I hated her." That thought seemed to be the most destructive of all. Wesley's eyes shone, and his breathing grew ragged.

Despite what had just transpired, Allison took her husband in her arms. "I know you loved her, Wes. It's fine that you did. She was your wife. Try to remember the good and let go of the rest. Everything is different now. I'm here, and it will never be like that again."

She pulled his head down and kissed his lips.

He remained rigid in her embrace, allowing her to move him but not responding in any way.

"I don't know what Samantha's demons were," Allison said, "but she's free from them now. She's at peace. Can't you let them go too? Find some peace for yourself?"

She kissed him again. This time, it seemed, she'd broken through Wesley's restraint. He scooped her into his arms and carried her up the stairs. As they passed the bedroom, she glanced at Melissa, where the child was obediently tucking her dolly into a pair of pink bloomers.

Then Wesley carried Allison though the bedroom door, pushing it shut with his foot and laying her on the bed. His fingers worked feverishly on the buttons of her shirtwaist, baring her to his eyes, to his touch. Her nipples rose eagerly against the thin, transparent fabric of her chemise. He gripped them between his fingertips and squeezed gently, exciting a flurry of half-pained pleasure.

"Oh, Wes," she moaned.

He pulled the flimsy garment from her body and set to work stimulating her breasts directly, plucking and rolling one while he nipped and suckled the other.

"Remember, Wes," she whispered, "no one has touched me but you. No one ever will."

In response, he released the nipple he was sucking and turned to the other. The soreness of the sensitive nubs faded to pure pleasure as he worked them. Meanwhile, his busy fingers opened the tapes on her skirt, shoving it away.

Eager to be bedded, Allison attacked the buttons of his shirt, pushing it from his body.

He rose to remove his shoes and trousers, and Allison hurriedly divested herself of her remaining clothing before reaching out to her husband and urging his naked body on top of her. She sighed, trying to wrap her legs around his.

On his knees, Wesley growled, pressing her hips down with one arm, and leaning back a bit. He reached down and with his free hand and sank his fingers into her drenched, ready folds. She let out a little, ecstatic whine.

"Mine," he rasped, slipping his fingers out of her and pressing them back in again. "All mine."

"Yes, darling," she whimpered. "All yours. Take me, Wes."

He pulled his fingers out and shoved his thick erection in, plunging with one hard thrust. She squealed in delight as he settled into a hard, fast rhythm that sent fire coursing through her body.

"I love you, Wesley," she told him. "I love you, I love you, I love you... oh!" Her orgasm overtook her unexpectedly and pleasured moans replaced her impassioned words.

"Sweet Allie," he murmured before applying himself to his own pleasure, spending himself in a flurry of vigorous thrusts.

Chapter 13

"That was kind of a turning point," Allison said, pouring more tea into her cup at the parlor table and returning to the rocking chair. "Don't tell anyone, please, Becky."

Becky perched on the sofa, sipping her unsweetened brew. "Of course not. So, he's better now? More relaxed?"

"Most of the time." Allison's voice darkened, even as she pasted a false smile on her lips. Then she swallowed convulsively a couple of times and ran her hand lovingly over her belly.

She's about four months now, and her baby's due sometime in late September. Allison's showing rather well, perhaps too much to attend my wedding in June. It isn't going to stop us though. As soon as I finish my own dress, she thought, visions of the deep-rose confection she loved, *I'm going to make a loosely cut one for Allison and the fusspots could all go to hell.*

Becky smiled at herself for thinking such uncouth thoughts. *It's a good thing James can't see what's going on inside my head. No doubt he'd run, screaming, if he discovered the 'perfect lady' he thinks he's marrying has a bit of a dirty mind. More than a bit, actually.*

She'd had a hard time not replaying over and over the events of the night of the fire when they'd lost control and given themselves to each other. While she still suffered paralyzing attacks of self-doubt over whether the wedding would take place, she knew she would cherish that memory forever.

They hadn't repeated their naughty behavior, but now the engagement had been announced, gossiped over, and accepted, James was able to soothe his fiancée with stolen kisses, which set her on fire. He had a freckle at the base of his lower lip that she liked to nibble...

"Becky? Are you still with me?" Allison waved her hand in front of her sister's face.

"Sorry, what?" Rebecca asked, forcing her mind back to the moment.

"Were you thinking about Mr. Heitschmidt again?" Allison asked.

She didn't answer, but if the heat in her cheeks was any indication, she didn't need to.

"Oh, sweetie, you have got it bad, don't you?"

"Yes," Rebecca admitted. "I love him so much, Allison. I can't believe he wants me to be his wife." She set her cup down and admired the amethyst and gold filigree ring he'd placed on her finger. The sight of the large, pretentious purple stone always made her smile. *It's like an advertisement hung in his store window, proclaiming 'This woman belongs to James Heitschmidt'.*

"I can," her sister replied. "There's no reason why he wouldn't. And he doesn't *want* to make you his wife, Becky. He's going to. I bet this time next year, you'll be the one stroking your belly and dreaming about your baby."

Rebecca's eyes stung. "I'm too old for that."

"Ha," Allison scoffed. "Mrs. Johnson just delivered a baby, and she's forty-three."

Rebecca couldn't help smiling. *I like the idea far too much, but what if James, whose daughter just turned twenty-four, doesn't want to start over again with a new baby? I'll have to find out.* "What's it like to be expecting, Allie?" she asked, a little dreamily.

"It's hard at first. I was really sick for a while there, but after the third month, I started to feel better. Now it's exciting. I can feel the little one wriggling in there. It's like a bowl full of minnows inside my belly, and I have the strangest pains at times, but I mostly like it." She touched her swollen stomach. "I can't wait to meet him... or her."

"Is Wesley excited?" she asked, and then cursed herself as Allison's face fell.

"Not too much," the younger woman admitted sadly.

"Why on earth not?"

"Well, I think," Allison said, setting her cup aside and rocking faster, as though to soothe herself, "it has to do with Samantha. You know what they say about... her." She indicated the corner near the window, where Melissa was sitting in a little patch of sunshine, coloring on some newspaper.

"Yes," Rebecca said cautiously.

"He doesn't trust... anyone because of that."

"Well I hope, for your sake," Rebecca said, "he gets over it soon."

"Me too, though it might be asking a lot. It's only been a few months since... since her death, and he never did get a chance to adjust."

"I know. How difficult that must be," Rebecca told her sister, rising from the sofa and kneeling to give Allison a hug. Allison placed Rebecca's hand on her belly, so she could feel the movements.

"That's so sweet," Becky said, smiling. Then she addressed her sister's abdomen. "Welcome to the family, little one. We're all so very glad you're here."

A knock sounded. Allison began the laborious process of rising from the rocking chair, but the unstable seat resisted her attempts.

"I'll get it," Becky offered. "I'm already up." Rising from her knees, she crossed the room in a few steps, admiring how much improvement the family had made to the formerly-shabby space in such a short amount of time. *Some of those scars and scrapes will never come off the walls, but they're only noticeable if I look for them. It's like a home now.*

She opened the front door. Kristina stood outside, her face twisted into lines of devastation. Rebecca hugged her without a word and urged her into the parlor.

Allison finally managed to gain her feet, groaned, swallowing hard and rubbing her forehead, and made her way to her friend. "What's wrong, Kris?" she asked, her voice a study in concern.

Their friend drew a shuddering breath and a tear streaked down her freckled face. Allison quickly joined the hug. The three women stood holding each other while Kristina shuddered with suppressed sobs.

"What is it, sweetie?" Rebecca urged.

"It's stupid," Kristina finally managed to sniffle.

"Nothing's stupid among friends," Allison insisted. "Tell us."

"It's about the... the train robber. We went to the hanging."

The other women gasped. "Why?" Allison blurted.

"We had to... I had to tell him... I forgave him... Oh Lord, that was hard." Her voice broke and she sobbed. Rebecca rubbed her back. "He's just a kid. I don't think he's any older than Cal… Cody offered to pray with him, but he refused. Cody's all broken up about it."

"And so are you," Becky observed.

"Why aren't you with Cody then?" Allison asked.

"He wanted to be alone," she replied, unsteadily.

Men can be awfully hard to understand, Rebecca realized, *even though it's women who have that reputation. Like fathers who are ambivalent about their wives' pregnancies and husbands who want to be alone when they really need their wives. It makes no sense.* She exhaled. *I'll have to deal with my own man's idiosyncrasies too. I hope I'm up to the challenge.*

A sudden, realization rose in her. *James needs me too… right now. The hanging will certainly have an impact on him as well. I wish he would come to me. Instead, he deals with his grief alone, shouldering the burden in silence. I'll have to make time to sit with him and try to get him to open up.*

Suddenly Rebecca felt a little out of her depth. *I've been on my own for years, despite still living in my parents' home, and now I need to get out of myself and take care of my man. Take care of James, even though he doesn't want it.* "You know," she told Kristina gently, "I'm not so sure that it's best for Cody to be left alone. I bet that man refusing to pray hurts Cody. I know how much he cares about people. I might be wrong—what do I know about marriage? —but it seems like you might want to insist he be the one to cuddle with you, not us. It will give him something to do, so he's not just brooding."

Kristina looked up, her face clearly showing that in her husband's arms was exactly where she wanted to be.

"Come on, Kristina. I'll walk you home," Rebecca volunteered. "See you later, Allison. Take care."

"I will," Allison replied, returning to her seat.

Kristina leaned rather heavily on Rebecca as they walked down the empty street Late afternoon sunshine filtered sideways between the buildings, at times dim, at other times blinding. Soon, all the workers would be heading home for their dinner, but right now, silence hung heavy on the town, save the whispering Kansas wind.

At last, they arrived at the vicarage, in the shadow of the church's steeple. Rebecca walked her friend to the door and knocked. Cody answered quickly. The young pastor looked almost as bad as his wife. His black hair stood on end, as though he'd been running his fingers through it, and it seemed he'd wrenched the collar from his wrinkled shirt. The white triangle hung haphazardly from the arm of the sofa. His reddened eyes told the rest of the story.

"What's going on?" he asked in a gruff, gravelly voice that sounded nothing like the smooth bass in which he enunciated their sermons each Sunday in a soft Texas drawl.

"Your wife needs you, Reverend," Rebecca said, urging her friend forward. He took her in his arms without pause. She snuggled against him, hiding her face on his shoulder.

"I don't know much," Rebecca dared to tell Cody softly, "but it seems to me that if you're both hurting, the place to be is together."

Cody nodded once and guided his wife inside, shutting the door. Rebecca headed back down the red brick path to the street, where she traversed the embedded bricks for half a block to the general store. *I need James, if only for a moment.*

There was no one there. The door of the mercantile was locked up tight. Through the window, she could see the corner they'd been setting up with several dress forms, a shelf for bolts of fabric, and a counter of her own. *As soon as the sewing machine he bought me for a wedding gift arrives, I can restart my business right there in my husband's store.*

She smiled. *James is such a conscientious man. Most would expect their wives to stay home, but he's not only willing to allow me to work, he's providing the space. I love him for that, along with so many other things.*

Her smile turned rueful. *If he's gone home, I can't really go there. I'll have to wait for another time. Drat.*

Sighing, Becky picked her way through the lengthening shadows up the street to her parents' house; the last place on earth she wanted to be.

Late that evening, Kristina Heitschmidt sat in a kitchen chair she'd pulled up to the window, watching the spring moonlight glitter on the streets. She'd been unable to sleep, despite passing an emotional evening with her husband.

A movement in her peripheral vision caught Kristina's attention. A figure swathed in black made his way down the street, movements furtive, sliding from one shadow to the next. Alarmed, Kristina stood, planning to wake her husband. *If the robber gang is planning something untoward, we need to do something to stop them.*

Then a gust of Kansas wind ruffled the figure, sending the black hood falling back to reveal the golden hair and delicate features of Rebecca Spencer. The woman looked to the left and right and, seeing no one, pulled the hood back up and hurried on in the direction of Kristina's childhood home.

The pastor's wife compressed her mouth in a disapproving line. *If Becky doesn't return in the next ten minutes or so, there will be hell to pay tomorrow.*

James sprawled on the sofa in his parlor, reading a book by the light of the oil lamp. Or trying to. Dark thoughts weighed on his mind. *Today, my son's murderer was executed. At one time, I looked forward to the dispensing of justice, but now I see it won't bring Calvin back. It will not give me the opportunity to make things right with my son, who died before we could talk, before we could forgive each other for the mess we made of our relationship.*

Cal died defending his sister, and she and Cody were there with him at the end, making sure he didn't die alone. Those thoughts, with which well-meaning friends tried to soothe him, provided no comfort at all. *I don't want platitudes. I want my son.*

A soft sound, a knock on the door, drew him out of his despairing contemplation. *How odd. It's late, far later than anyone should be up, let alone knocking on people's doors. Who could it be?*

He opened it to see the petite figure and glowing golden hair of his fiancée.

"Rebecca?" James asked, startled.

"James, I… I need… can I please come in?"

Blinking, he ushered her into the parlor and shut the door.

"What's going on, love?" he asked, turning to face her.

"I couldn't sleep. I… I'm sorry. I hope I didn't disturb you."

She looks… desperate, nearly hysterical. James approached quickly and took her in his arms. No matter how often they embraced, it always amazed him how warm and sweet she felt. Tonight, it appeared, she also felt needy. She slipped her arms around his neck and pulled him down for a hot, wild kiss. It was exactly what James wanted, and he shared his love with her for long moments, until fiery arousal left him on the edge of his control.

"Stop, love," he urged, pulling back a few inches and studying her face in surprise.

"Oh please, James, don't stop me. I need you." She guided his mouth back to hers and nipped his lower lip.

"Rebecca?"

"I'm burning up. I can't stop… thinking about you, about what we did. Can't we please, please do it again?"

He blinked. *Where did this eager creature come from? Oh, I've seen the heat in her eyes more than once, and I know, once our marriage vows are said, I'll be getting a passionate wife. I want that, but I never expected this.* "Let's just be very clear here. You're asking me to make love to you?"

She nodded, biting her lip. "I feel like such a hussy, but I can't help it. I want you. I need you. Please, James."

He kissed her forehead. *I should send her home. Make her wait until our wedding night, but I can't. I need her just as badly.* "Listen, love. You're not a hussy. Everyone needs to be close to the one they love sometimes. Never be ashamed to ask me for what you need, darling."

"I do love you, James," she said fervently.

The words resounded like music in his heart. "Come on," he said, taking her hand and leading her up the stairs to his bedroom.

Unlike the previous time, when they'd come together in a mad rush, this evening James undressed his lady slowly, kissing and caressing her as he bared her body. Her busy hands worked feverishly at his buttons, stripping him down as he did her until they stood naked. Then he reached out his arms and engulfed her in a crushing embrace, feeling the intense pleasure of her soft skin.

He pulled the pins from her hair, freeing the silky, golden strands to tumble around her shoulders and down her back. He laced his fingers through it at her scalp, pinning her in place so he could ravage her mouth. She acquiesced to his plundering with a soft, breathy moan.

James's heart pounded. He released Rebecca's mouth and stepped back, holding her hands and looking over the entire length of her body. Slender shoulders, small, upright breasts crowned with erect nipples, much darker than he would have expected on her pale skin, tiny waist, softly curving hips... she was a study in delicate beauty. *It seems almost wasteful that her gorgeous body has been hidden away all these years with no one to enjoy it.* Determined to make up for lost time, he stepped close to her again, kissing her and then trailing his lips down her neck. He cupped her breasts and leaned down to kiss each one.

The difference in their heights made it difficult for him to continue while standing. She seemed to realize it because she stepped away, walking to the bed, pulling down the covers and stretching out on the cream-colored sheets.

James grinned at her eagerness and quickly joined her, kneeling to straddle her hips and continuing what he had begun. He touched his lips to her nipple and opened over it, treating her to a long, pleasurable suck. Her fingers laced into his hair, holding him against the soft flesh as he nipped and tugged the tender peak. She moaned and squirmed.

"Hmmm," he hummed, "you are so sweet." He left the glistening nub and turned to the other, lashing it with his tongue.

"Oh, James," she sighed. "Oh yes."

"Does that feel good, Rebecca?" he asked. "Does that please you, darling?'

"Oh yes. I had no idea."

"So innocent," he teased, smiling as her eyes lit up. "Let me teach you." He kissed her between her breasts and followed the line of her sternum down, then down lower again, trailing his lips over the convexity of her lower belly, nibbling the edge of her navel, and at last pressing his lips to the golden curls between her thighs.

Rebecca drew in an unsteady breath. "James?"

"Trust me, love. Bend your knees."

She did, and he moved her, positioning her legs on the outside of his thighs, so she lay splayed open before him. He ran his thumbs along the edges of her cleft and pressed gently, parting the folds and revealing the wet pink flesh between.

He glanced up at her blushing face and smiled.

"So pretty," he whispered, stroking the length of her womanhood from top to bottom with the tip of one index finger. She gasped as he touched her clitoris, and then sighed as he slowly eased into her opening.

He lowered his mouth then and kissed her, snaking out his tongue to tease her sensitive, throbbing pearl. Rebecca whimpered.

"That's it, darling," he murmured, "I want to make you feel so good."

She seemed to be beyond coherent answers, but her sobbing breath and the clenching of her passage told him all he needed to know. He built her pleasure slowly, taking her to the edge of ecstasy and letting her slip back, playing her body with skill until she squirmed. Then, and only then did he bring her over. She cried out. Her body twisted, and she clamped down hard on the finger inside her.

James stretched out on top of her and whispered, "That's it, darling. Enjoy it."

"Oh! Oh!"

The sight of her flushed, beautiful face, lips parted, eyes closed in ecstasy tempted him beyond resistance. James withdrew his finger from her and shoved his erection in, taking her with a powerful thrust. She was all wet, clinging heat and soft, yielding sweetness as her body clasped his in the most intimate embrace.

"I love you, Rebecca," he said as he pulled back and pushed in again. She arched and spasmed around him a little longer, and then her body went soft and acquiescent under an onslaught of passionate plunges until at last he reached his own peak and spilled his hot seed into her waiting belly.

He kissed her as their ardor cooled. When he lifted his face from hers, her sapphire eyes opened, shining with tears.

"What's wrong, love?" he asked tenderly, not wanting a replay of the previous time.

She shook her head. "I just can't believe this is really happening."

"Believe it, Rebecca. I love you. In just a few short months, you'll be my wife."

She smiled and pulled him down for another sweet kiss.

Cody woke suddenly from a deep sleep at the sound of a soft gasp. The bed beside him felt empty and cold. "Kristina?" he said softly, his voice uncooperative. He opened heavy eyelids. In the bright moonlight, he could see her standing by the window.

His sleepy body resisted the command to move, but eventually, he managed to lever himself upright and cross to her, taking her long, lean body in his arms and kissing her cheek. "What's wrong, darlin'? Why are you up?"

Then he glanced outside the window, where a couple stood in the street, locked in a passionate embrace. The difference in their heights and matching light hair told Cody everything he needed to know. "Maybe they didn't..." he began, trying to give his father-in-law the benefit of the doubt.

"They did," she replied. "She went to him over an hour ago."

Cody shook his head.

"It's not right, Cody," Kristina said, her voice catching.

"I know," he replied. *Really, Lord? Do I really have to deal with this? With James? Why James?* He shook his head again. *I really do not want to confront the head of the elder board, my friend and the father of my wife.*

Sighing, Cody pulled Kristina away from the window and back into the bed. "Enough spying, love," he told her. "I'll deal with it. Try to get some sleep." He kissed her forehead and cuddled her close, wishing his warmth could melt away the image of her father's sin.

Chapter 14

"Do you call this lemonade?" Mrs. Fulton asked sourly, regarding the pale, yellow liquid in her glass with an expression that could have curdled cream. Her perfectly groomed, steel gray eyebrows lowered to the top of her steel-rimmed spectacles. Her thin lips pursed into a prune-like pucker. Even her metallic-gray curls seemed to quiver with disapproval.

Allison raised one eyebrow and took a sip. *Pleasant, tart and sweet, and the floating ice makes it even more refreshing.* "As a matter of fact, Mother," she replied, "I do. What's the problem?"

"Oh, nothing," Mrs. Fulton harrumphed in a tone that implied just the opposite.

Allison sighed. *Wesley and I have been getting along better in the main, but his mother's another story. We've never liked each other, but she and Wes have been alone, just the two of them, since his father left when he was seven. They're very close.* So close Mrs. Fulton could hardly stand him being friends with anyone else, let alone marrying.

Now he's married again to someone she's never approved of. Married and about to be a father for the second time. Allison couldn't help smiling, her free hand drifting toward the side of her belly, where Wesley's baby pressed back against her touch.

"What are you smirking about?" Mrs. Fulton snapped.

"Nothing," Allison said. "It tickles, is all. Would you like to feel?"

Her mother-in-law rolled her eyes in disgust and muttered what sounded suspiciously like 'uncouth hussy'.

Allison grinned and quickly suppressed it. *I said I didn't care that Wesley's mother doesn't like me, and mostly I don't. Though she doesn't come around much, the animosity does make her rare visits awkward.*

Mrs. Fulton set her cup on the floor with a frown as sour as the lemons Allison had laboriously squeezed. Then she regarded a plate of cookies on the parlor table and sighed in ostentatious disgust.

I'm quite sure she has to work hard to be that obnoxious.

"Hello, Mother." Wesley banged the door open and strode into the room, pecking Mrs. Fulton on the cheek before crossing to Allison and placing his hands on her shoulders. "Hello, darling. How are you feeling?"

"I'm fine, dear," she told him sweetly, appreciating him making such a show of affection in front of his mother.

"That's good. What have you got there?" He scooped her drink out of her hands and took a big gulp.

"Hey," she protested, laughing and swatting at him.

He grabbed her hand, restraining her. "I was going to give this back, but since you're acting that way..." He downed the whole glass.

Allison dissolved into helpless laughter. *Sometimes, Wesley gives me flashes of the carefree boy I fell in love with years ago.* She looked up at him and humor faded to affection as they shared an intense gaze.

"Humph," Mrs. Fulton snorted, shattering the mood. "If that's how you two are going to behave, I'll go. I would hate to interrupt your little honeymoon."

"Bye," Allison said cheerfully, waving.

Mrs. Fulton stormed out of the house in a huff.

Allison looked back up at her husband, suddenly doubting herself. *Even as a child, Wesley was fiercely protective of his mother. I hope that little tease doesn't make him angry.*

He scowled at her. "You're a bad girl, Allison," he said sternly.

"Sorry," she said, trying to feel contrite.

"Where's Melissa?"

"Napping. I'll get her up in a minute."

"Let her sleep," Wesley said, his frown turning to a naughty grin. "I'd like a private word with you, Mrs. Fulton."

She smiled and let her husband lead her out of the parlor and towards the stairs.

"James, we need to talk."

James Heitschmidt turned in the church aisle to see his son-in-law approaching him from the door, where he'd been shaking hands after service.

"What's going on, Cody?" he asked, reluctantly releasing his fiancé's arm with a gentle squeeze. "See you at lunch, Rebecca."

Her pink lips curved into a sweet smile. She took his hand for a moment, giving him a lingering look. "See you then."

He watched her leave, unable to tear his eyes away from her retreating figure until she disappeared behind the church door.

"James," Cody said, trying again to capture his attention.

"Sorry, Cody. Yes, I'm listening. What did you need?"

"Let's sit." The young pastor indicated a pew and James sank into it, his thoughts still on Rebecca.

"James!"

"Sorry," he said, his facing heating, "but you remember what it's like, don't you? I mean, after all, you've only been married a few months. I still catch you with that distracted look on your face." He gave his son-in-law a fond look. *Now that I've adjusted to Kristina being married, I'm glad she's joined her life with a man who adores her.*

"I have no problem with you looking, James, not even with a few kisses, but really, you should have stopped there," Cody stated, his voice firm but his tanned cheeks bright red in a ferocious blush.

A cold sensation shot through the pit of James's stomach, but he managed to say mildly, "You really shouldn't listen to rumors, Cody. Rebecca is a lady." Then he ruined everything as an image of his lady, naked and whimpering, shot through his mind, making his own face burn.

"Rumors? No, James. Not unless your daughter has taken to spreading malicious gossip about her own father. Not unless my own eyes deceived me. We saw you. Is this how you treat a woman you care about then? For shame."

He's not backing down. James sighed. "Fine. You're right. But make no mistake, there's nothing casual about this. I love Rebecca. I'll be marrying her June first. Is it really such a terrible thing?"

"Yes," Cody replied. "Do I have to remind you that you're head of the elder board? After me, you should be the person in this town most above reproach."

This is going badly. I hope no one is gossiping. Rebecca wouldn't like that. "Does anyone know other than you two?" James asked.

"I haven't heard, and of course I have no intention of saying anything that would damage Miss Spencer's reputation, but as your pastor, I have a responsibility to let you know your behavior won't be tolerated. James, you know what I have to do if you persist." Cody gave him a pleading look.

James closed his eyes. *Scripture is clear on this; those who willfully continue in sin are to be cast out of the fellowship.* He tried again to reason with his son-in-law. "Come on, Cody, isn't that a little harsh? I'm not hurting her, and we would hardly be the first couple to..."

Cody cut him off with a sharp gesture. "You're making excuses, James, and you are hurting her. I know a bit about her... history, and I can't imagine being used in this way does her any good."

James's jaw clenched. "I'm not using her. I love her."

"You might know that, but does she?"

James wanted to say yes. He really did, but he couldn't. *Rebecca's trust is so fragile, and the way she clings to me makes it plain she still doesn't really believe in my commitment.* "Cody, surely you remember how difficult it is to wait..."

"I remember," Cody replied. "I remember every day before the wedding. I don't regret holding out."

"Of course not, but neither of you had any experience."

Cody just looked at him.

This is getting much too personal. I don't want to talk or think about Cody's intimate life with my daughter. James changed the subject. "What should I do?"

"Stop," the young pastor replied simply. "Wait. June isn't so far away."

"I doubt I would succeed," James admitted. "I seem to have little willpower where Rebecca is concerned."

Cody considered his words. "Well," he said, "I've been scouring the scriptures for a solution, and what I came up with was from Leviticus, where it says couples who anticipate their wedding vows should go ahead and get married. Since you won't stop, how about just moving up the wedding? Y'all have a small one planned. It shouldn't be that hard."

And why not, really? James thought to himself, relieved at such an easy and appealing solution. "I'll talk to Rebecca."

"Preferably in a public place," Cody urged.

James made a face. "All right, Cody. I'll seriously consider everything you've said."

"Do that," the younger man urged.

Shaking his head, James left the church and hurried through the spring sunshine to the Spencer home.

He knocked.

"Come in," Mrs. Spencer's muffled voice called from beyond the closed door.

He obeyed, closing the door behind him. Following the sound of clanking pots and pans to the kitchen, he found the ladies preparing lunch.

"Mrs. Spencer, may I borrow Rebecca for a moment, please?" he asked.

She glanced at him and nodded. "I think I have things under control here."

He grinned. Once Rebecca's parents had gotten over the surprise of their spinster daughter's engagement, they had become quite supportive of it.

His beautiful lady shot her mother a beaming, breathtaking smile. "I'll set the table," she said, gathering up a load of plates and set forks and knives on top.

James collected the drinking glasses and followed her into the dining room. As often as he'd eaten there, he scarcely took in the scarlet tablecloth, the matching draperies framing the bay window that overlooked the street, or the china cabinet in the corner.

He set his burden on the table and moved swiftly, plucking the plates from Rebecca's hands and depositing them before grabbing her in a tight embrace and planting a wet kiss on her mouth.

When he lifted his head, she smiled at him, her eyes sparkling.

"I love you, Rebecca," he said, and her grin widened further. "Do you believe that?"

"Yes, James," she replied automatically, but her tone contained less conviction than he would have liked.

"And do you believe that I'm going to marry you?" he pressed.

Her smile faded. "We're planning the wedding. It won't be long."

The words are right, but she still doesn't believe. He shook his head. "I think we're going about this the wrong way."

Her delicately arched golden eyebrows drew together. "What do you mean?"

"I mean," he explained, trailing his hand down her arm until he could grasp her hand. "Why are we waiting until June to have our wedding? Why are we waiting at all? It's too hard to resist temptation and I don't know about you, but I'm about to jump out of my skin wanting to be with you all the time."

Her eyes grew misty. "What brought this on?"

He touched his lips to her forehead and then drew close to her ear and whispered, "I haven't done right by you, and I feel guilty about it. Sooner or later, people will find out what we've been up to. I don't want your reputation to suffer. I also don't want to wait to have you in my bed every night."

The cheek pressed to his grew warm. He turned and kissed her there too.

"You haven't done anything I didn't want, James," she said.

"I know," he replied, "and I love your eagerness. We're going to have a wonderful marriage, but we're not married yet, Rebecca. To me, that seems like a waste. Do you think we could... hurry things up a bit? I mean, what are we waiting for?"

"For my dress," she replied. "It's not finished."

"And nothing else?"

She shook her head. "Planning a wedding with only ten guests is relatively simple. It could be put together in a week, once the dress is done."

"And how long do you think it will take you to finish it?" he asked.

Her eyes widened. "A few days, if I work hard. But, James..."

"Ten days, Rebecca. No more."

She gasped. "But…"

He took her face in his hands and looked deeply into her eyes. "I can't wait. Please?"

She blinked. He sweetened the request with another kiss.

"My mother is going to throw a fit," Rebecca said.

James grinned, recognizing her oblique comment as acceptance. *Now everything will be all right.*

Ten days later, Rebecca sat in the church's office, off the main sanctuary, where elder board meetings took place. She had dressed in her rose silk gown, and her sister, for once, was brushing her hair, weaving spring flowers into the corn silk strands. The soothing caress of boar's bristles did nothing to comfort the nervous bride.

Her parents, who should have been here with her, were protesting the rapid pace by sitting in the pew instead of assisting the bride.

"I think I'm going to be sick," Rebecca said softly.

"You'll be fine," Allison replied. She moved around the chair and the small swell of her belly brushed her sister's arm.

"Weren't you scared at your wedding, Allison?"

"Of course," her sister replied, patting her shoulder. "I knew Mother would throw a tantrum, and then Mrs. Fulton would throw a bigger one, but Wesley is worth all that." She dropped her hand to her tummy.

She does that constantly now, Rebecca thought idly, gulping down a wave of nausea. "Were you worried he wouldn't show up?"

"No," Allison replied. "I knew he would be there, and you know Mr. Heitschmidt will be here. He loves you, Becky. Why would he not come to his own wedding? The wedding he nearly started a war to ensure would happen immediately?"

Rebecca shook her head. Her hands shook… her whole body did. She laid her arms down on the table and rested her forehead on them.

"Becky?" Concern filled Allison's voice, but Rebecca couldn't reply. Her world seemed to be closing down on her. "I'll be right back," her sister said, laying the brush down on the table and hurrying from the room.

Rebecca didn't pay her any mind. She focused on not fainting, though her stays were not laced particularly tightly. Consciousness faded and wavered. She tried to breathe. *In and out, Rebecca. In and out. Keep on drawing air. Don't hold your breath.* She knew she was being silly, but she couldn't help it.

"What's going on in here?" a deep voice cut through her haze and she lifted her head. It felt heavy as a sack of flour, and about as animated.

Freckles swam in front of her face. "What's wrong, Rebecca?"

"James?"

He turned her chair and crouched beside it, wrapping his arms around her. His warmth dispelled her frantic, panicky state somewhat, but she still couldn't answer. Her fractured thoughts made no sense to her. How could she express them to him?

"I think she's got the worst case of bride nerves ever," Allison said. "She's talking nonsense like you were going to jilt her or something. I thought she needed to see you were here waiting. Can you keep her busy so I can finish fixing her hair, please?"

James nodded. At least that's what Becky assumed the strange, wavering movement meant. He pulled a chair around the table, so they could sit knee to knee, and he took her hand in his.

"Rebecca," he said gently, "I'm here. It's our wedding day. In a few minutes, you'll be my wife. Nothing is going to happen to prevent me from marrying you. Try to relax, love. I'm here, and I'm going to stay right here beside you today and for the rest of our lives."

He kept on talking, stroking her hand with his, sometimes squeezing her reassuringly. At last, Allison set the brush aside again and grabbed a tiny daisy, tucking it away somewhere in Rebecca's hair. "There," she said. "You're ready. Let's get this over with before you pass out."

James stood, pulling Rebecca to her feet. He placed her arm on his bicep and covered her hand with his. Then they walked out. Instead of processing down the aisle, James led her across the front to the pulpit, behind which Cody stood.

The organ crashed out a loud note, and Rebecca started violently. James patted her hand.

Rebecca wavered. *I'm not going to make it.* Her high-heeled white boots bit into her feet and she swayed. James's hand left her arm and snaked around her waist, supporting her.

She closed her eyes and opened them, looking up into his face. *This is real. Sandy hair, silvered at the temples. Warm brown eyes. Masses of freckles. Snub nose. Full, sensual lips.*

Cody's soft drawl sounded, but the words were garbled beyond recognition, so she focused on James instead. *James and breathing. Nothing more is needed.* His lips twisted, forming words. She furrowed her brow, trying to understand. *What did he say? Oh yes, 'I will.*

She gulped and bit down hard on her lower lip. The sudden sting woke her up enough that Cody's words at last gelled. "... until death do you part?"

James gave her a little squeeze.

"I will," she said.

He nodded, and his worried expression gave way to a smile. His face drew closer. His lips touched hers. The world narrowed down to his eyes, fixed on hers, shining with joy. His smile broadened. She blinked. The world rushed back into existence in a roar of sound.

They turned to face their 'audience'. Wesley sat holding his daughter on his lap. Her parents stared, stony-faced and silent. From the choir loft, Kristina regarded them with an unfathomable expression. Only Allison, seated beside her husband, smiled, and even she looked strained, though Rebecca figured that was because Wesley had shifted subtly away from her.

Marriage to Wesley is nothing like Allison had expected, and she's still reeling from it. Poor Allison. And poor Wesley. I know he hoped for a better outcome. I need to do something about that. The random thought threaded through her mind, though what she could do to help her sister's floundering marriage, she wasn't sure. *I want to give Wesley Fulton a piece of my mind, for making Allison pregnant and then acting as though she's done something wrong. As though married couples were not supposed to make babies together. Clearly, he didn't hold back.*

Pressure on her back. James leading her again. *James, my husband.* Slowly a bright smile spread across Rebecca's face. *I did it. I actually managed to get married. Now I have a husband, and it's James. What could be better?* They stepped out into the sunshine as a married couple.

Two hours later, Rebecca sprawled on James's bed—their bed—in her chemise and bloomers, her dress draped over the back of the chair. She pulled pin after pin from her hair until it tumbled free in a shower of gold and white flowers.

James froze in the process of removing his tie and collar. "Pretty," he said, and heat bloomed in her cheeks. He shrugged off his black suit jacket and tossed it aside, slipping his suspenders from his shoulders before joining her on the bed.

"So, Mrs. Heitschmidt," he said.

"So what, Mr. Heitschmidt?" She giggled.

"You seem better. I was worried about you." He scooted close to her and slipped one arm around her waist.

"I was acting like a ninny," she said, a little embarrassed. "I hope I didn't hurt your feelings."

"Well, love, I wasn't thrilled at how little trust you have in me, but under the circumstances, I did understand. I'm just glad the day is done." He grinned. "I bet you are too."

"Relieved is more like it," she replied, trying not to think about the part where he felt she didn't trust him. "I don't exactly know what came over me, but I think I nearly fainted."

"I'm sure you nearly did. I'm so glad you stayed on your feet through the wedding." He touched his lips to her forehead. "And now?"

"Now I'm waiting for reality to sink in that I'm really your wife and have every right to be in this bed with you in my unmentionables." She smiled.

"If they're unmentionable, love, we'd better get rid of them," he replied solemnly. "I can't have my lovely wife embarrassed by wearing garments that cannot be named." He reached for the hem of her chemise and lifted it over her head. "There," he said, as though proud of his accomplishment. "Is that better?"

The heat in Rebecca's face spread down to the parts of her he'd just uncovered. Her skin prickled with tingling arousal.

"It's somewhat better," she replied. "I'm only half unmentionable now."

He winked and reached for the ribbon that held her bloomers in place.

"Cody?" Kristina said softly, cuddling her husband. He rolled in her direction and snuggled up against her.

"Are you awake?" she asked.

"No," he replied, resting his forehead against the full softness of her bosom.

"If you're not awake, why are you answering me?" she asked, her tone ironic.

"I'm talking in my sleep," he replied.

Kristina dug her fingers into his ribs.

"Argh," Cody shouted in protest. "What are you doing, woman?"

"Just making sure," she replied smugly.

"You are evil and cruel, Kristina," he said. "What did you want? I hope after that rude awakening, it's something pleasant." He took her in his arms and kissed her.

She let him for a while. Then she wriggled out of his grip and said, "I heard a rumor."

"Kris, I just got through telling your dad you don't listen to gossip."

"Well, normally I don't," she replied, "but in this case, it comes from a reliable source."

"What source?" he asked.

"Allison."

Cody stuck his lips out in an expression of exasperated amusement. "What rumor?"

"Well, she doesn't know for sure, but she thinks Rebecca is expecting. She said she saw signs in her sister she recognized from when she first conceived."

Cody sighed and raked his fingers through his hair. "I don't know what you want me to do about it, darlin'. They're married. I can't prevent the gossip if that's true."

"Oh, it's not that, Cody. If there's gossip, well, so be it. I'm just thinking… I mean… well, Allison and Wes are expecting and now if Dad and Rebecca are too… well, I'm not."

"Is that a problem, Kristina? We've only been married a few months. I'm enjoying having you all to myself." He rubbed his nose against hers.

"I don't know," she replied. "I'm not really worried exactly. I just didn't know how you felt about it."

Cody let the thoughts settle in silence for several minutes. When he spoke, it was in a calm, serious voice. "Kristina, if the Lord sees fit to bless us with children, I'll welcome them. If not, well, this life we have—each other, the church, your father, and visiting my folks and sister sometimes—it's a good life and I wouldn't regret keeping it just this way. You're enough for me, darlin', all by yourself."

"I love you, Cody," she said, hugging her husband.

Chapter 15

A loud clank woke Allison from a deep sleep. Her eyes fluttered open in the late afternoon sunshine and she shook her head, feeling groggy. Melissa still snoozed beside her, more trusting now, after several months of stability.

If only adults could heal as quickly as children do, she thought ruefully. *It seems like Wesley's wariness is rubbing off on me, rather than the other way around. I knew it wouldn't be fast or easy, but I expected things to be a bit better by now. Instead, we seem to be at a stalemate—no animosity, but also no progress. I wonder if Cody can offer any insight.*

Soft clinking sounds echoed through the house in an irregular rhythm. *What on earth is that? It sounds like someone is inside. Dear Lord, are we being robbed? Have the train robbers come to my house with some nefarious plan? I don't have anything worth stealing, though that hasn't seemed to be their goal in a while.*

Quietly, she rose from the bed and tiptoed to the wardrobe, carefully avoiding the boards that squeaked the most. She eased the creaking door open and reached to the back to retrieve the shotgun. *It's not loaded, with Melissa so nosy and curious. Do I go for the shells in the spare bedroom or just rely on bravado? What would make a robber most likely to react the way I want—by running out of the house?* Though she knew herself to be a crack shot, most men, especially strangers, would never believe it. *The shells then,* she realized with a stifled sigh.

Moving softly despite her bulky, unbalanced shape, Allison moved through the upstairs, shutting the bedroom door as though it could shield Melissa from harm. The spare room seemed to mock her, filled as it was with Samantha's still-undealt-with possessions, but she braved her former rival's ghost and entered anyway.

A sheet had been thrown carelessly over the bedframe, another over the mirror. Stacks of abandoned clothing lay in messy profusion in the corner, but it was the bureau Allison wanted. She gritted her teeth against the hiss of the drawer, and every rustle of papers as she dug to the bottom made her heart pound harder until her stomach threatened to upend itself. She opened the weapon and slid shells into both chambers. The click as she reassembled it sounded like a roar in her ears. *It would be a miracle if the robber didn't realize someone was awake by now.*

Grimly, nearly ill with fear, Allison approached the stairs, the shotgun hanging by her side. *I can have it raised and fire it in a second. If I can get the jump on this intruder, I can fire a warning shot that should fill him with pellets. That ought to be enough.*

Refusing to consider what would happen if it wasn't enough, she eased her way down one tread after another, ears straining for some sign her unwanted guest was approaching. The clinking from the kitchen continued unchanged. *What on earth can it mean? Are they stealing all the dishes and silverware? It's not valuable, just sturdy everyday pieces.* At the foot of the stairs, Allison turned toward the kitchen, whose door stood partially ajar. She was able to make out a short, stocky figure with gray hair.

What on earth? She raised the gun, sighting along the barrel, and then paused. *There's something familiar about that shape.* Her breath caught, and her finger began to compress the trigger. *Oh, no. Damn it, no.*

At last, she understood what she was seeing. Her mother-in-law stood at the kitchen sink, apparently washing dishes.

Allison eased her finger off the trigger and set the shotgun against the wall outside the kitchen door. Her belly swooped, and her face tingled as terror gave way to rage.

"Mother, what are you doing?" Allison asked sharply, striding—or rather waddling purposefully—into the kitchen.

"The dishes, of course," Mrs. Fulton snapped back, not bothering to turn. "Even a slattern like you should recognize the activity, though you're terrible at it."

Allison paused, drew in a deep breath and counted to ten. "I don't share your opinion," she said bluntly, "but I actually meant to ask just what the *hell* you're doing creeping into my home uninvited and meddling in my silverware."

"I came to visit *my son's* home," Mrs. Fulton sneered, "to see if you're taking care of him properly. I see you're not. Sink full of dishes. Dust everywhere." She ran her finger ostentatiously over the sparkling countertop.

"I hardly think two lunch plates and two forks are anything to worry about," Allison replied. "I also think none of it is any of your business. This is my home too. You need to wait to be invited, not just turn up and let yourself in—how did you get in anyway? The doors are locked."

"This is my Wesley's home." Mrs. Fulton finally turned, a fierce scowl on her face. "He gave me a key in case of emergency, and the state of these dishes *is* an emergency." She indicated a pile of plates and forks on the counter.

"Are you washing my *clean* dishes?" Allison demanded. Suddenly, her face felt hotter than the sweltering July weather could account for.

Triumph flared in Mrs. Fulton's face. "Not sure why you'd think they're clean," she cackled.

Allison's jaw went slack. For a moment she stood frozen, not sure what her next step ought to be. Then her anger, which had burned fire-bright a moment before, sizzled like lightning, and like lightning, it struck. "Get the hell out of my house, NOW!" she shouted, taking a threatening step toward her adversary. "Don't ever let me catch you in here again." She took another step so that she towered over the smaller older woman.

Mrs. Fulton's bravado wavered as she considered Allison's size, strength and youth. "My baby will hear about how you've treated me, and you'll be sorry," she threatened as she dodged to the side, circling Allison with an agility that belied her age.

Allison turned with her, keeping her fixed in a furious glare. "Go right ahead and tattle, bitch, but for your own safety, keep out." She stepped heavily, her pregnancy adding weight to the noisy stomps she landed on the floorboards. With deliberate aggression, she drove her mother-in-law back down the hall, and out the door, which she slammed shut almost hard enough to break the glass in the nearby parlor window.

Aggravated, Allison sank into the rocking chair, unable to believe what had just happened. "What in the world? Who does things like that?" Over a long stretch of moments, her pounding heart began to slow back toward a normal pace. Her ragged breathing calmed. Inside her belly, her baby squirmed and wriggled.

"I'm sorry, love," she told the child. "I hope that didn't upset you too much. I imagine it was scary. I was scared too."

It occurred to her that the bitch she'd just evicted would be her baby's grandma. The thought brought tears to her eyes. "Not on my watch," she vowed. "That . . . that creature will never sink her claws into my baby. Never."

She rested her hands on her belly, receiving her child's gentle touches as though they were intended to comfort. "No matter what, I will protect you. I don't care who or what happens. You and Missy mean more to me than my own. I always thought people were exaggerating when they said things like that, but it's true. No harm will befall you or your sister, I promise." She leaned her head back against the rocker and studied the ceiling, tracing the crack in the plaster Wesley had repaired the previous weekend with her gaze. "Our home is sacred."

A knock on the door startled her out of her contemplations. "Who is it?" she called.

"Ally? Allison Spencer? Are you in there?"

Relieved that the voice was that of a man, she rose from her seat and made her way to the door. "Allison Fulton," she corrected. "Who is this?"

"It's Jesse, Jesse West."

"Jesse?" Allison yanked on the door handle and revealed the familiar face of her childhood friend. Her anger over her mother-in-law's rude intrusion faded to the background in the face of her delightful surprise. "Jesse, it *is* you! What are you doing here?" She stepped over the threshold and threw her arms around him—or tried to. Her belly bumped into his hip.

"Well, well, Allison. What have we here?" he laughed, indicating the swell where her nearly-formed baby jutted out. "I knew you and Wes would be the first. Congratulations."

"Your turn will come, Jesse," she replied. *After all, a handsome blond man with tanned, rugged features and whip-smart mind is sure to appeal to any number of women. . .* she began mentally running down the list, only half attending to the conversation even as her mouth chattered on unheeded. "Are you here for the sheriff's deputy position? I know Wes has been trying to get ahold of you for months. It was so sad about poor Deputy Charles, but it will be so nice to have you home to stay. Have you talked to Sheriff Brody yet?"

Jesse laughed. "Yes, Allie, I have. Say, do you mind if I come in for a minute? I know you're not expecting visitors, but I promise not to examine any undusted corners. There's someone I want you to meet."

His words cut off her chatter and refocused her attention fully on him. She took a step back, allowing the young man to cross the threshold. *Oh, yes, that's right,* she recalled. *Kristina, Becky and Lydia all mentioned meeting him... and the woman he's going to ... to marry. A stranger he brought to town. Why is it so hard to remember things these days?*

"Allison, I'd like you to meet my betrothed... soon to be my bride, Adeline McCoy," he announced, drawing a young woman into the room. "Addy, this is Allison Spencer Fulton. She and her husband, along with the church organist you met yesterday, were my best friends growing up."

Allison studied the new arrival, a young woman with rich red-brown hair, who clung nervously to Jesse's arm, even as she assessed Allison with shrewd brown eyes. Petite in stature, the slim young woman's ragged travel clothes failed to conceal the conspicuous curve of her own belly.

Oh, dear, Allison thought. *Looks like they put the cart before the horse.* "Pleased to meet you," she said, reaching out to take Addie's hand.

Addie grasped it, her palm moist. "I've been looking forward to meeting Jesse's friends. I've heard so much about all of you," the young woman said softly.

Allison smiled. "Thank you. Welcome to Garden City, where the sun scorches all summer and the wind never stops blowing."

Addie laughed. "With an introduction like that, how can I resist?"

"So, are you from around here?" Allison asked, trying to make conversation. "Oh, or, wait, won't you sit? Can I get you anything? I mean, I can make tea, but it's mighty hot for it..."

"I'd love a glass of water," Jesse suggested. "Addie, you should have some too. It's beastly out. I don't want you to have any problems." He stroked the curve of her belly, a subtle gesture, but Allison noticed.

Wes never does things like that, she realized. *He's still willing to kiss and make love, of course, but to pay special attention to the baby... never.* She frowned. "Two waters, coming right up. You two make yourselves at home," she said. Though the words sounded right, she knew her tone had turned stiff and unwelcoming. *Today has just been too much. It's a strain to remember basic manners.*

She hurried into the kitchen, where the sight of all her double-washed silverware brought back in a rush just how much too much the day had, in fact, been. Scowling, she retrieved a silver tin of cookies she and Melissa had made the previous evening and added two glasses of cool spring water. *I'll have some myself once the visit ends,* she thought. *I shouldn't get too dry either, even though everything is uncomfortable in my belly these days.*

Carrying the items awkwardly, as she had more objects than hands, she returned to her guests who had perched side by side on the sofa. Jesse had his arm around his intended, and her head rested comfortably on his shoulder—or rather on his upper arm, so different was their height even when seated.

"Here you go," she told them, offering the glasses, and then she popped the lid off the tin and extended it.

The couple regarded the contents, and a grin crossed Addie's face. "That looks delicious."

"Thanks," Allison replied, though her overwhelmed emotions swirled up in choking profusion. "My daughter and I cooked them yesterday." *And afterwards, we washed the dishes together, and swept the floor, and made the beds... Stop it, Allison. There's no truth to Mrs. Fulton's accusations and you know it, so stop thinking about it. She was just being nasty, trying to prove who's boss. I think she realized today it isn't her. Not in my home.*

Leaving the tin on the end table beside her guests, Allison retreated to her usual perch on the rocking chair and tried to force her mind to concentrate on the conversation, though it proved a struggle, now that the surprise of Jesse's arrival had worn off.

"So, um, Allison," Jesse began, suddenly sounding more nervous than Allison had ever heard before, "I know it's short notice, and I'll understand if you can't make it, but Addie and I are... um... we..." His arm slid down from her shoulder to her waist, and his hand flattened against the side of her belly.

Interesting, Allison thought, though for some reason the sight made the sour feeling incited by her encounter with her mother in law return full force. The added discomfort of an attack of heartburn did nothing to improve her mood.

"Spit it out, Jesse," Addie teased, looking more relaxed than she had a few minutes before. "We're getting married this afternoon." She giggled. "Not a moment too soon, I'm sure you've noticed, and as Jesse's oldest friends, we'd love you and your husband... and daughter?" At Allison's nod, she continued. "We'd love it if the three of you could come."

"Where is Wes anyway?" Jesse demanded. "It's Saturday. Is he still at work? I thought the bank would be closed by now."

"It is closed," Allison replied. "He had a deacon's meeting."

The couple regarded her, clearly noting the sudden strain in her voice.

Stop it, she ordered herself sternly. *You're being inhospitable.*

"Will he be done in the next hour or so?" Jesse asked. "We hope to start at three."

"I don't know," Allison replied, struggling to control her urge to snap. *Not their fault. Calm down.*

Addie suddenly looked less comfortable. She snuggled closer to Jesse's side.

"Maybe this isn't a good time after all," Jesse commented. Then he regarded his old friend curiously. "Is everything all right, Allison?"

She inhaled deeply and released her breath in a sigh. "Yes. I'm sorry. This late in things..." she touched her belly lightly. "Well, it's not very comfortable. I'm sure you'll find that out soon enough."

Though she meant it to be a joke, the edge in her tone made it sound harsh and rude.

Addie recoiled, eyebrows lowering. "You know, maybe we should go, Jesse. I think we've popped in long enough."

"Please, no," Allison urged. "I'm sorry, I..." she trailed off, not sure what to say next, but at that moment, the door banged open and Wesley stormed into the room, his face set in a harsh scowl.

"Just what in the devil is going on, Allison," he demanded.

Allison closed her eyes in embarrassment. Then, determined to turn the tone of the visit around, she pasted a bright smile on her face. "Hello, Wes. I'm glad you're home. Look who's stopped by." She indicated the soft.

Wesley turned, confused, and then froze.

Jesse shot to his feet. "Hello there, old man," he said jovially, his smile a bit forced.

"Jesse," Wesley replied, his voice a study in neutrality. "I'm glad you decided to come back. Did you take the job?"

"I sure did," he replied. "Thanks for reaching out. It couldn't have come at a better time." He extended a hand to his lady and helped her to her feet. "This is Addie. We're getting married this afternoon, in about two hours. We stopped by to invite your family if you'd like to come."

"Congratulations! We'll certainly be there," Wesley promised. "Listen, I hate to be inhospitable, but I need to talk to my wife in private..."

"We were just leaving," Addie replied firmly. "It's nice to meet you, Mr. Fulton." She shook his hand and then turned to Allison. "Mrs. Fulton."

Then she steered Jesse out the door.

Embarrassed, Allison closed her eyes. "That went well," she said dryly.

A swishing sound suggested her husband had taken a seat on the sofa across from her. "What's going on, Allie?" he asked, though this time he sounded more tired than angry.

"What do you mean?" she asked. "Surely you're not objecting to me entertaining our *best friend* and his betrothed while you were out."

"Of course not," Wesley snapped. "They're more than welcome, naturally. I'm talking about Mother. Did you really yell at her, *swear* at her, and chase her out of the house?"

Oh, Lord. Here we go. "And if I did, Wes?"

Wesley's teeth ground together.

"If I did," Allison continued, schooling her voice into the blandest, calmest, most neutral tone she could manage, while her heart pounded, and the contents of her stomach attempted to reverse their direction, "would it not be reasonable to conclude there was a valid reason for it?"

"I don't know what possible reason you could concoct for such rudeness, but I'm willing to listen." He leaned back against the sofa, arms crossed over his chest.

A flicker of her earlier anger rekindled. "Concoct? Interesting word choice," she pointed out. "So, you've already decided I'm going to lie? If so, then why should I bother explaining anything?"

"I said I would listen. I'll decide what to believe on my own, thank you."

"Will you, Wes?" she shot back, "or will you believe whatever *she* told you to believe? What did she tell you anyway?"

"Nothing earth-shattering," he replied, glaring at his wife. "She said she stopped by, wanting to lend you a hand, since you seemed overwhelmed, and you blew up at her."

The gall of that bitch. I can't believe it. "Well, that might be one way to interpret it," Allison conceded. "Though I imagine she failed to mention that she let herself in, uninvited and unannounced, while I was *sleeping*, and took it upon herself to wash the dishes without asking. Wes, I thought there was a burglar in the house, maybe one of the train robbers that almost killed my sister. I nearly shot your mother with the shotgun. What she did was incredibly dangerous."

Wesley's angry expression changed to confusion. "What?"

"Do you believe me?" Allison sneered, too angry to remain calm. "Do you trust that I'm telling you the truth, or will you run to your mommy and demand she explain? She'll lie to you, you know. She lies all the time."

"Don't talk about my mother like that," Wesley snarled. "I'm sure she just didn't think… she was trying to help. You know, you might try to be a bit more understanding."

Allison stuck her neck forward in astonishment. "Under– No. No, Wesley, no. I understand. I understand better than you do. She's not trying to be nice. Nice would be coming for tea and bringing cake. It's not at *all* nice for her imply—to straight out say—that my clean, freshly washed dishes are, in fact, so disgusting that she needs to break into the house and rewash them. Do you really think that sounds nice? It sounds like a street-dog dominance pissing match to me. All over my home. With you standing by, watching and doing nothing."

"It does sound like that," Wesley muttered, breaking eye contact and studying the fists he had clenched in his lap. He crumpled his lips so hard his nose wrinkled. Then he lifted his head. "Allison, are you sure..."

"She called me a slattern, Wes. Do you really think I'm overreacting?"

"No," he admitted. "No, I think you're right. She does hate you." He sighed, lowering his guard and letting her see the real Wesley he normally kept locked up tight. "And her frenetic cleaning...and making comments about the house... that sounds exactly like something she said... would say."

Allison caught the correction immediately. "Did say, isn't it?" She challenged her husband with raised eyebrows. "She talks about me, doesn't she?"

"Yes," Wesley admitted, frowning mightily. "But I told her it wasn't true. I told her... told her our life is beautiful and I'm happy and I couldn't ask for more."

Allison relaxed her scowl enough to show approval. "Thank you."

"I tell her every time."

Allison drew a deep breath as the deeper meaning dawned on her. "So, you stay and argue with her, let her call me names and only offer a token protest? Why don't you walk away from her and teach her a lesson? Refuse to talk to her until she can be polite?"

"Don't you think that's asking a bit much?" Wesley protested.

"No, I think it's the bare minimum," Allison replied. "You're my husband, Wes. It's your job to defend me, to refuse to associate with people who disrespect me."

"I've tried," he protested. "What more do you want from me?"

Allison considered. *What would fix it? What do I want?* The answer bloomed clear as sunrise over the prairie. "You tell her I'm done with her. I will not see her again. She's not welcome in my home..."

"Wait just a damned minute. It's my home too!"

"And you're welcome to entertain her in your home. You, Wes. Not me. Not Missy or the baby either. I won't have her trying to turn my children against me behind my back. Fight me on this, Wes, and it's not going to go well for you. Is it my home, or is she right, and it's your home, and I only live here as an unpaid maidservant—who happens to share your bed?"

"Of course, it's your home," Wesley protested.

"Then this cannot be negotiated. I will never host your mother in my home. She is not welcome. If she comes in, I will leave."

"Leave! You would leave me because you don't like one guest?"

Well, that escalated quickly. "How strangely your mind works. I mean, if she's over I'll take Missy and visit my sister or my parents. You may not get dinner that night, but I'm not going to loiter while she insults me."

Wesley sagged. It looked like relief. "Fair enough. Agreed."

"Oh, and, Wes?"

He raised his eyebrows.

"Get the damned key back."

Allison lay on her side, trailing her fingers over Wesley's bare chest. A sheen of sweat dampened her body, but she didn't mind. *It's a hot, nasty summer, so I'm going to be sweaty anyway. At least I had fun getting that way.* Her body ached and tingled, a pleasant reminder that, despite quarrels and tension, marriage had plenty of compensations.

Wesley stroked her back. "That was nice," he commented blandly.

She rose up on one elbow and saw the mischief twinkling in his eyes.

"I suppose," she replied, matching his falsely bored tone with one of her own.

"You suppose? So, all that squealing and gasping was for what? Just for show?"

"Well, I didn't want you to get discouraged," she replied, tweaking a tuft of his chest hair. "You know if you practice a bit..." Then she shrieked as he dug his fingers into her ribs.

Oho, Mister Fulton. Two can play at this game. She tickled his belly.

"Argh" Wesley captured her hands in his. "Don't torture me, you evil woman."

"No fair," she shot back. "If I can't tickle you, you can't tickle me either."

"Fine," he conceded. Then he leaned over her enormous belly and lavished a long, wet kiss on her mouth. "This is more fun anyway," he added.

"I agree, she murmured. The tingling aftermath of their just-completed relations increased. Against her lower belly, she could feel a suspicious firmness in the region of Wesley's sex. "Again?" she asked.

"Maybe," he replied. "Interested?"

"Maybe..." She broke free of his grip, but instead of teasing him, she planted both hands on the back of his neck and drew him down for another kiss.

This time, she intentionally seduced him with a teasing driving of her tongue against his lips.

"Why, Mrs. Fulton," he claimed in teasing surprise. "Could it be that milady fancies another ride?"

She grinned. "It depends on the steed's stamina, I suppose," she replied.

At that moment, the baby punched sharply, directing a firm outward pressure against its father's penis.

Horror crossed Wesley's face and he drew away, his tumescence instantly shrinking.

"Are you all right?" Allison asked. "That was a strong one."

"Yes, I'm not hurt. It startled me is all." He shuddered.

And it startles me, Allison realized, *how little interest Wesley takes in this pregnancy. It almost seems as though he's disgusted by it.*

She hadn't understood, until earlier in the week when Addie and Jesse paid a visit, that men might actually have a positive feeling about the signs of pregnancy in their women. *They weren't even married yet,* she thought. *All in a rush, on the brink of disaster, and he couldn't keep his hands off her, even in front of people.*

Wes never does that. He goes out of his way to avoid touching me there, and every invitation to feel the baby moving results in similar expressions of distaste. Does that mean Wes isn't comfortable with pregnancy... or that he truly doesn't want this baby?

That she had no answer was the worst part of all.

"Good night, Allison." Wesley leaned over, careful not to touch her belly, and kissed her forehead, before rummaging under his pillow for his nightshirt.

Well, I suppose marital relations are done for tonight, Allison thought, but the bitterness of yet another disappointment lodged deep in her heart and began to fester there.

Chapter 16

"Get up, Allie," Wesley urged, taking her hand and tugging gently.

"Hmmm?" Allison shook off the lingering urge to fall asleep on the sofa in the comfortable warmth of the sunshine.

"Come on, Mama Allie," Melissa urged, tugging her other hand. "It's time for the picnic."

"Picnic?" Allison looked from her daughter to her husband in confusion. "What picnic?"

"Weren't you paying attention?" Wesley grumped, instantly annoyed.

"Paying attention to what?" Allison snapped, irritated by his irritation. She set her jaw in a pugnacious line and challenged her husband with a fierce glare. "Tell me what's going on or forget it. I'll take a nap."

"Today, after the service, Lydia and Dylan invited us, your sister and brother-in-law and Cody and Kristina for a picnic at the river. I believe Jesse and his wife also mean to be there," he enunciated in an insulting drawl. "You were standing right there and nodding the whole time."

"I was standing right there, nodding off," Allison shot back. "Remember that I was up half the night with leg cramps and a backache when this little one wasn't kicking the hell out of me."

Wesley shrugged. "That's normal, isn't it?"

"Perhaps," she replied, "but that doesn't mean it's comfortable or pleasant. Add to that the insult your mother shot me under her breath as she passed, I was a bit distracted."

Wesley scowled, as he always did when Allison reminded him of his mother's continued bad behavior. "I don't know what you want me to do about that. I took back the key—and you can't imagine what I had to go through to get it—and now she only visits when I'm home and you're not. We have freedom of speech in this country. If she says something, it's her right to do so."

Allison frowned. *No, I won't get drawn into that nonsense. Not again. It's his favorite go-to whenever he wants to score some kind of point against me.* "So, there's a picnic. All right, that's interesting, but what makes you think I want to go? I just told you I'm so tired I can barely stay awake, and I'm not in a good mood."

"Clearly," he muttered under his breath, "but what's new in that?"

Allison sat back against the sofa, resisting his pull on her arm. "Care to say that out loud?"

"Well, Allison, I think your bad mood may just be permanent until, you know, after… but does that mean we shouldn't enjoy the first nice day in months? Our friends have invited us to spend time with them, and I'd like to go."

"So go," Allison replied. "Take Missy and go see them. I'll stay home and nap."

Wesley shook his head. "Don't you think it might be a good idea to be a bit more welcoming toward our best friend's bride. After all, you missed their wedding."

Allison dropped her head back against the upholstery. *Here we go again.* "I wasn't feeling well. You know that. I had a massive heartburn attack that made me throw up. I was in no condition to go anywhere, let alone a wedding. It wasn't personal." *At least, not in a way I'd care to explain to you.*

"And yet, within hours you were better enough to…" he trailed off, suddenly remembering his daughter stood beside them, taking in the conversation with wide brown eyes.

"I can't help that," Allison replied. "The sickness comes and goes. But, seriously, Wes. Are you really implying that I was faking sick, like a school kid, to play hooky from the wedding? I wanted to go. I meant to."

"Good. Now you can come to the picnic since you aren't currently sick, and since tired and grumpy is your regular mood these days."

While she processed his comment, he drew her to her feet.

"It will do you some good to get some fresh air," he added. "Let's go."

"Yes, please, Mama," Missy begged. "Can't you please come?"

Unable to resist the child's begging, Allison sighed. "Let me get my hat. It's still mighty sunny out."

Squealing with delight, Melissa pranced away to retrieve Allison's wide-brimmed straw hat and her own sunbonnet. Then the family set out, leaving their house and heading south along the town's red brick street, past the train depot and out onto the prairie, where the stuffy closeness of the buildings gave way to a tepid breeze that blew through the drying grass, setting it rustling. A soft splashing reached Allison's ears as they drew near to the bridge. In the summer heat, the river had receded, leaving a cracked mudflat that had moistened to a quagmire in last night's rain.

Allison's brief foray into acquiescence died a quick death at the sight of Jesse and his bride, seated on a blanket under a small, withered tree, their hands busily exploring the contours of her belly. She giggled. "Did you feel that?"

"I did," Jesse agreed, a broad grin spreading across his face. "I can't wait to meet him… or her."

Addie beamed. "Me either. This winter is going to be amazing, isn't it?"

"Oh, yes." Jesse leaned forward. "Keep on growing, little one. Your mama and papa are excited to meet you, so you just grow up big and strong, so you can be born healthy."

Addie laced her fingers into Jesse's golden hair. He claimed her lips once, briefly. "I love you, Mrs. West," he murmured.

Allison's heart clenched at the sight. *How long has it been since Wes said he loves me? I can't even recall the last time.*

Turning to her husband, she saw a look of disgust and horror on his handsome face. "In public, no less," he muttered.

"What?" she hissed, nudging him in the ribs. "You used to kiss me in public all the time."

"Not the kiss," he replied in an undertone, eyeing the newlywed couple with a sour frown. "It's bad enough all you pregnant ladies waddling around with your… everything showing. But to put his hands all over it, out where anyone can see? It's trashy."

Allison tutted. "Every now and again, Wes, when you open your mouth, I hear your mother's voice. Don't turn into an old lady, please."

The look on her husband's face could have pulverized rock. Without another word, he scooted forward, greeting the couple with a loud exclamation that badly startled Addie. Her face darkened until it almost matched her hair. Grasping Jesse's hand, she laced their fingers together and moved them to her knee, safely away from the more intimate public touching.

Wesley drew a small, leather-bound book from his pocket, along with the stub of a pencil, sank to a sitting position, and began scratching away.

Allison regarded Jesse and Addie. *So in love. So happy. I wanted that with a man who used to make me feel that way, but it all went wrong. Is it me? Am I really so grouchy and demanding that I can't expect decent treatment? Or is it him, still hurting from the years he spent with Samantha? I know his mother still plays a role. Perhaps it's a combination of all those things. I don't know. All I know is, when I see all the happy couples around me, it hurts like hell.* "Come on, Missy," she urged. "Take your shoes and socks off. That mud looks mighty inviting."

"Really?" The child's eyes widened. She plunked down on her bottom, eager to obey. Allison regarded her own footwear and sighed. *What have I gotten myself into?* Groaning, she crouched down to examine her boot laces.

"Um, hello, Mrs. Fulton," Addie said tentatively.

Allison's head shot up, and she looked around wildly, dreading to see her mother-in-law. No sign of the disapproving face crowned with tight gray curls appeared, and it slowly dawned on her that Addie had addressed her. "Call me Allison," she said sharply.

Addie nodded, and an uncomfortable silence fell. As quickly as she could manage, Allison stripped off her footwear and struggled to her feet, letting Melissa tug her toward the mud.

She sighed in relief as the cool moist gooeyness oozed up around her swollen ankles. *Feels wonderful.*

Melissa squealed with laughter and waddled around in the shallow puddles.

Allison watched, envious of the child's freedom to relax and play. *If Wes married me for his daughter, he made a wise choice. She's thriving. At least I can handle being a mother so far. Being a wife apparently isn't something I'm good at.* Though she tried to remain matter-of-fact, the thought brought tears to her eyes. *Now stop it,* she urged herself. *Don't make a scene. Try to enjoy spending time with your friends. Be thankful they're not fussing over you being out and about so late in pregnancy.*

It took her several long minutes to calm herself, and by then the rest of the party had arrived and taken their places on the blanket. The sight of so much love—of Cody lying with his head in Kristina's lap, sound asleep as she smiled down indulgently; of Dylan approaching with his arm around Lydia, finally making a declaration of their connection; even of her own sister, who sat hand-in-hand with the husband she'd never dared imagine she'd have—drove home the contrast with painful sharpness.

Wiping her feet in a patch of low-lying grass, she tiptoed back to the blanket with Melissa in tow. Wesley sat a bit apart from the group, still scribbling away in his bank book. She rolled her eyes. Then she took in the last couple. Jesse and Addie.

Again, her childhood friend had drawn his bride as close to him as he could without her actually sitting on his lap. He had his hand splayed on the side of her belly, a funny smile on his handsome face. The sight almost undid all her efforts to calm herself. Only this time, instead of sorrow, a thread of cold, ugly rage flared in the neglected corners of her heart, fed by the discomfort of pregnancy. She narrowed her eyes. *Damn them for making everything worse.*

Though she knew the thought was irrational, she could in no way dispel it. *Damn Addie for bringing my misery into such sharp focus.*

But such thoughts could hardly be expressed, so she made a weak attempt at courtesy. "Hello, Lydia, Sheriff. Wes, can you put that away, please? Everyone is here now."

"Just a minute," he replied. "I'm almost done."

"I'm not waiting on you, Fulton," Jesse teased, giving his wife a gentle squeeze and reaching for the food as Allison lumbered to a seat, awkwardly far from her husband.

I wish I'd stayed home. She groaned in discomfort. *Getting up and down from chairs is hard enough. I may never be able to rise from this position.*

"I'm starving. Let me at that chicken!" Jesse continued, bringing his usual humor to the situation.

Lydia laughed. "Of course, Deputy West."

"Here you go." The sheriff dropped the basket near Jesse, who pretended to attack it like a starving coyote.

Between hungry men and Allison's own sour mood, conversation lagged, though not into the comfortable rapport of friends. *I really should have insisted on staying home. I'm not lending anything positive to this gathering,* she thought as she tugged a snippet of meat off a chicken wing. The breading set her stomach immediately churning.

Oh, come on, she whined internally. *It's not even greasy. Please, let's not add heartburn to everything else.* But the burning rose up in her throat, nonetheless. She swallowed hard and considered her options. Tart, acidic lemonade. Tart, acidic cherry pie and greasy fried chicken. Nothing she could use to quench the fire. She selected a biscuit, which she nibbled in desperation while she considered the other contents of the basket. *Grapes might work. Deviled eggs might also, but neither one is guaranteed not to make things worse.* She frowned. *Some days anything and nothing sets this off. It's a misery, and still so many days to go.*

Glancing at the assembled group, her scowl deepened at the sight of Addie, one hand clutched in her husband's, the other holding a chicken breast to her mouth as she tore off a generous bite. Watching this interloper enjoy a tasty meal without apparent discomfort did nothing for Allison's mood. *Come on, don't be nasty,* she urged herself.

"Are you feeling poorly, Allison?" Lydia asked.

Thank goodness. A distraction. "There's no room left in my stomach. I'm hungry, but when I eat, it gives me heartburn. The midwife says I should just nibble whatever sound appealing and hang on." She showed her friend the biscuit. "I only have a couple of weeks left. I'll be glad when this is over."

"Sounds terrible," Addie commented. "I'm sorry you're having a hard time." Though she spoke kindly, the woman had long since become a symbol of everything that was wrong with Allison's life.

"You're next," Allison snapped. "We'll see if you do any better." Her face burned at her rudeness and she shut her mouth, setting her biscuit aside.

"Allie," her husband admonished, speaking at last, "that wasn't called for. Look, everyone already feels sorry for you. Don't milk it."

Milk it? Oh, that man! "You have no idea what you're talking about," she hissed at him. "Men never do. Think this is easy, Wesley? Do I look like I'm having fun?"

"You look like you're whining," he replied. "What do you think, Jesse? Shall we leave the hens to their clucking and put a line or two in the water?"

Allison ground her teeth in frustration, finally stemming the flow of uncontrolled words. *Sometimes, I think I hate him.*

"Sounds good to me," Jesse replied. "You don't mind, do you, Addie?"

Addie's expression turned nervous as she regarded Allison. "I don't mind. See if you can catch a trout for supper, okay?"

"I'll try." He kissed her lips gently, and the comparison between his tender leave-taking and Wesley's grumpy retreat galvanized Allison's anger even further.

"Would you like to go?" Lydia asked Dylan.

"Don't mind if I do," he replied. For some reason, when he kissed Lydia, Allison felt nothing but a blunted echo of wistful happiness. *I hope they get what they both want.*

"What about Cody?" Allison asked, indicating the sleeping pastor.

"He's out cold," Kristina replied. "Sometimes the Holy Spirit just sort of... takes him over. He loves it, and he always preaches the best sermons, but then he passes out afterward. I don't expect to see him move for at least an hour." She smoothed his dark hair back from his forehead and gazed tenderly on his face.

"How cute is that," Addie said. "I love how comfortable all you couples are together." Her gaze skated away from Allison, unconsciously excluding her from the compliment.

Lydia blushed.

"Mush," Allison muttered, losing control of her mouth again. "We'll see how long any of it lasts."

"You know something," Becky said mildly, "your husband has a point. You're not being your usual friendly self, Allison. What did Addie ever do to you?"

"I agree," Lydia added. "She's a nice girl and she's new in town. I remember when I first arrived. You, your sister and Kristina made a point of coming to my café, talking to me, telling everyone how nice I was and how great the food was. Why welcome me and not her?"

Oh, no. They heard me. I didn't mean it, not really. It's just so... so hard. Her face burned, and her lip trembled. "So, everyone's going to gang up on me? Kristina?"

Kristina wrinkled her freckled nose as she searched for words. "I think, probably, that you've got a lot going on, and you aren't feeling your best. I can see you've decided Addie is to blame. You haven't given her a chance. I'm not sure what that's based on, though I'm willing to listen if you want to talk about it."

Melissa jumped up from the blanket and ran to her father. He plunked her down on his lap and let her pretend to hold the fishing pole.

Poor sprite can feel any hint of tension, and it upsets her badly.

"Skittish little thing," Lydia commented. "She's never liked me either."

Allison heaved a huge sigh. The movement seemed to excite the baby, who responded with a heavy kick to her left lower rib. "Stop that, you. Come out, and you won't be so crowded, but there isn't any more room."

Time to face the music. I think maybe I've been acting like a brat. She turned to look at each of her friends, gauging their reactions to her unkind comments. *Have I lost everyone I love along with my dreams?* Becky looked back steadily. *She understands better than anyone, but she's not going to give me an inch of leeway.*

Kristina's eyebrows lowered in concern, *but is it for me or for Addie? As the pastor's wife, it's her job to make sure we welcome the stranger.*

Lydia glared, not in fury, but with the threat of unleashing an Italian temper tantrum that would leave Allison smarting for days.

Allison quickly turned to the object of her frustration. Addie curled up, her arms around the knees she had drawn toward her chest, trying to appear invisible, as though debating whether she should stay or bolt. The roundness of her belly transformed her defensive shape into a ball.

She looks vulnerable, and why not? She just arrived in a new town, barely married, visibly pregnant, and ready to be judged. Sadly, I'm the one who did the judging. That isn't like me. Argh. What's wrong with me?

She struggled to find some kind of acceptable, understandable reason for her dislike of her childhood friend's wife. *One that doesn't reveal too much of my own inescapable pettiness.* She cast about and at last hit on a single, lame excuse. One that made her cringe even as she voiced it. "Doesn't it bother anyone else that Jesse went out into the wild world and came back with this one? And her pregnant out to there, no less, but no sign of a wedding ring. Oh, no. They had to hurry up and marry before anyone could get to know her. That bothers the hell out of me. Lydia," she turned and their eyes locked, "you, I understand. You never knew Jesse. You only know how to be hospitable. Kristina, I'm surprised at you though. I know how you used to feel about Jesse."

Kristina smiled kindly. "Used to. It's been years. Yes, I was sweet on Jesse when we were seventeen. I dared to hope, when Lily passed away, that he might find me acceptable, but, Allison, why on earth would I hold on to that now? Look at what I have. What am I supposed to regret that I would begrudge him his happiness? I want him to be happy and now we both are. Cody loves me. I'm first in his heart. That's as good as it gets and much more than I expected. So, in honor of years of friendship, I affirm Jesse's choice. This is the girl who taught him to love again. I won't say a word against her. Not unless she shows me by some action that she's hurting our friend. So far, she seems to be helping him."

Of course, she's right. Why would she regret not being Jesse's second choice when the pastor loves her with all his heart? It was a stupid question that got just the answer it deserved.

Becky spoke into the awkward silence. "Before you dig any deeper into that hole, if you condemn her for going to the altar pregnant, you'll have to condemn me too. Don't forget that."

"I would never condemn you," Allison told her sister fervently.

"Then, Allison, how can you say a word about Addie? Things happen. They're married now. You can't deny he's happy, and she seems nice so far." Becky's gentle voice left no room for either anger or mistaking her meaning.

"Allison?" Addie's soft voice cut through the sound of wind whispering through the grass to reach unwelcoming ears. "I didn't marry Jesse to hurt you, and I have nothing against you. I'm glad he had wonderful friends growing up, especially you and Kristina. You two taught him to listen to women. Most men don't know how to do that. I knew about you both. He told me so many stories. I was looking forward to seeing this town, to meeting his friends. This seemed like a place for a person to start over with no one judging them. A place to fit in and make a life. I wanted that. I had hoped his friends could be my friends. If you won't accept me, well, there's nothing I can do about it, but I hold no anger toward you."

Allison bit her lip. "Why do you have to be nice?" she demanded.

"Why do you have to choose her for a target?" Lydia shot back. "Why not be angry with the people who actually hurt you? Start with your evil mother-in-law. Leave Addie alone if you can't be her friend."

Allison sighed and fell silent, contemplating. *I should stop this stupid argument. It's only making me look even more like an ass.* She tried to say something kind, but the words abandoned her. *The contrast between what she has—what I wanted—and what I have is too great. I can't look at her. They're right that it's not her fault, but that doesn't mean I can be rational about it.* The most she could manage was blunt honesty. "I'm not apologizing until I have a better handle on how I feel about anything. It's probably best to give me a wide berth until after the delivery. I'm not in a good state right now."

"You're not," Kristina agreed. "I do feel sorry you're so uncomfortable, but it has been affecting your mood."

Stung, Allison burst out, "I can't control it. I feel so horrible. My feet hurt. My back hurts. When I try to sleep, my hips hurt and my legs twitch. I'm never doing this again."

Becky rose and went to her sister, wrapping an arm around her shoulders. "I'm sorry, honey."

Allison gave her sister a tight pseudo-smile and stretched out on her side on the blanket. *Maybe a nap will improve my mood. Probably not, but I have to try something.* Within moments, she drifted off into a restless and uncomfortable sleep.

Chapter 17

Hold up, cuz!" Edgar Fulton called to Wesley as he passed the post office on his way to the end-of September deacons' meeting. *I love being able to attend these meetings without hearing fussing about it when I get home. Allison approves, which makes a task I enjoy even more enjoyable. Besides, being at the house isn't as fun as it used to be.*

The thought brought with it a sliver of guilt. Don't be unkind, man. It's not Allie's fault she's in a bad mood. She's so huge I don't know how she stands up anymore. The thought of why his wife was so swollen set his insides squirming uncomfortably. As did the thought of her crabby, whiny demeanor, which only seemed to worsen with every passing week.

If you're honest, you'll admit that even her worst is nowhere near as bad as what you once knew. Yes, she's in a sour mood and can be a bit unreasonable, but this is Allison. She's never violent, doesn't scream and doesn't hurl insults. She only whines and complains a bit. It didn't stop him from resenting her thought. *Is a peaceful home too much to ask for?* "What's up, Ed?" he called to his cousin, squashing down resentment and focusing on the conversation at hand.

The young man hurried across the street. Summer rain had turned the dirt between the stones into a quagmire, and he slipped and skidded, finally grabbing Wesley's arm for support. Thankfully, Wes had seen the move coming and strengthened his stance to compensate.

"You have a letter," Edgar replied, waving a rectangle of paper in front of him.

Bank business, Wesley thought, remembering he was expecting correspondence on a shipment of gold bars due to arrive next month. *As if the train robbers weren't bad enough when all they wanted was revenge. If they knew we were getting...* He didn't finish the thought. Didn't have to. Edgar tucked the letter into his hand and one glance at the envelope revealed to Wes that he had been completely wrong. Heart-stoppingly,

164

gut-wrenchingly wrong. The name 'Andrew Fulton' headed the return address.

Wesley blinked, not knowing what to think or feel, moments before a wave of irrational terror washed over his insides like the swollen Arkansas River.

Oh, grow up, he chided himself. *It's a piece of paper. It can't hurt you.*

"It's from your dad," Edgar crowed, oblivious to Wesley's inner upset. "Don't that beat all? After all these years."

"I know," Wesley replied, forcing wooden words past paralyzed lips. Thanks, Ed. I have to go now. I have a meeting."

His cousin waved and sauntered back across the street, wiping his forehead as a wind stale with the rankness of overripe summer sent a few crispy blades of dried grass waving south towards the Oklahoma panhandle and the whole of West Texas. Wesley turned, facing into the wind. Clutching the letter in one hand, he fought his way through the gusts toward the church.

"Don't read it," he muttered to himself. "Why the *hell* should I care what he has to say now, almost twenty years later? I was only a kid when he took off. What must I have been, seven?"

Seven, yes. And why do I not remember it? Losing a father should be a memorable event. I don't remember much of anything from before that time. He didn't want to remember either. The very thought had his stomach and jaw clenching.

"So, don't read it. Tear it up and throw it in the river!"

But do you really want that? What would it hurt to know what the old bastard has to say? You sure don't have to respond.

By the time Wesley reached the church, he was still of two minds about the unexpected missive and just what he should do about it.

"What have you got there, Wes?" Allison asked, hefting herself out of the rocking chair and waddling across the bedroom floor to her husband. He hugged her awkwardly and kissed the top of her head.

"It's a letter," he said.

She gave him a look. "I can see that. So what? You get letters every day. Why is this one special?"

"It's from my father," he replied.

"Your... but... wow!" Allison stuttered.

"I know. Why is he writing to me now? I haven't spoken to him in years. He abandoned us. I'm tempted to throw it in the fire."

"All right, Wes," Allison agreed easily, "but you might read it first. See what he has to say."

He already had the envelope ripped open. After a quick scan of the contents, he handed it to her.

Dear Wes,

I know you probably don't want to hear from me anymore. All the unanswered letters should tell me that, but it's not easy for a father to let go of his son, so I had to try one more time.

Soon I'll be relocating overseas, and I don't think I'll have the opportunity to return. Before I lose the possibility of making things right with you, I need to try once more for contact.

There are so many things I need to tell you, I hardly know where to begin. If you have any interest in talking to me, meet me on the first of October at the New Long Branch Saloon in Dodge City at noon.

I will wait until nightfall. I hope to see you then.

Dad.

Allison set the note on the bedside table and turned to face her husband. He'd stuck his hands into his pants pockets, in a gesture of false casualness.

"You're not going," she said, more as a statement than a question.

"Why not? I'm curious to know what it's all been about. So many years I've wondered what happened. He says I've ignored his letters, but he hasn't sent any. I want to know what that means."

"Wes," Allison said gently, though inside she wanted to rage and scream, "I understand your desire to know more, but you really can't leave. What about the train robbers and their threats? Can you really leave me alone? Do you want to risk your safety for no good reason? Besides, the first of October is tomorrow, and our baby is due to be born any day. I can't have you just hop on the train to Dodge City and be gone. What if I go into labor?"

"Well, Allison, I don't really know what difference that would make," he said mildly. "I wouldn't be around during the labor anyway, and I'd be home either late tomorrow night or early the next morning."

"You won't be around for the birth of your child?" she asked, incredulous.

"No, of course not. Delivering babies is women's business. I would just be underfoot. Tell you what. I'll ask Mother to stay with you."

"Your mother?" She raised one eyebrow. "How is that supposed to be an improvement on being alone? Have you forgotten I'm not speaking to her? I'd prefer my sister since Mom has gone with Dad on that getaway." *It seems everyone's intent on abandoning me at my most vulnerable moment.* She blew out a sigh between her lips. *Oh, don't be a grump, Allison. Dad and Mom deserve their getaway after the year they've had. And this...* She stopped berating herself. *There's no excuse for this. He shouldn't go, and I have every right to complain.*

Wesley spoke again. "My mother has been through delivery, Allison. Your sister is barely expecting. It would be better to have someone who knows what's happening. Mom can get the midwife if it comes down to it."

Allison opened her mouth to protest, to insist, in no uncertain terms, that the woman's evil presence would not be tolerated, but her husband cut her off. "I'm going. Probably nothing will happen, but even if it does, you'd be doing this without me either way. Men don't attend childbirth, and I need to know what he wants. Now it's late. Let's go to bed."

He headed for the water closet as Allison slowly pulled off her dress. Her body, heavily distorted with the weight of her nearly-due baby, ached constantly. The squirming limbs sometimes felt as though they were about to tear open her flesh. *This hurts so much. I want the delivery over with. And now my husband isn't even going to be around.* Allison stood naked beside the bed, running her fingers over the huge swell that threatened constantly to topple her. *How long can it be? Days? A week? Couldn't be than that. I'm huge. I never imagined my body would stretch so far. Surely Rebecca, in her fifth month and sporting a tiny, concealable bump, will not grow so large.*

Wesley returned for bed before she could pull on her nightgown.

"Allison?" he approached her slowly. Angry as she was, she turned her back on him, reaching under her pillow for the last nightgown she could get into.

Wesley's hands slid down her back and around her hip, carefully avoiding the heavy curve of her belly. His other hand went to her breasts. "Don't be angry with me, Allison. You read it. I have one chance to meet him. How can I say no?"

"I don't know, Wes," she replied wearily. "I had hoped your wife, the woman who waited for you while you married another woman, who picked up the pieces after your world fell apart and tried to put them back together—for you and your daughter— who has loved you since you were a child and loves you to this day, and who puts up with your lingering problems, the woman who is carrying your baby and is about to deliver, would mean more to you than a father who disappeared so long ago, none of us remember what he looks like."

"Allison," Wesley said, his voice serious, though his caressing of her tender nipples was far from innocent, "the only person on earth who means as much to me as you do is Melissa. I'm sorry I haven't been the husband you hoped for, but this is my one chance to find out what it was about. Please, Allie, don't make this a problem. Let me go. I'll come home to you as soon as I can." He turned her around and looked down at her, heat flaring in his eyes.

"How can you want me when I look like this?" she demanded.

"How could I not? Come on, love. Who knows how many chances we'll get before...?" he trailed off.

"Wes?"

He led her to the bed, pulling back the covers. She flopped onto on her side. "What is it, Allie?" he asked, angling his body so he could kiss her.

"Do you want this baby?"

He went still, considering his words.

He doesn't know, she realized in despair.

"It's not the baby, Allie, and it's not you. I can't forget how hard it was before, with Sam. She... well, you know. And Missy... I don't know... I'll never know."

"So, I'm suffering, and so is your little one," she captured his hand and placed it on her belly, forcing him to face what he'd tried too hard to ignore, "because you bedded an easy girl. That's not fair."

"I know," he said.

"Melissa is yours because you love her and because you've claimed her. This baby is yours in every way," she pointed out.

"I know that too, Allie. I know." He petted the straining skin, even as his expression twisted with discomfort.

"But do you believe it? Not just with your head, Wes. Do you know it deep in your soul? Do you have faith in me? I've never betrayed you, Wes. These are the only hands that have touched me." She grasped his fingers and slid hers between them. "I love you, Wes. Only you. Do you not love me anymore?"

"My goodness, expectant mothers are dramatic," he replied, distracting her with kisses as his hands escaped her and fled to the sensitive places on her body.

She let him because she was too tired to fight.

When Wesley attempted to lower her on her back, she protested. "I can't do it like that. The baby's too heavy."

"That's all right, love," he replied, lying back himself and extending a hand so she could straddle him.

He guided his sex to her entrance and slipped through the pregnancy-moistened passage to her fullest depth.

It feels good, she admitted silently. *Of course, it does. Wesley knows what I like.*

He held her in place, his hands on her hips while he glided gently in and out. Eventually, her snug sheath tightened in pleasure and a soft gasp escaped her lips, but the intense closeness sex had brought in their early marriage did not rise with the orgasm, and even as her body tightened, her mind remained aware.

Wesley has rejected intimacy with me, so I withdrew from him to protect my heart. The two of us live side by side, our bodies touching, but our hearts shielded from contact. How did we come to such a place?

She didn't know, and in the aftermath of a climax, a quarrel, and ongoing frustration, she suddenly felt exhausted. Wriggling away from Wesley, she flopped down on her side and quickly fell asleep.

Chapter 18

The following morning, Wesley slipped out of the house while his wife slept. *I don't want to continue arguing with her about whether I should go. I said what I intended to say.*

He made his quiet way through the early morning stillness to his mother's house, the bank, and then the train station, where he purchased a ticket to Dodge City. *I'll be there well before noon and have time to gather myself before I confront the man who made my childhood so difficult.*

Allison woke up feeling sore and grumpy. She had an ache in her back, another in her hip, and her shoulder was more than half numb. Bright sunlight seemed to assault her senses. She hauled her heavy body into a sitting position.

"Mama Allie?" a little voice chirped from the bedroom doorway. "Mama Allie, I'm hungry."

The mention of food made Allison's stomach heave. "I'll get you something in a moment, baby."

"Please hurry. My tummy is rumbling."

Allison groaned. "As quick as I can," she replied. Smoothing a scraggly wisp of blond hair out of her eyes, she gripped the bedpost and used it to haul herself to her feet. Her calf knotted in a painful cramp. She whimpered, flexing her foot to soothe the ache, and reached down, trying to dig a knuckle into the charley horse, but couldn't reach past her enormous belly.

The muscles of her abdomen tightened as well. Allison clung to the post, waiting helplessly for the pains to stop.

"Mama Allie!" Mellissa yelled, hurtling into the room.

"Missy, stop!" Allison shouted.

The little girl pulled up short, her lip quivering.

"I can't pick you up, baby. I'm sorry."

"Why are you so fat, Mama Allie?" Melissa asked.

Allison cautiously released her stranglehold on the bedpost and took a step. Her calf ached, and so did her back, but she moved forward anyway. "Remember how I told you I'm going to have a baby, Missy?" she replied. "That baby is right here." She patted her belly. "Any day now you'll have a little brother or sister."

"Oh." Melissa considered this. "What's for breakfast? Can I have cinnamon rolls?"

"Sorry, I don't have any dough ready for that," Allison replied. "I can try to make some for you for tomorrow. How about eggs?"

"I hate eggs!" The child stuck her nose in the air so that her messy golden hair fluttered down her back.

Allison sighed. The food games her stepdaughter played sometimes exasperated her to the point of exploding. "I can offer you oatmeal with cinnamon," Allison said, "but nothing else."

"I s'pose," Melissa replied, apparently acquiescing to Allison's exhausted expression.

Allison descended the staircase, groaning as she stepped on each wooden tread. In the kitchen, she stirred the oatmeal with one hand. The other remained fisted against her lower back. It ached so intensely she wanted to cry. *Not to mention the smell of the oatmeal makes me nauseous.* Plunking a bowl in front of Melissa, she splashed cool milk on the hot cereal and staggered out of the kitchen to use the necessary.

"Hello," a voice called from the other room as she finished.

"Becky?" she called through the door.

"Yes, Allie. Where are you?"

"Just a minute," Allison replied. She settled her nightgown back around her. "Um, James didn't come with you, did he?"

"No," her sister replied. By the sound, she now stood outside the bathroom door. "He's at the store."

"Good." *I can come out in my nightgown if only Becky is here.* Opening the door, she saw her sister standing before her, dressed in a pretty calico frock that only strained slightly around the curve of Becky's pregnancy. "Hi there. How's my favorite little niece or nephew?" Allison asked, pressed her hand to her sister's belly.

Becky took in the sight of Allison, swollen and disheveled, still wearing her nightgown. "You look like hell," she said bluntly.

"I know," Allison replied. "I feel like it too. At least I'm consistent."

"Tell you what. Why don't you go get dressed? I'll play with the munchkin for a while."

Allison tried to smile, but she could feel it was little more than an unhappy grimace.

"Actually," Becky said, "maybe I should just take her with me. Would that help?"

"/Becky," Allison said, "you're an angel." Tears of gratitude stung her eyes. Then another vicious cramp tightened down her spine and she moaned softly.

"On the other hand, maybe I should stay. I don't think you should be alone. Honey, are you in labor?"

"I have no idea," Allison replied, leaning her head weakly against the door frame. Her swollen feet throbbed. "Is Mother at home?"

"Sorry," Becky replied, smoothing a strand of hair out of Allison's face. "She and Dad went out of town, remember?"

Tarnation. I did know that. Why can't I think straight? "It's hard to remember anything," Allison said. "My head feels like it's stuffed with cotton."

"I know what you mean," Rebecca replied. "I'm not looking forward to this winter."

"At least it won't be so *hot* for you," Allison replied, panting.

"Are you having pains?" Becky laid a hand on her sister's belly. "I can't tell if you are or not."

"I don't think so. It's my back that hurts." *Hurts is an understatement. It feels like a fist clenching down on it.*

"Help me out here, Allison," her sister pleaded. "I don't know what to do. Should I get the midwife?"

"I don't know, I... owwwww!"

"I can't, I mean I don't... I'll get help. Come on, Melissa!" she grabbed the toddler, who had just wandered into the room, and hurried out the door.

The intense, painful sensation eased, and Allison moved cautiously out of the door frame of her water closet, hoping to make it to the sofa before anything else happened. One slow, painful step at a time, she inched her way into the parlor.

About halfway across the open space, her muscles locked again. With nothing to grab, she crumpled to the floor, rocking on her hands and knees while her pelvis ached and throbbed. Somehow, being in this position helped, so she stayed.

The clenching returned, but this time, it felt right to lower her chest to the floor, so she did. It eased the horrible pressure considerably, no matter that she looked like an idiot. She sighed, shifting her hips to one side and then the other. *If this is labor, I want no part of it.*

A strange swooping sensation rolled through her body, forceful enough to take her breath away. The next time her body tightened, it clearly came from her belly. It hurt, but not as intensely. Cautiously, Allison raised herself up from the floor. *I don't want to sit,* she realized, pondering the internal signals, *but leaning forward helps. Maybe on the arm of the sofa?* Shifting her weight from foot to foot, she struggled to remain calm through what she now realized was the beginnings of labor pains.

Beyond the window of the train, the golden stalks of autumn grass waved across the landscape from horizon to horizon.

Endless, the grass, Wesley thought. *Like life. Everything changes. A person, like a blade of grass, is born, matures, and eventually shrivels and dies without disturbing a blade no more than ten paces away. Each lives out its own existence, mostly alone, mostly not affecting those nearby.*

Some are cut short, disease or natural disaster truncating their lives, but even those who arrive at maturity are cut down in their time, and no one is unique or different. All experience much the same existence. Like a grain of wheat, I've propagated again, spread my seed and borne fruit. Or maybe it isn't again. Who knows? Allison's right that it doesn't matter who Melissa's birth father really was. She's mine by my choice. Mine legally. What difference does the rest make at this point?

A new thought occurred to Wesley. *Out of all the boys she fooled around with, Samantha chose me to be the father of her baby, to provide the home they needed. In a twisted sort of way, it's flattering. Allison would say to keep that with my other good memories of her.*

Maybe she's right. That realization spurred another. *I did the same with Allison; chose her to be the mother of my child, and to provide the home we need. She rose to it the best she could, gave her all, even her heart, to keep me happy. I repaid her about as well as I was repaid.*

Depressed by the similarities, Wesley turned his attention back to the dying grass.

"What are you doing?"

Allison, in the midst of yet another pain, didn't immediately respond to her mother-in-law's arrival. She hummed low and deep, not quite a groan, but almost. She'd been doing that for a while. It gave her something to think about and helped her take her mind off her discomfort.

At last, Allison lifted her head to take in Wesley's mother. Her steel-gray, curly hair was escaping its pins, hovering around her head like a halo. Her eyes, also metallic in color, peered suspiciously through wire-rimmed spectacles. Her thin lips compressed into a sour expression.

"I'm in labor," Allison explained simply. "I'm all right so far, but would you please go and get the midwife?"

"Bah," Mrs. Fulton dismissed the request with a wave of her hand. "It's too soon. You don't need that yet." She challenged Allison with a direct stare, one Allison tried to meet with her own firmness.

Just what I need, this bitch interfering. Labor is hard enough without her meddling.

Somehow, in her vulnerable, inward-focused state, Allison could not muster the strength to kick the woman out. Then, another cramp, this one harder than any previous pain, tightened Allison's belly, and she moaned.

Triumph flared in the older woman's eyes.

I can't worry about her now, Allison thought frantically, concentrating on turning her moan into a hum, like she had before. It still worked, but not as well. *This is a definite change over the previous hour.* "Please," she begged. "Please go get the midwife."

"Soon," Mrs. Fulton replied. "In the meanwhile, stop that infernal racket. Don't you know you'll wear yourself out moaning and groaning? You've barely started. It gets much worse than this."

"Wonderful," Allison muttered. Another pain seized her, and she leaned against the arm of the sofa, rocking her hips and trying not to make a sound.

An hour later, Allison's contractions were right on top of each other and had strengthened to the point where her soft toning, which she had quickly given up trying to conceal, no longer sufficed to distract her. She still tried, but at the peak of each one, the pain overcame her concentration, making her cry out sharply.

As the contraction waned, she whimpered, panting. "I can't do this, Mother. Please go get the midwife."

"Settle down, Allison," Mrs. Fulton snapped, "you're acting like a baby. You have hours to go."

Allison began to cry. *Being here with my mother-in-law is worse than being alone. I want Wesley... or Becky. Someone, anyone who cares. I want my mother.*

"Oh, stop your blubbering!" Mrs. Fulton snapped.

Allison couldn't stop, and when the next pain tightened her belly, the tension of her emotional discomfort prevented her from riding the wave. Her moan rose to a scream. At the apex, she felt as though something had burst inside her. Warm liquid ran down her thighs. She glanced at her mother-in-law, who regarded her with deep disgust.

"I told you to settle down," Mrs. Fulton groused, her lips tight. "Now you've gone and pissed yourself."

Alison didn't say a word, though she felt quite sure it wasn't urine. *Didn't the midwife mention this? Too bad it isn't an indicator of where my labor is at.*

Another contraction began to build, and Allison turned her attention inward, struggling to maintain herself in the face of it.

Wesley stalked into the saloon. The original had burned a few years ago, and this was the owner's attempt to resurrect his business. The place showed signs of shoddy workmanship; with warped floorboards. The leaky roof created water stains on the dark red wallpaper and wainscoting. Many tables had matchbooks or other objects wedged beneath, to stabilize wobbly legs. As though in response to the shabby environment, few patrons graced the place with their presence. *Of course, it's barely after noon*, Wesley reminded himself.

Meeting each set of eyes, Wesley dismissed one after another. *Too young. Too old. This one's an Indian. That one's blond. None of them resemble me in any way.* That only left the man sitting at the bar with his back to the room. He wore a substantial black hat, which concealed his features from questing eyes.

At the sound of the door swinging shut, the man turned. Wesley found himself staring into a face rugged with exposure to the sun. Grizzled stubble coated the cheeks, but the features beneath the surface could have been seen in his mirror. He gulped, a maelstrom of contradictory emotions swirling inside him. Slowly he crossed the dimly lit space to sit on an empty barstool beside the stranger he should have known.

"What can I getcha?" the barkeep demanded in a harried voice.

Oh please, Wesley thought. *As if you're so busy.* "It's too early for booze. I'll take a sarsaparilla."

The lukewarm, foamy mug slid in front of him a moment later. Through all this, he'd not turned once to look at the man behind him. *No more delaying, Wes.*

He turned and met eyes the exact color of his. "Andrew Fulton?" He was pleased his voice sounded completely neutral.

"Yes, that's me. Hello, son."

Slowly, one agonized step at a time, Allison climbed the stairs. Her labor pains had grown so intense, she could think of nothing else. It was as though she'd been submerged in a red ocean of agony, barely able to float. An intense pressure had begun in her lower body. *It feels like… something unmentionable. I want my bed.* She couldn't have explained why if she'd tried. She only knew she had to get there, and so she made her painful, precarious way up one tread after another.

The intensity peaked, and she gripped the railing with such force she could feel the paint cracking below her hands. "Ohhhhhh" she groaned, expelling her air in a low, barely-controlled and endless tone, dreading taking a breath. She was right to worry, as the moment it took her to suck air into her lungs ratcheted the intensity up to unbearable. Her tone turned to a screech, and then a groan as the pain finally eased.

"Oh, shut up your caterwauling," a sour voice commented.

"If you're not going to get the midwife, *you* shut up!" Allison snapped, panting. As soon as she was able, she scrambled up the last few stairs to her bedroom, grateful to make it off the stairs. *That must have been dangerous. I could have fallen.*

She shuffled quickly but awkwardly down the hall to her and Wesley's bedroom and stretched out on her side on the bed, just as her belly tightened again. *No! Oh, no.* She sobbed, and then, with her last moments of strength forced herself to draw in a deep breath and release the low, loud moan that was the only remaining defense between her and hysterical screaming. The pressure in her pelvis increased. It burned in places she couldn't even imagine. *Why is it so hot in here? It's October. It should be cooling.* Sweat beaded on Allison's forehead. Her molars ground together. Suddenly, something inside her seemed to shift. The agonizing pressure changed to a sensation she could not have described, though her subconscious seemed to understand it. *I have to push NOW!*

"Well, Wesley," his father said, after regarding him in silence for several seconds, "I imagine you have things you want to tell me and ask me. We might as well get that out of the way first."

Wesley stared at his father without speaking. It *seems unreal that the face I forgot in childhood looks as familiar to me as the one I see while shaving every day. Older, more haggard to be sure, but familiar, nonetheless.* The questions that had bubbled in his head since the previous night, stealing his sleep, that had occupied his mind on the train here, all left him. He had no idea what to say.

"Or," Andrew said with a chuckle, "I could go first, I suppose." He took a swig of his drink. "So, how are you these days?"

"Fine," Wesley replied in a monotone.

"Are you married?"

"Yes."

A smile spread across his father's face. "How is Allison?"

Wesley lowered his eyebrows. "How did you know?"

The question produced a rough guffaw. "As if you'd have married anyone else. Thick as thieves, you two, since you were toddlers. How your mother hated that. She thought the Spencers were trash, but they're good folks. It's no surprise."

Oh. "Allison's expecting. She's due any minute." Still that flat tone. *I don't know how to feel, though perhaps anger might appear at some point.* It wasn't there yet, so he wallowed in his numbness.

"Expecting! Congratulations. So, I'm going to be a grandfather, eh?"

"No," Wesley replied. Andrew regarded him with a surprised look on his face. "You already are. Yes, I'm married to Allie now, but she's not my first wife. I was married for a few years before, but my wife passed away. I have a little girl by her."

The confused expression intensified. "You didn't marry Allison the second you were able? Who was your first wife?"

Wesley lowered his eyes to the bar. "Samantha Davis," he mumbled.

"Sam… oh wow. But she's… and… Wesley, *why*?" his father stammered.

He sighed. "She was pregnant."

Understanding dawned. "Is your daughter all right?" Andrew's eyes bored into his.

Wesley nodded. "Smart as a whip. She gives Allison and me both a run for our money. And now that Allie's so heavy and tired…"

Silent communication passed between the two men. When Wesley spoke next, it was to voice the question that had haunted most of his life. "Why did you leave, Dad? I would never let anything separate me from Melissa. How could you just walk away from your only son?"

Now Andrew looked confused again. "I didn't. Surely you remember? You were seven years old."

Wesley stared at him. None of the words made sense, though a strange feeling of impending doom hung heavy in his belly.

"I didn't leave you," Andrew stated at last. "I took you with me."

Allison groaned and wiped a strand of sweaty hair off her forehead. Lying on her side no longer felt right, so she shifted, rising onto her knees again. "I need a towel," she snarled, feeling more liquid running down her legs.

For once, Mrs. Fulton didn't argue. She hurried to the linen closet and returned with a pile of towels, which she stacked on the bed. "Lie down," she ordered.

Allison shook her head. "This feels better. Owwww!" The burning pressure began again, and Allison pushed with all her strength. It felt like fire in her innermost places. Something seemed to be spreading her body outward. She stopped, panting, and the outward push retreated. The urge intensified, stealing her will. "The baby's coming," her mouth babbled without any conscious decision of her will. "It's coming." She bore down. *I have to do this. It will all stop if I can just bring this baby down.*

Gripping the bedpost with one hand, she remained kneeling and pushed hard again. This time a large object stretched her obscenely wide. Crackling sounds and sparkling lights crowded around her—real or imagined, she had no idea. Black spots swam in front of her eyes, and she closed them. All this took seconds, and then the pressure eased with a pop. *What in the world?*

Still clutching the bedpost in one hand, she reached down with the other and touched something warm, velvet-soft and wet. Allison whimpered, an incoherent sound as her brain finally fired something sensible. *A head. It's the head.*

A new contraction tightened. She bore down once more with a shriek as the shape one shoulder and then another passed from her into the world. She instinctively guided a small body to rest on the towel.

Abruptly the pressure ceased. Her legs buckled, and she directed herself backwards, away from the tiny body, to lie on her back, a position that no longer felt too heavy on her spine. *It's over. Thank God.* She tried to reach for the baby, tried to open her eyes to see it, but the spots had returned in her vision. Now they began to spin, joining together until black crowded her vision and unconsciousness dragged her down.

"What the hell do you mean?" Wesley demanded. "Took me with you where? What are you talking about?"

"I'm talking about when we left your mother. I couldn't stand her behavior anymore. She was always a bit moody and clingy, but it wasn't too bad… until you were born. Then she became a completely different person. She was so possessive, she wouldn't let me touch you. She had all these ideas, some of them nonsense, others dangerous, about how you had to be raised. When you were about six, she had some kind of breakdown, screaming and cursing, hitting us both, throwing things. I… I knocked her away from you." Andrew's cheeks darkened. "I wasn't trying to hurt her, but she fell, and her head hit the floor. While she was unconscious, we grabbed some clothes and lit out. You don't remember any of this?" He peered at his son.

Nausea gripped Wesley's innards. A confused mélange of images and sounds rolled across him. Screaming. Hazy, unformed visions of adult-sized people circling him as he looked up in terror.

"I've tried not to," he said, swallowing hard. Wesley took a deep breath through his nose. The scents of the bar; tobacco, liquor and sweaty men washed over him. Adult smells, they steadied his reality.

"You really don't remember what happened?"

Wesley shook his head. Focused on suppressing the dizzying memories, he couldn't see his father, or take in his tone of voice at all.

"We were on the run a year, you and me. We went from farm to ranch, town to city, doing odd jobs and trying to keep body and soul together, but all in all, it was a good time. I felt like, if we could keep away from her for seven years, the marriage would be over, and I would be free. I didn't want you exposed to her instability any longer."

Images swirled faster in Wesley's mind. *Holding onto the reins with Dad, as I sat on his lap on the back of a galloping horse. Sneaking into a train car and hiding among sacks of wheat. Mucking horse stalls, far to the north. Gathering eggs out west.* He forced his eyes to focus on Andrew. "What happened?"

His father slowly shook his head. "I don't know. Somehow, she found us. I woke up in the middle of the night, in a hotel room in St. Louis, feeling something wasn't right. She was there, holding a knife to your throat." Andrew's own throat convulsed. "She said… she said she wouldn't let me have you. She would… kill us all before that would happen. Starting with you. I…" Andrew broke off, shuddering.

"What would you do for your daughter, Wesley, if her safety was threatened? What would you sacrifice to protect her? I knew, if your mother won, you would be safe. If I ran again, she would find us, and I would watch you die. I couldn't let that happen. She didn't want to hurt you, only me, so I let her. I agreed to her terms. To leave and let her keep you, on one condition. I had to receive regular reports on your well-being. If I heard from my sources that you had been harmed, I would have ended her, and the consequences be damned. Maybe it was wrong, but I didn't know what else to do. Can you possibly understand my position?"

Wesley nodded without reflection, numbly reacting to the question without contemplating it.

"To keep you safe, I had to let you go. However, my spies, the Spencers, have kept me informed about you all these years. Your mother had to let Allison play with you, let you play at their house, so I could get regular reports. I even sent them money sometimes, when I heard your mother overspent her allowance."

Overspent? Allowance? He must have looked puzzled because his father hurried to explain. "Your mother's parents once owned a large cattle ranch. When they passed on, her father arranged in his will for the property to be sold, but the money was placed in the care of a lawyer from Wichita. Your mother was to receive payments each month for her comfort and support, and she did. When we were… together, she was able to spend that money on herself. After the separation, it was still enough for the two of you to live on, if she was frugal, but she didn't like it. I think having her income restricted offended her."

Wesley nodded. At last, words dropped from his mouth, random as rain. "She hated it. Although she never discussed money with me, which I thought was bizarre, given my profession." His thoughts turned, taking his babbling gush with them. "She always called the Spencers trash. I figured it was because Mr. Spencer drove the train. She loved to talk about her daddy, the landowner, the cattle rancher."

"I'm sure that played a role," his father concurred. "Charlotte always was a bit of snob."

"Why did you marry a snob?" Wesley asked.

"Why did you marry a..." His father trailed off. "Never mind."

Wesley lowered his eyes. *It seems being swayed by the lusts of the flesh into marrying unsuitable women is a family tradition.* Squashing down his emotions, he focused on the conversation.

"At any rate, they would have been trash to her regardless, but knowing they were reporting back to me made them intolerable, except she had to tolerate them. She must have come to hate them more than anyone, in time. No wonder she despised the idea of you marrying Allison." He grinned.

"So that's the long answer to the short question. I kept an eye on you through them, until you stopped living in her home. Until you were a man and could care for yourself. That's when I tried writing to you. I don't know why my letters never got through, but I've been writing to you each month since you turned eighteen. Wesley, I hated that I had to leave you, but under the circumstances, I didn't know what else to do."

All the jagged pieces of Wesley's childhood fell into place with a nearly audible jangle. *I can't quite remember the events Dad's describing, or maybe I just don't want to, but it all makes terrible sense.* Trying to come to grips with years of suppressed memories, Wesley buried his face in his hands.

An eerie silence descended on the Fulton house. *Silence is wrong.* Allison dragged herself out of the deep place she'd gone and tried to make sense of her surroundings. The red crazy quilt, still crumpled from not having been made up that morning, lay wadded at the foot of the bed. A pile of multicolored towels, stained with an unholy mess, protected the white sheets. Allison looked up at the plaster of the ceiling, tracing one slender crack from the window to the door frame. *Wesley needs to patch that, but... I've given birth. I know I did. Where's the baby?* Last she recalled, she'd been kneeling by the bedposts. Now she lay on the pillows, an uncomfortable bunch of fabric under her hips. *What's happening?*

"Mother?" she called. "Mother? Mrs. Fulton?"

"Yes, what?" came the cranky reply from the next room.

"What's happening?"

"What do you mean?" Mrs. Fulton's bespectacled face interposed itself between her and the crack, and she glared.

"Where's my baby?" Allison placed her hand on her belly, feeling the slackness. "Are you cleaning him… or her? What did I have?"

"You had a boy," Mrs. Fulton replied, and her face contorted into an expression Allison couldn't read.

Allison smiled despite her exhaustion. "A boy. Maybe Wesley will like that. I hope I can call him Peter. I like that name. Where is he?"

"He…" Mrs. Fulton broke off, and an even stranger look crossed her face. "I'm sorry, Allison."

"Sorry?" Allison asked, instantly alert. "Sorry about what? Where's my son?"

"He…" The woman gulped. "He was stillborn."

Wesley and his father sat in silence for the longest time. After a while, Wesley raised his burning eyes from his hands and slowly sipped his drink. *I wish I'd ordered a beer, or better yet a whiskey shot… several shots. I need it, but all I have is this mug of warm, sickly sweet soda, and no voice to order something different.* He frowned at his drink, unreasonably irritable at its lack of soothing power. *So, Mother really is crazy. People say it often. I've gotten in fights with them many times, but this makes sense.* Long-suppressed memories rose up, minute by minute. *Dad isn't lying to make his abandonment seem more palatable.* Wesley could feel the sharp steel touching his throat now. Could hear the screaming.

Suddenly, it was all too much. Abandoning his drink on the counter, he staggered out the door into the alley, between the saloon and the shoddy rooming house next door and vomited.

"Son?"

Wesley raised his head to see his father extending a handkerchief in his direction. He took the square of fabric and wiped his forehead and then his mouth.

"I guess you finally remembered," Andrew said softly. "I didn't realize you'd forgotten so much."

"Yeah," Wesley replied. He straightened and stepped away from the mess back into the street, eager to feel the sun on his face. It scorched him, and the sharp sensation chased away the ghosts, allowing him to breathe again.

"Are you all right?" his father asked. "I'm sorry I upset you."

"No, I needed to know the truth," Wesley replied, after several slow deep breaths. "I needed to understand why I grew up the way I did. No wonder Mother hates Allison."

Andrew nodded. "I'd be amazed if she didn't. I'm also amazed you came today. Did you say she was about to give birth?"

Wesley nodded. "She was pretty mad. I haven't been the best husband to her. She may not get over this for a while."

"Why did you then?" Andrew asked.

Wesley shrugged. "I wanted to see you, to know what it was all about, what I've been avoiding thinking about my whole life. I'm not sorry. Besides, I didn't leave her alone. I let Mother know to check in on her. I'm sure if anything... happened, Mother was to get the midwife for her."

Andrew's jaw dropped.

"What?" Wesley demanded.

"Think, son. What did you just say? You left *your mother*, who hates the Spencers, who thinks they're trash, who disapproves of your wife—she does, doesn't she?"

Wesley nodded.

"A woman with a history of violent and unstable behavior—in charge of looking after Allison in her most vulnerable moment?"

Realization dawned on Wesley. Two seconds later, both men ran hell-bent for leather towards the train station.

186

Allison lay in her marriage bed, on her side, staring blankly at nothing. Slow tears ran from the corners of her eyes. They already soaked the pillow, but it didn't matter.

Dead. He was moving and squirming in my belly this morning, such a short time ago. How could he have died between then and now? What happened? Why did my baby die?

Even sobs were beyond Allison's reach. She could only stare, breathing slowly and letting aimless tears run across her face. She touched her slack, empty belly. Blood trickled from between her thighs. She felt like a battlefield.

What will Wesley say? Will he be relieved? Will I ever be able to forgive him if he is?

A soft, muffled sound shattered the silence of Allison's lonely vigil. Her eyes narrowed.

You're dreaming, Allison. That or grief has pushed you over the edge. It must have been a bird… or maybe a cat outside the window.

Allison closed her eyes and willed sleep to come.

Rebecca Heitschmidt woke with a gasp, pulling away from her husband. She blinked twice, and then bolted from the bed where they'd been enjoying a late-afternoon nap.

She pulled on her shift and tied her bloomers loosely around her belly. Tossing her dress over her head, she patted James on the arm. "Wake up," she hissed urgently.

He mumbled and rolled to his side.

She grabbed his shoulder and gave a rough shake. "Wake up, James."

"Wha…" He yawned hugely. "What is it, Rebecca?"

"Allison needs me," she replied. Come on, get up."

"Allison? How do you know? Did someone come?"

Rebecca shook her head sharply. "Listen, James. We need to go NOW! Come ON! Something's wrong, I can feel it." She tugged on his arm and he rose from the bed, quickly pulling his underwear over his freckled thighs, and then adding trousers and a shirt.

"What about the sprout?" he asked, waving toward the room across the hall, where Melissa was also napping.

"Grab her. We need to move!" Rebecca insisted.

"I don't understand," James said, taking hold of Rebecca's hand and pulling her to a stop.

At last, she ceased tugging and fretting and met her husband's eyes. "Trust me."

Even though the train ride from Dodge City to Garden City only took about an hour, to Wesley it seemed like a year. For the first time since well before Christmas, the fear of train robbers—the source of murmured conversation from many of his fellow passengers—found no foothold Wesley's thoughts.

Unable to remain seated, he paced nervously up and down the aisle, upsetting several passengers, until his father snagged his arm and dragged him into a seat.

"You can't make the train move faster by fussing, son," Andrew said.

"Nothing's going to be wrong, you'll see," Wesley replied. "We'll get there to find Allison making dinner and arguing with Mother, and Melissa playing with her dolls."

"I'm sure you're right," Andrew replied. "I'm sure you are."

There was a lurch as the brake slowly engaged, beginning the gradual process of stopping the hulking iron beast in the as-yet invisible Garden City train station.

Wesley concentrated on staying calm. *Everything will be fine. It has to be fine.*

There's that sound again. Groggy and disoriented, Allison opened her eyes to a strange, kittenish mewling. *It sounds as though it's coming from inside the house… and under a pile of fabric.* Despite her lethargy, she hauled her aching body from the bed and went to investigate. Blood trailed unnoticed down her thighs as she approached the spare bedroom.

This door should not be ajar. No one wants to deal with Samantha's things. Why is it open? She tiptoed through.

Inside, a drawer had been removed from the dresser, filled with blankets, and placed atop a cosmetic-smeared vanity table. She looked at it, tilting her head. There seemed to be a shape to the top blanket. Cautiously, she approached and placed both hands on the textile. *There* is *something underneath.* Heart pounding, she yanked back the blanket and stared. One of Melissa's dolls regarded her with expressionless button eyes.

Allison's lower lip quivered. She considered just sinking to the floor and crying until she died, but before she could really work herself up to it, another squeak sounded, this time from downstairs.

Oh well, you can always fall apart later. She took a step towards the door of the bedroom, crossed the threshold, and turned to face the stairs. In her weakened state, they looked taller and steeper than normal, and she hesitated to take a step.

The mewling sounded again. Steeling herself, Allison placed one bare foot on the cold, unwelcoming wood.

The train took an eternity to come to a stop. Wesley already stood at the door, long before the wheels ceased turning and the great hulk's momentum died. Not even waiting for the step to be lowered, he flung himself to the platform and raced towards his home, his father close at his heels.

At the base of the stairs, Allison considered sitting down. She felt bruised all over but feared she would never be able to rise. She did stop briefly, leaning against the wall, and at last, became cognizant of the fact that she was bleeding. Regarding the messy pool at her feet, she shrugged. *What does it matter anyway?*

"Allison!" A sharp voice arrested her attention and she stared dumbly at her mother-in-law. "Get back to bed right now. You can't be up yet."

Allison's stubbornness hardened into determination. *I've heard all I care to hear from this woman.* "What is that noise?" she demanded.

"What noise?" Mrs. Fulton didn't look surprised in the least. She met her daughter-in-law's hard-eyed glare with one of her own.

"It sounds like… like crying," Allison replied.

"My dear girl," Mrs. Fulton drawled, in a tone that completely lacked even a hint of sympathy, "I told you what happened. Your poor son did not survive. If you're hearing crying, you're losing your mind."

From outside the door, the quiet squeaking started up again, this time in earnest. Allison turned in that direction. "What *is* that?"

"I don't hear anything," Mrs. Fulton insisted, but she also ran for the door, escaping before Allison could grab her.

Something's wrong. Very wrong. What is she doing? Trying to make me think I'm crazy? But if that's the case, the baby could still be…

Allison raced after her mother-in-law, as fast as her legs would carry her. Outside, she could just see the woman's back as she disappeared between two houses. Allison ran after her, heedless of the fact that she was running barefoot through the streets, clad only in a bloody nightgown.

Her painful steps brought her to the edge of town and beyond, to the wild place between city and prairie; rough uneven ground, with sharp bits of broken grass that tried to impale her feet as she passed. Ahead, she could see the plump figure of her adversary running straight towards the river. Her movements revealed a bundle wrapped in a white blanket, clutched precariously in one arm. A soft keening split the air from time to time.

Oh, dear God in heaven, WHAT is this crazy woman doing?

At the uneven bank, Mrs. Fulton paused, her eyes scanning the swollen torrent. Recent thunderstorms had swelled the Arkansas past its natural banks. It submerged the mudflats that normally formed its borders and rushed around the pylons of the bridge in angry gushes of swirling white water. Mrs. Fulton turned and shot Allison an ugly, triumphant grin before proceeding onto the planks. Even now, the water washed over them. She picked her way over the sodden boards to the center and turned again, daring her son's hated wife to follow.

Allison took a deep breath and approached, her feet sinking deep into the mud before she finally arrived at the bridge. Steeling herself, she stepped onto the first slippery board.

When Rebecca, James and Melissa arrived at the Fulton house, an eerie silence had descended. The two adults glanced at each other, and then another of those odd flashes of intuition had Rebecca stumbling off the street onto the lawn and skirting the side of the house. She could hear her husband's footsteps as he cracked and shattered the dying grass under his feet.

Along the west wall between the Fultons' property and their next-door neighbors, a small pile of refuse lay waiting to be burned. Mostly leaves and grass clippings, it also contained some smelly kitchen leftovers and a wooden spoon with a broken handle. There was also a strangely shaped bundle wrapped in a blanket. Rebecca stared as the bundle stirred. It wriggled, squealed like a kitten, and then the blanket fell away and a chubby pink fist popped out.

"Oh, my heavens!" Rebecca exclaimed, scooping the blanket into her arms and unwrapping it to reveal the red, wrinkled face of a newborn baby.

James drew nearer. "What on earth, Rebecca?"

She shook her head. "This must be Allison and Wesley's baby. I can't imagine what this means. James..." She lifted her eyes to her husband. "Who would put a baby in the trash?"

"Someone unstable. Do you think Allison…"

"No," Rebecca cut off her husband with a sharp gesture of her head. "Not Allison. She wanted this baby." Then her eyes widened. "Oh no. I sent Mrs. Fulton to watch over her. I thought she might be in labor and I didn't want her to be alone."

"Rebecca, Mrs. Fulton is more than half crazy," James pointed out. "Plus she and your sister don't like each other. Her being here would upset Allison badly."

"I know, but my parents are away, and I didn't know what else to do. Wesley told me to get her if ever Allison needed help and he wasn't available. But… but that still doesn't explain why the baby is in the garbage pile." Rebecca cuddled the tiny boy to her chest.

"Come on," James suggested, still frowning mightily at his wife's questionable decision. "It's cold out here for that little one. Maybe inside we can find the answers."

They trailed back around the house to the front door. It stood open. Another curious look passed between husband and wife as they mounted the steps and entered the silent house. It was clear the moment they passed the threshold that no one was inside.

Melissa scrambled down from James's hip and ran to her room, her little shoes stomping on the stairs as though she weighed twice her tiny size.

James slipped his arm around Rebecca's waist and together they approached the staircase. On the bottom tread lay a vile, black pool of half-congealed blood the size of a saucer. Rebecca gagged. Smaller drops led the way back up to the landing and around the corner, to disappear behind a partially closed door. With great trepidation, the couple entered Allison and Wesley's bedroom.

"Oh, Lord!" Rebecca exclaimed in a harsh whisper. It looked as though a murder had been committed on the bed. The comforter lay in a heap, half hanging off the foot of the bed. A wad of ruined towels, completely soaked in blood, covered the mattress at pelvis-height. Beside the bed, another pool of blood slowly spread out to fill the grain of the floorboards. Rebecca swallowed convulsively, willing herself neither to vomit nor to cry. She did manage to quell the gorge, but the tears escaped. "James, what's happening?" she asked.

"I don't know, love," he replied, "but I aim to find out. Come on, let's get out of here."

They descended to the parlor, careful not to track the mess around, and Rebecca sank onto the sofa. She carefully unwrapped the blanket and looked down into the face of her nephew.

"Someone wanted this baby to disappear," James said. He didn't sit but rather leaned against the wall beside the front door. "What purpose would that serve?"

Rebecca spoke without tearing her eyes from the child in her arms. "It would hurt Allison. Mrs. Fulton hates Allison. She would want to hurt her."

"I can see that," James replied. "She would pretend something had happened to the baby to make Allison sad. But then what? Where are they?"

Rebecca shook her head. "Allison is strong and stubborn. Those blood drops suggest she got out of bed and came down the stairs. Would Mrs. Fulton have tried to lure her somewhere?"

"To what end?" James asked.

"I don't know," Rebecca replied. "I just don't know."

At that moment, the door burst inwards and Wesley Fulton barreled into the house, sweaty and breathless. "Rebecca? James?" He looked from one to the other, confusion crumpling his features. "Is everything all right?"

"No, Wesley, it's not," James replied. "Rebecca took Melissa earlier today because Allison seemed to be going into labor." He spared the younger man a disapproving glance. "She called on your mother, who promised to come over and help. We stopped by a few minutes ago to see how everyone was doing, and we found… we found your son outside in the trash pile."

"Son?" Wesley blinked. He approached Rebecca and looked down, first at her and then at the baby. "Oh, gracious. Is he all right?"

"He seems to be," Rebecca replied softly. "He's sleeping now. He was cold and crying when we found him."

Wesley scooped the baby into his arms. A crooked half-smile spread slowly across his face.

"Not now, Wes," James snapped. "Your wife is missing. So is your mother. We have no idea where they've gone, or why they even left the house. Allison just gave birth. She shouldn't even be out of bed."

Wesley's head shot up. "Gone?"

"Yes. There's blood everywhere and the front door was open. Think, man. What kind of mischief could your mother be up to?"

Another pair of boots pounded up the stairs and Wesley's father burst into the room. "Any kind of mischief," the man replied grimly.

Andrew Fulton is back? Rebecca thought numbly. *What a day for strange occurrences. I haven't seen him since I was fifteen.* Ignoring the irrelevant musing, she forced herself to stay on topic. "How do we find them before something terrible happens? We have to get my sister back to bed before she injures herself." *If it's not already too late. Please, God let it not be too late.*

"Charlotte can be dangerous and violent. I don't doubt she could kill, if she was angry enough," Wesley's father said.

"I think she may already have killed once," James added. The eyes of the others swiveled to him. "Think. She's unnaturally possessive of you, Wes. So, when you married Samantha, didn't she do everything in her power to torment your wife?"

Wesley nodded.

"And we've all wondered what the hell Samantha was doing on the river in the winter. Even though she wasn't right in the head, she knew better than that. It might have been suicide, but what if she was tricked? Wouldn't that also make sense?"

"Oh, Lord," Wesley groaned.

"Highly likely," his father added.

Rebecca nodded. *It does make terrible sense.* "Allison is in full possession of her senses. She's strong and she knows Mrs. Fulton isn't trustworthy. Why would she let herself be lured?"

"Why was her baby in the trash?" James retorted. "What other motivation could get your stubborn sister out of her childbirth bed? Only a threat to someone she loves."

The three men looked at each other. "Would she risk the river a second time?" James asked.

"Probably, since the first time succeeded," Andrew replied.

Wesley gently returned his son to Rebecca's arms. The sound of his shoes clattering down the porch steps reverberated before she realized he was moving. Andrew stared for a split second and then pounded after his son.

"James," Rebecca snared her husband with a glance. "You bring my sister home safe to me, you promise?"

"I'll do everything I can," he replied, and then he left her alone with her sister's children.

Tears streaming down her face, Rebecca began to pray as she'd never prayed before.

Over the roar of the water, a faint mewling remained audible, emerging from the squirming bundle clutched in Mrs. Fulton's arms.

"Mother, please," Allison said in a calm, soft voice. "What are you doing?"

"Getting rid of something unwanted," the older woman sneered. The moisture in the air had caused her steel-colored hair to escape its pins and curl into a wild nimbus around her head. A manic light shone behind the metal frames of her glasses.

"He's not unwanted," Allison replied. "I want him."

"Wesley doesn't."

The truth of those harsh words tore at Allison's heart. When she met the mad eyes again, it was through a veil of tears. "That might be true, but he's my son too. Please, Mrs. Fulton, don't do this. Give me back my baby."

Mrs. Fulton regarded Allison for a long moment, head tilted as though considering. She took a deep breath and said, "No, I don't think I will." Then she tossed the bundle over the waist-high railing, into the swirling river.

The men raced out between the houses on the edge of town and arrived at the Arkansas River bridge, just in time to see Wesley's mother toss a white bundle into the river. Time seemed to slow as Wesley took in the terrifying scene of his wife, clad in a red-stained nightgown, taking a step towards the railing, and then another. Her screams echoed across the landscape, audible despite the roar of the water.

The swollen river churned against the pylons of the bridge and the surrounding rocks. *If she goes in, there will be no finding her.* Panic strapped wings to his feet, and he raced toward his wife in a burst of previously unknown. He flew across the muddy, uneven ground toward the bridge, his shoes slipping and skidding in the mud, and then on the wet boards as he skated across a film of water to reach her. Just as she placed one foot on the waist-high rail, he snagged her around the waist and dragged her back, tumbling both of them to the ground.

"Allie, no!" he shouted.

She struggled in his grip.

He tightened his arms, pinning her. "Stop!"

"Let me go! Let go!" she shrieked, trying to wrench herself free.

"Stop it, Allie. Allison, listen to me!"

"The baby! She threw the baby in the river. Let me go, Wes!" She fought him, desperate to get to the railing.

"She didn't," he said gently into her ear. Still, she flailed. "Allison!" She scratched heedlessly at his hands. *I'm no getting through. Her panic is too great.* He sat up, lifting her into his lap. Gripping her shoulders fiercely, he gave her a little shake hoping to break through her hysteria. "Allie, listen. The baby is fine. He's at the house with your sister. Mother tricked you. The baby is fine."

At last her eyes began to focus. "Wesley?" Though she'd said his name a moment ago, it seemed as though she was realizing for the first time that he was there.

"Yes, Allison. I'm here." He relaxed his crushing grip and enfolded her in a warm embrace. "I've got you, love."

"The baby's fine?" Allison asked in a tiny, wavering voice.

"Yes, honey. He's perfectly well. Rebecca has him and Melissa at the house, and they're both fine."

Allison inhaled, and it sounded like a sob. "She had something. It was making sounds like a baby. I thought..." At last, great, choking sobs overcome her. She was soaked and shivering.

Wesley cradled her against his body.

"It was probably a cat."

At the sound of another masculine voice, both Wesley and Allison looked up.

Andrew stood over them, his features grim. "She always did hate cats."

Movement caught Wesley's eye and he turned to see James approaching. Wesley turned Allison in his arms, shielding her body from his brother-in-law's sight. The thin white nightgown, wet as it was, provided nothing like decency.

"Andrew?" Heads swiveled towards Mrs. Fulton. In the commotion, Wesley had forgotten she was there.

"What kind of mischief are you up to, Charlotte?" Those eyes, which looked so much like Wesley's own, narrowed in anger as his father glared at his mother.

Wesley's gaze went from one to the other. *Can I remember ever seeing them together? Perhaps, but it's vague.*

"What were you hoping to accomplish? Have you become a murderer, Charlotte?"

"She has," James said. "I bet she orchestrated Samantha's death, didn't you, Mrs. Fulton?"

"She deserved what she got. That stupid slut made my Wesley miserable." The venom in each word could have poisoned a buffalo.

"Whose choice was it to marry her, Mother?" Wesley asked. "She didn't put a pistol to my head. Did you really kill her?" *I hate to think it, though it does make some sense. It would explain why Samantha out by the river at all.* "How did you lure her out onto the ice?"

Mrs. Fulton ignored the question.

"Allison is a good woman," James said. "She doesn't deserve this."

"She's a slut, just like the other one. Did you notice how quickly she got with child? Bet she already was. Wesley, can't you leave the tramps alone, darling?"

The sudden syrupy sweetness of his mother's voice set Wesley's teeth on edge.

"She must be a witch. She must have cast a spell on my baby boy, to make him act this way."

Wesley shook his head. "No, Mother. Allison is no witch. I love her. I've always loved her. You know that. Come on, gentlemen, let's go."

Wesley rose to his feet, setting Allison down for a moment to adjust their positions. *I would no more let her walk barefoot through the mud than I would let her go into the river.*

Mrs. Fulton pounced, grabbing Allison by the arm and dragging her back in the direction of the railing. In an act born of pure instinct, Wesley tightened his hold on his wife's waist and pivoted, shielding her body with his own and thrusting one arm outward. His movement caught his mother across the throat and sent her reeling backwards.

Her high-heeled boots skidded on the wet wood and she stumbled. Her movement brought her in contact with the railing of the bridge. In an instant she inverted, feet up, head down, screeching as she tipped into the eddying water below. Her screams abruptly cut off. The water closed over her and she could be seen no more.

Wesley stared at the place where his mother had disappeared. *In this flood, it's unlikely she'll be found, and any attempt to retrieve her would endanger the rescuer.* It only took a second to decide what to do. Agony speared through his heart, but he scooped his wife into his arms, nonetheless.

"James, please get the doctor. Allison has lost a lot of blood and I'm worried about her. I'm taking her home to bed. Father… would you please get Sheriff Brody? He's going to need to search for… for the body." Wesley's voice wavered, but he stiffened his resolve and stalked back towards town, carrying his wife home.

Chapter 19

Seven days after Allison's ordeal—a week she had spent almost entirely in bed under the doctor's strict supervision—she lay asleep late into the morning, following a restless night with little Peter. Rebecca and James had taken Melissa to their house for a few hours, so Wesley had a quiet moment alone with his wife and son. Sadly, Allison was out cold. His son, cradled in the curve of Allison's body, watched him with solemn blue eyes. Wesley couldn't help gathering him up and taking a seat on the rocking chair.

"Now then, my good man," he said formally, in a murmuring undertone, "your mother has earned this nap, and you and I are going to let her take it. A gentleman always takes care of his lady, and you've been a bit hard on mine lately."

Peter blinked. He had a knowing expression on his funny little-old-man face.

"I hope you grow some baby fat soon," Wesley quipped. "I've seen handsomer fellows."

The baby sneezed.

"Bless you. Well, I can see I was wrong about you. I wasn't sure if I'd be able to open my heart to more people, but clearly, I was. I can see myself in you, and my dad too. You're a Fulton man, and it's going to be my job to teach you what that means. I hope you have a head for numbers. I have expectations of you. You're going to get a good education and I hope you'll take over my place at the bank someday."

Peter regarded him solemnly.

"Of course, you might prefer a different profession. That would be fine, too. Maybe someday, you'll have a brother who can be a banker if you don't want to. That is if your mother will forgive me. I've been… a bit of an ass lately, and I would deserve it if she didn't."

"Yes, you have," Allison said in a quiet, neutral voice.

"I know," Wesley replied, meeting his wife's eyes and deliberately lowering the wall he'd erected between their hearts. *It never did serve you well. Being open with Allison feels right. Shutting her out was worse than losing her.* So he finally spoke the truth. "You deserve better than what I've done to you and I regret it."

"I understand," Allison said, but there was not one hint of softening in her voice.

"What can I do to make it up to you?" he asked. "Please tell me."

"Tell me what you did wrong, Wesley, so I know you aren't just trying to get back in my good graces with nice words. Tell me what you're not going to do again."

"Forgive me, love. I need a moment to think about how to say this the right way."

She nodded.

From his perch on his father's lap, Peter squealed.

"Argh," Allison growled, crossing her arms over her chest.

"What's wrong?" Wesley demanded, alarmed.

"Nothing. Please bring me the baby."

Wesley positioned his son on his shoulder and carefully rose, crossing the room in a few long-legged strides and handing Peter off to Allison. She fumbled with the front of the nightgown Rebecca had made for her and opened the buttons to bare her breast. Wesley watched in unabashed fascination as milk beaded on the rosy tip. She positioned the baby and Peter opened wide, covering his mother's nipple and clamping down eagerly. Allison sighed in relief.

"Does that hurt?" Wesley asked, taking a seat on the bed beside his wife and stroking a strand of tousled golden hair from her forehead.

"It did at first," she replied, "but not so much now. It tingles when…" She looked away.

"When?"

"When the milk comes in. It feels like needles. Don't you already know this?"

He shook his head. "Samantha was embarrassed to let me see her this way. She didn't want me to look. She also weaned Melissa to cow's milk as quickly as she could." He thought about saying something else, something uncomplimentary, but decided against it. *Samantha's gone, and Allison was right when she reminded me to keep the good from my first marriage and let the rest go. It's part of my life, of my past, of mistakes I made, of the lessons I've learned. We both did our best under bad circumstances, and now Samantha is as at peace. It's time to allow some to come to me.*

He slipped his hand behind Allison and cuddled close to her side, watching their son eat, just as she was doing. As one they reached out and traced the soft, downy hair. Their hands met. Wesley laced his fingers through Allison's and lifted her hand to his lips, kissing her knuckle.

"What I did wrong," he said slowly, measuring his words, "was to let my past get in the way of our life together. I let my mother's view of you influence my behavior. I should have married you when I was twenty and found some way to make it work. It would have been fine. I should have chased Samantha away. I should have taken my time with you after Samantha's death. Instead, I let a series of decisions snowball into a colossal mess, and you had to bear the burden."

She looked up at him through her eyelashes. He nudged even closer to her, and his arm tightened around her. She leaned her head over, resting her cheek on his shoulder. He smiled. *This feels right.*

"All those things were in the past and couldn't be changed, but after our marriage, I should have put the ghosts away. I should have made myself remember that you are not Samantha. You kept reminding me, but I let old habits creep into my new marriage. I kept hearing things in the back of my mind. My mother telling me you were trash. I never knew why she said that, but I've heard it my whole life. Even though I never believed it..." he didn't know what to say next.

"Why did she say that, Wesley?"

Peter finished and let go. One tiny fist remained clenched tight, the other relaxed.

Allison extracted her hand from Wesley's and positioned the baby on the other breast. He continued eating eagerly.

Wesley shrugged, grief spearing his guts again. *She was a crazy, mean-spirited excuse for a woman. That doesn't make her any less my mother.*

"Mom seemed to have lost her mind when I was born. She became dangerous and unstable. I didn't remember until my father told me, but he took me away when I was seven. Do you remember that time, Allie?"

"Remember the year when my best friend disappeared? How could I forget?" Allison replied. "I was so happy when you came back, but my mother told me in no uncertain terms that I was not to ask you a single question about it, on pain of a lashing." She smiled ruefully.

Mrs. Spencer's lashing are nothing to take lightly, Wesley thought. *Goodness knows I got a couple myself.*

"But why…"

"She found us," he replied, amusement fading to grimness. "Threatened to kill me if she couldn't have me back. Father agreed—reluctantly—on the condition that your parents keep an eye on the situation and report back to him."

"So, they were his spies?" Allison gawked, thunderstruck.

He nodded.

"Well that explains it all, doesn't it?" She rolled her eyes. "What a disaster."

"It was," he agreed. "It's no wonder she both hated you and let me play with you anyway."

"And all the while, said condescending things about me and my family when you were alone?"

Wesley nodded.

Allison considered for a moment. "So, you let your mother affect your opinion of me and your experiences with Samantha color your expectations. Is that right?"

"I think so," Wesley replied.

"And what about Peter? Why did you not want him? Why did my being pregnant make you pull away from us both?" she demanded.

Wesley lowered his gaze from his wife's angry blue eyes to his son's face. Wrinkles, turkey neck and all, Peter still looked angelic.

"I was stupid," Wesley said bluntly. "I didn't want the complication. I was just settling into life with a normal wife. Melissa was improving, acting like a normal child. I thought maybe, just for a while, I could take a breath and adjust to being happy. Then you got pregnant," he squeezed her, "and you weren't your usual sweet, forgiving self. Sorry, honey, but you were a bit... grumpy. I know!" he protested in response to her evil look. "I know you were sick and miserable, and I know my attitude didn't help, but I was just hoping for a moment to be selfish and bask in your affection, and suddenly all your focus turned inward." He exhaled in a sigh that ruffled the baby's wisps of hair. Peter released his mother's nipple, looked up at Wesley cross-eyed, and then lowered his eyelids.

Unable to resist, Wesley leaned down and kissed his son's forehead. "I was wrong to get impatient with you. I think I forgot who you are, I was so wrapped up in what I expected, but that was foolish. I must have the strongest wife in all of Kansas. Who else would have gotten up an hour after giving birth and chased a crazy woman through the streets? Allison, you're amazing. You risked your life to protect our baby." He kissed her cheek. "I don't deserve you, or Melissa, or Peter, but I love all three of you more than words can say. Will you please forgive me, Allison? Let's bury the past and work towards being a family again, can we?"

Allison looked up into Wesley's eyes with a fathomless, unreadable expression. The moment uncoiled, stretched out in silence as the pain of the last year, of the last several years, passed over her face. Every flash of sorrow lanced through Wesley's heart, each like the blow of a bowie knife.

She sniffled and at last spoke. "All right."

Wesley beamed, hope welling up in a wild spring that showered down joy on the darkened, shattered parts of his soul, washing away a lifetime of pain. A cautious smile spread across Allison's face. He leaned down and touched his lips to hers, sealing the promise with a perfect, tender kiss.

Dear Reader,

Thank you for taking the time to read *High Plains Promise*. If you enjoyed it, please consider telling your friends and posting a short review to Amazon. Word of mouth is an author's best friend and much appreciated.

You may have noticed that the denouement of this story is on the short side, but of course, that's because Wesley and Allison's story is far from finished. There's more to come in the rest of the series. For a preview of Book 3, *High Plains Heartbreak*, please read on!

If you enjoyed this book, I have more. More historical, contemporary and paranormal romance, all just as sweet… with heat! Check out my web site http://simonebeaudelaire.com/ for information about my current and upcoming projects.

You can also check out my page at Next Chapter Publishing https://www.nextchapter.pub/authors/simone-beaudelaire-romance-author

Best wishes and love always,

Simone

Books by Simone Beaudelaire

When the Music Ends (The Hearts in Winter Chronicles Book 1)
When the Words are Spoken (The Hearts in Winter Chronicles Book 2)
Caroline's Choice (The Hearts in Winter Chronicles Book 3)
When the Heart Heals (The Hearts in Winter Chronicles Book 4)
The Naphil's Kiss
Blood Fever
Polar Heat
Xaman (with Edwin Stark)
Darkness Waits (with Edwin Stark)
Watching Over the Watcher
Baylee Breaking
Amor Maldito: Romantic Tragedies from Tejano Folklore
Keeping Katerina (The Victorians Book 1)
Devin's Dilemma (The Victorians Book 2)
Colin's Conundrum (The Victorians Book 3)
High Plains Promise (Love on the High Plains Book 2)
High Plains Heartbreak (Love on the High Plains Book 3)
High Plains Passion (Love on the High Plains Book 4)
Devilfire (American Hauntings Book 1)
Saving Sam (The Wounded Warriors Book 1 with J.M. Northup)
Justifying Jack (The Wounded Warriors Book 2 with J.M. Northup)
Making Mike (The Wounded Warriors Book 3 with J.M Northup)
Si tu m'Aimes (If you Love me)

About the Author

In the world of the written word, Simone Beaudelaire strives for technical excellence while advancing a worldview in which the sacred and the sensual blend into stories of people whose relationships are founded in faith, but are no less passionate for it. Unapologetically explicit, yet undeniably classy, Beaudelaire's 20+ novels aim to make readers think, cry, pray… and get a little hot and bothered.

In real life, the author's alter-ego teaches composition at a community college in a small western Kansas town, where she lives with her four children, two cats, and husband—fellow author Edwin Stark.

As both romance writer and academic, Beaudelaire devotes herself to promoting the rhetorical value of the romance in hopes of overcoming the stigma associated with literature's biggest female-centered genre.

Excerpt from High Plains Heartbreak, Love on the High Plains book 3

Garden City, Kansas 1885

"Jes...se?" A broken voice penetrated Jesse West's focus for the briefest of moments. He lifted his head. The rarest of commodities, a gentle breeze warmed by a kind late-April sun seemed to kiss the tears streaming unceasingly down his cheeks. Then his gaze dropped back to the raw mound of earth at his feet. All around him, under the partial shade of wind-blasted oaks, other freshly dug graves, too many of them, clawed the earth apart. Earth like hearts. He dropped his eyelids.

Warmth penetrated the shoulders of his shirt. It was no surprise, and he did not react to the touch except to murmur softly, "Kristina."

"Jesse, I'm so sorry. So sorry." The grip of her capable musician's hands became a full-bodied hug as she crushed him from behind. *She's so strong.*

But not strong enough to stem the flow of tears, or to stop his heart from bleeding. *Can a heart bleed to death?* He wondered idly, staring at a furrow in the upended soil. *Just bleed and die and leave a shell of a man who eats and breathes but isn't really alive?* "I wish it had been me."

"Oh, Jesse!" Kristina began to sob, and her tears soaked into the back of his shirt.

Reluctantly he turned his back on the grave. *Not like it matters. She's with the angels now, not in the cold ground. And it's not like I'll ever forget the sight.* "Kris, I..." his voice broke. It was just as well, as he had no idea what to say.

"I'm so sorry," Kristina sobbed again. "Lily was such a good girl. I was so happy for you both..."

Her words cut fresh lacerations in the bleeding wounds on his soul. *The best girl,* he replied silently. *Every man's dream of a woman. How could this happen? Tomorrow was supposed to be our wedding day!* The unfairness of life clogged Jesse's throat so badly he felt he could choke on it. *I wish I would.*

But here was one of his closest friends, standing five feet from her mother's equally fresh grave, trying to comfort him.

"I know, Kris. I..." He took a shuddering breath. "You're no better. Your poor mama..."

At his words she went completely to pieces, shuddering as she cried.

"Hey," he said, lifting her face so he could look into her ocean-green eyes. She had been so ravaged by grief, every inch of visible skin between her heavy freckles had tear stains. Her snub nose ran unchecked. He handed her a handkerchief. She wiped without the slightest attention, her eyes locked on his. "Kris, I'm sorry about your mama. But at least you'll be away from all this grief soon. You'll be glad to get back to school, won't you?"

She shook her head. "I'm not going."

Jesse's jaw dropped, the shock of her words cutting through his sorrow. "Kris, what?" His eyebrows drew together into a solid line. "You're the most talented musician I've ever known. How can you even consider not going back to the conservatory? How can you stay here in this gossip-factory of a town with all these memories?"

"I have to," she replied, her lip quivering. "I can't leave Dad alone."

"Cal can stay," Jesse insisted. *Let those two stallions battle it out. Cal can help at the general store.*

"Cal left. When we woke up this morning, he was gone. Left a note on the table." Her full lips, her prettiest feature after her eyes, twisted into a wry parody of a grin. "He said he'd had enough of Dad's bossy ways, and with Mom gone, he was going to seek his fortune." She sniffled.

Why that little... "I'm sorry, Kris." This time the pain lashed her features. *And rightly so. Poor Kris. With those freckles, who knows if she'll ever find a husband? And then to lose her career too. Life's unfair.* At the thought of just how unfair, another tear escaped him, trailing down his wind burned cheek and moistening his stubble.

"You should go back anyway," he told her with brutal honesty. *Go and live, Kris. You can't stay here. This town is a dead end. You'll never have a future here. Go and finish school and play your music all over. Don't let your dreams die.*

"I can't." Desolate despair weighed down her pugnacious features into the caricature of a bulldog. "But at least I'll have my friends around me." There was a pleading in her turquoise eyes. *I know what she wants, what she'd never admit to, standing here over Lily's grave. But it won't be. I can't marry Kristina. I don't love her enough, and that's worse than being alone.*

Slowly, his soul burning as badly as his eyes, he drove another nail into the coffin of her future. "Not me. I'm leaving in the morning. I don't think I'll ever come back."

For more information and purchase, please check:
https://www.nextchapter.pub/books/high-plains-heartbreak

Made in the USA
Middletown, DE
10 September 2020

19420903R00128